WHENEVER
I'M
WITH
You

WHENEVER
I'M
WITH
You

X LYDIA SHARP

SCHOLASTIC PRESS · NEW YORK

All rights reserved. Published by Scholastic Press, an imprint of Scholastic Inc., *Publishers since 1920.* SCHOLASTIC, SCHOLASTIC PRESS, and associated logos are trademarks and/or registered trademarks of Scholastic Inc.

Library of Congress Cataloging-in-Publication Data available

ISBN 978-1-338-04749-3

10 9 8 7 6 5 4 3 2 1   17 18 19 20 21

Printed in the U.S.A. 23
First edition, January 2017

Book design by Yaffa Jaskoll

FOR J2 & J3,
THE NORTH AND SOUTH POLES OF THE AXIS
ON WHICH MY WHOLE WORLD SPINS

WHEREVER YOU GO, LET YOUR
HEART LEAD YOUR FEET.

CHAPTER ONE

The sun is dying.

Every day it surrenders another piece of itself to the lengthening nights, and soon these rainy autumn days will freeze over. I'm not exactly eager to experience my first Alaskan winter, but I would think being cold is preferable to being cold *and* wet. Preference is relative, though. If I had my choice, I wouldn't be cold at all. I'd be sunbathing on the pool deck at my mother's mansion—minus her and her current leading man, the reason Dad and I were forced to trade in our very public life in LA for a nearly anonymous one in Anchorage.

Today is the first rain-free day we've had all week, so naturally we're taking a dunk in a lake. Wouldn't want to get too dry, or be too smart. The air is thirty-four degrees, cold enough to see my breath, and the water temperature is who-cares-I'm-not-doing-it. Roughly.

"Your turn, SoCal," Jase says through chattering teeth. Someone hands him a blanket and he makes a burrito out of himself with it. He wriggles for a second, then his underwear lands at his feet with a soggy slap, and he kicks it away. "Time to show us what you're really made of."

SoCal. I'm so far out of my element here that Kai's friends nicknamed me after the place I came from. "I'm made of common sense," I tell him.

Kai snickers at that. "You don't have to prove anything, Gabi," he says to me while looking at Jase, a protective glint in his dark eyes. "I'll go next." He's the only completely dry one left besides me.

"Wait." I grab Kai's hand, and warmth transfers from him to me, loosening my chest. My next breath is a little deeper. "You don't have to prove anything, either." Swinging from a rope tied to a tree branch that hangs over a lake is a cheap thrill in summer, but in mid-October in Alaska, it's a temptation Death might find too hard to resist. So far, Death doesn't seem to be paying attention to us, but that could change in a blink.

Kai gives me a smile meant to put me at ease, but all I see in it is a dangerous mischief. His confidence and persistent optimism were what first drew me to him, but sometimes I question his judgment. Like the last time we went hiking and he walked along the edge of a sheer drop as casually as though he were walking along a broad, flat shoreline. Humming a song while doing it, even.

"I'll be fine," he says. "Hold my clothes under your coat so they're nice and toasty when I put them back on." He takes off his knit cap, revealing unruly waves of black hair, and hands it to me.

"Okay." I won't tell him not to do it. That's his choice. The same as it's my choice not to do it. One thing I learned pretty quickly after I met Kai was that he does respect my opinion—even if he doesn't always agree with it.

A few other guys and a couple of girls are huddled together by the trees, back in their dry clothes and coats but still shivering. And they're looking at me like I'm the crazy one.

We've all got a mild case of cabin fever after the wet weather, so when Kai said he was going out today, I joined him without question. Then I realized the rains had left behind a twelve-degree drop in temperature. But apparently this is a tradition they have every year on the first frosty day of October. Like shaking their fists at the coming winter, saying, "You're nothing to me. I can handle the cold. Watch this!"

They all grew up here, though. I moved to Alaska from Southern California only just this past July. I've survived earthquakes and wildfires and storms of paparazzi, but none of that has prepared me for the months of arctic misery I'm about to face.

I fold Kai's hat, shirt, and pants inside my coat and almost can't get it zipped back up. He stuffs his socks inside his boots, and then he's down to nothing but his boxer briefs. Not that I'm not enjoying the view of his lean, muscled body—all those square inches of bare skin in a shade that more closely

5

resembles his Canadian mother than his Tlingit father—but this is not the scenario in which I imagined seeing him next to naked for the first time.

He's already shivering and not a drop of water has touched him yet. But everyone else seems okay now, even Jase, whose lips aren't so blue anymore. They've pulled some dry wood from the back of Jase's truck and are about to light a campfire. They'll roast hot dogs and marshmallows, and laugh like they didn't all just give Death the finger. Maybe Jase is right. Maybe I do need to prove I haven't been spoiled by my rich Californian roots.

I watch Kai brace the thick rope in his hands, and I try to put myself in his place as he goes through the motions. I took acting classes for years, even had a bit role in one of my mother's films when I was sixteen, just last year. This is no different from stepping into a new character. Maybe if I think this through, step by step, I'll find it's not as bad as I assumed.

Kai heaves a breath, and I copy him. He backs up a few steps, then launches into a run. I imagine the soles of my feet smacking dirt and stones. My heart rate increases. Kai swings over the lake and goose bumps pop up over my whole body. He plunges into the water with a magnificent splash. I hold my breath, my muscles tightening as they would if I were under-water, the stinging cold pricking like needles on my skin.

He hasn't surfaced yet, so I keep holding my breath like I'm right there with him. *Is he okay?* I wait, numb with cold and anxiety, the voice of reason in the back of my mind now roaring, desperate for control: *Kai, get out of there!*

I've counted to four-Mississippi when he comes up for air and shouts in triumph. I melt in relief. He swims to the bank easily, water gliding over his back. Jase hands him a blanket, and he wraps it around himself, grinning. Everyone's looking at me with anticipation, urging me to give it a try.

But I'm certain now—I can't do it. My muscles will lock up and I'll drown. I just wasn't made for this. Give me sunshine and scrub, baked earth and salty shores. Give me a life that doesn't require layers to survive.

I say nothing to them, just shake my head.

The disappointment among Kai's friends rolls over me. They wanted a show, and I let them down. One of the other guys gives Jase a couple of bills.

He *bet* on me? I understand him thinking I spoiled his fun, but I didn't think I was so different from everyone here that Jase would put money on what I'd do or not do.

Not that I consider Jase a real friend, more like an acquaintance by association, but seeing that stung. I turn away from him, muttering where I think he should shove those dollar bills.

"Don't let him get to you," Kai says between chattering teeth. "You're not doing anything wrong by not doing what everyone else does."

"I know." I've never been one to be swayed by peer pressure, but that doesn't mean I like being the odd one out.

I reach up to tug Kai's hat down over his reddened ears.

"My bet?" he says, his tone warmer. "Jase wouldn't last a day in LA."

His words hit their mark, and for one delicious moment, my inability to withstand the cold and my being too cautious in their eyes don't matter anymore. Jase and his stupid bet don't matter anymore. Everything melts, and it's just me and this boy. This boy who always knows what to say, how to say it, and when. This boy who, three months ago, saw me at my worst and didn't let that scare him. Instead, he stepped into the darkness of my soul and turned the lights back on.

Everyone is dry now, circled around the crackling campfire, exchanging stories about bear encounters, some of which are obviously exaggerated to be funny but not entirely made up. Black bears rummage through garbage at night like raccoons. I don't see the humor in it. Facing a hungry bear in the dark sounds like the stuff of nightmares.

The closer the sun gets to kissing the horizon, the closer I huddle against Kai to stay warm. He drapes an arm across my shoulders and pulls me closer. I imagine what it would have been like if we'd met under different circumstances, if we'd met in SoCal instead of Alaska. Kai would have fit in there better than I do here. His poise, easy smile, and natural charm would have made him the life of every party. Swap his basic tee and jeans for a suit and tie, and have him escort me to a movie premiere, and the cameras would never stop flashing. We'd spend nights on the beach, splashing through frothy waves, lying on a blanket in the warm sand, instead of sitting on a flimsy fold-up chair by the fire, my face roasting and my back freezing.

"What about you, Gabi?" Jase's new girlfriend, Mel, says, pulling me out of my reverie. In the three months I've known Jase, he's had a different girl with him practically every other week. Mel pierces another giant marshmallow with her stick and then holds it over the fire. It quickly browns. "You got any fun stories from LA?"

Stories? Yes. Fun stories? Only if you consider people trying to take your picture for the sole purpose of ruining your life *fun*. "No," I say, "not really."

"Nothing?" Jase shoots me an incredulous look. "Not even a celebrity sighting?"

"I've seen a few," I say. Like my mom and her boyfriend, the most talked-about couple in the media right now. But I can't tell them that. "It's not that big a deal."

"Maybe not for you, Miss Hollywood." An unamused grin snakes between Jase's cheeks. "Us nobodies don't get to see famous people every day."

"So what?" Kai says. "We get to see better things. Things you can't see anywhere but here." Going by the light tone of his voice, I don't think he's stepping in just to get Jase off my back this time. He turns to me, eyes glittering with pride. He loves this place. "Outside the city, Gabi, it's a different world. There's Denali National Park, the mountains and wildlife, there are glaciers *everywhere*, and the northern lights—"

"We've also got mosquitoes the size of birds in summer," Jase says.

I instinctively shudder, remembering my first mosquito plague. I still carry a bottle of insect repellent in my purse, right next to the bear mace I hope I'll never have to use.

Jase starts whittling his stick with a pocketknife and tossing curled shavings into the fire. "Seriously, Kai, you sound like one of those wilderness guides we make fun of at my summer job. They're as bad as the tourists, the way they romanticize this place. And then people die out there, searching for some idealistic life they think Alaska promises but that doesn't actually exist."

Everyone hushes. Even the fire seems to crackle in a whisper. Then something takes hold of Jase's expression, an unspoken realization that morphs into a dreadful remorse. "Sorry, I didn't mean . . ."

"It's okay," Kai says. "Forget it." He offers a wan smile and scratches the nape of his neck. I have no idea what just passed between them. Between all of them. One of the perks of being the new girl—I have no history here.

"Who cares about fame, anyway, Jase," Mel says, breaking the ice that had thickened around us. "Can you imagine being that rich?" She raises a brow at me, as if citing me as an example of what she means.

I've been pegged as the rich Latina from LA, because no one here except Kai knows much more beyond that. They don't know my mother is a household name, and her latest scandal is the reason I'm wearing a coat over a sweater over a thermal top while my friends in LA are probably lounging poolside tonight, flaunting their half-naked, sun-kissed bodies at one another. Same coastline, different world.

Mel pulls at the charred outer shell of her marshmallow, leaving a gooey white glob on the end of her stick, and then pops the crunchy part into her mouth. Jase watches her chew, his whittling forgotten until she swallows and asks him, "What would you do with all that money?"

"Buy a one-way ticket from Alaska to Hawaii," he says. Laughter rises up, and the conversation turns to lighter topics again. Even Kai smiled at that comment, and although Jase is not my favorite person, I can relate to his desire to ditch the cold.

"You wanna get outta here for a minute?" Kai whispers to me. "We can see the sunset better over there."

"Over where?"

"Over anywhere but here."

"Sounds perfect."

We excuse ourselves from the group and say our good-byes. Jase reminds us about his Halloween party coming up, and Kai mutters something in response, never slowing his steps.

"We'll be there," I say over my shoulder. We already have our costumes set, and the colder it gets, the less we can do outdoors. Going to a party, even at Jase's house, is better than doing nothing.

Kai tugs me along through the woods until the voices behind us are barely audible. We can't see the sunset at all over here.

But I do see an animal peeking out from behind a tree trunk up ahead and watching us with curious eyes. It has big pointy ears, a pointy snout, and red fur. It's about the size of a small dog, but it isn't a dog, or anything domesticated.

"Is that a fox?" I say, planting my feet.

Kai stops at my side and follows my gaze. "Yep. It probably smelled our food."

"Will it hurt us?"

"Not if we don't hurt *it*." He starts to move again, but I don't, and our arms stretch between us, hands still held tightly together. My eyes are locked on the fox, though, whose movements have become skittish, head snapping one way then the other, foot lifting then dropping, like it can't decide if it should go or stay.

Well, it isn't the only one. "Shouldn't we wait for it to leave?"

"Gabi, look at me," Kai says.

Slowly, I turn my head to face him. As soon as the fox is out of view, I let out a breath and relax. Kai instills a natural calm in me that I've never had around anyone else.

"I would tell you if it wasn't safe," he says. "Do you believe me?"

"Yes." I believe he understands this place better than I do, and I believe he wants what's best for me. Since the day we met, I've known those two things without a doubt, the same as I know the sky is blue and grass is green.

"And if we ever did get into a sticky situation," Kai goes on, "I trust you have good instincts, and you'd do the right thing."

"Except this time," I say, only half joking. "Just standing here wasn't the right thing."

He smiles at that. "I wouldn't call this a sticky situation. Either way, you didn't freak out and scare the thing into thinking it needed to protect itself, like some people do with wildlife—even Alaskans. You kept a level head and asked me what to do. That's what I mean when I say you have good instincts."

He has entirely too much faith in me, but okay. I follow his lead, looking for the fox as we pass the tree it was hiding behind, but it's gone now. Even animals have to make the decision to keep moving forward, I suppose.

After about twenty more feet, we stop. Kai leans his head back and stares straight up through the trees, so I do the same. This part of the park is more secluded, so it's quieter, but not completely silent. Nocturnal critters let the world know they're waking up now, and somewhere in the distance, a creek burbles over stones. The stars are just starting to become visible in the darkening bruise of the sky, twinkling between wispy clouds. Crisp air tingles in my throat. Away from the fire, the tip of my nose quickly cools. I lower my gaze and meet Kai's. He's got that look in his eye, the one that makes my mouth water and my throat go dry. Like he's been traveling through the desert for days and finally found an oasis. Me.

"I feel blasphemous," he says, "for thinking you're more beautiful than the sky."

"Is that all I am to you?" I tease, thankful for the breeze cooling my heated cheeks. "Just a pretty face?"

"No." His smile lights up my insides. "You're a pretty face and a strong will and a complex, intelligent mind and the best thing that ever happened to me. So there." He cradles the back of my head and draws me close to him. We breathe each other in and tangle our lips. He tastes like sweet promises and spicy heat, feels like where I belong. Alaska disappears, leaving only us.

Then he pulls away, gasping, little puffs of mist mingling between us before they dance away on the breeze. "There's actually something I wanted to talk to you about, away from them."

"Okay." I will my head to stop spinning so I can focus. Of course I'd love to keep kissing, but Kai is the first guy I've been with who likes having a conversation with me, doesn't just want to use me to get close to my mom to further his acting career.

Those things don't matter to Kai, but my opinion does. "What's on your mind?"

"I've been thinking about what's going to happen after graduation. Everyone's talking about college and majors and . . ." He sighs. "That's just not for me."

"Yeah, I don't like the idea of being stuck inside a classroom all day, either." Right now we're both homeschooled, with flexible schedules and the freedom to set our own pace. But my college tuition is already paid through the first year, and my mom insisted a degree would open more doors, even in the arts. I don't care what school I go to, though. I just picked USC because it was close to home. Or it was, at the time.

"It's not even really about that," Kai says. "Online classes are an option in college, too, and that's no different from the homeschooling we're doing now. I just want to be done with school after this. It's enough."

"So what do you want to do?"

Kai's smile flickers toward his eyes. He takes my hand and we make our way toward his car, shuffling through wet, fallen leaves on the forest floor. "I've been thinking about going to visit my dad."

The man who abandoned their family? Why would he want to see him? "Where is he?" I say instead. Kai hasn't talked about him much, and there has to be a reason for that. His dad is probably just as much of a sore spot for him as my mother is for me. I'm not going to prod his open wounds.

"North of here," he says.

There isn't much more of the world that qualifies as "north of here." But at the same time, Alaska is huge, and we're near the southern coast. "North of here" doesn't narrow it down, either. I wonder if maybe Kai doesn't know his exact location.

"I haven't seen him since he left last year," Kai goes on. He's speaking slowly, like he isn't sure how to put words to his feelings. "And I don't know when I'll be able to see him again. I can't leave home long enough to take a trip. Mom and Hunter need my help."

It's never seemed fair to me that he has to pick up the pieces that his dad broke, but I get why he feels responsible. Both he and his twin brother, Hunter, switched to homeschooling after their dad left almost a year ago, so they could help out more with their brothers and sisters while their mom works double shifts to make up for the income that left with their dad. Kai and Hunter are the oldest of seven kids, there's a nine-year gap between them and the next one, and the youngest is only two. There's always something to clean around their house, or someone to feed, or some errand to run.

My mind clicks into a new gear, trying to figure out a way to make this work for him. "What if you went during summer break? After you're done with school but before Hunter is too busy with college to handle things without you around. How long would you be gone?"

"Depends on the weather. Also depends on if I find him . . . It's been so long since we talked."

I swallow down the memory his words wrenched up from my gut—the last time I saw my mother. What was said. What wasn't said. The lies she told before that. The lies I refused to tell from that day on.

"Okay, so. Totally doable if you go right after graduation. We can talk to Hunter about it tonight, start getting everything in order that needs to be done before you go."

"Don't worry about all that. I can handle it, okay?" He squeezes my hand and swings it between us. "I'll figure it out. I just needed to vent, talk about it with someone who won't tell me I'm crazy for wanting to go."

I get it, but that doesn't mean I can't help. He's always quick to help me. Why can't I do the same for him? I bump my shoulder against him, forcing his next step sideways. "Remember what you told me the day we met?"

A boyish grin slides onto his face. Of course he remembers.

"I dropped one of my bags in the driveway—"

"One of your *many* bags—" he teases.

"And you picked it up for me and said—"

"'Welcome home,'" he finishes with me. "You looked so lost, Gabi."

"That's because I *was* lost. I didn't know which door was mine." Kai and I live in the same side-by-side duplex along one of the many creeks and rivers running through the outskirts of Anchorage. Some would call that fate. I call it an extremely well-timed coincidence.

He didn't just help me find the right door, though. He helped me turn a bad situation into a good one. He pulled me out of my self-pity and showed me how to have fun, over and over again.

"I was lost and you helped me," I say. "So whatever I can do to help you prepare for this, I will. If you want to see your dad, you're going to see your dad. Got it?"

"Yes, ma'am," he says through a laugh.

"Be careful," I tease. "I could get used to hearing that phrase. You'll spoil me."

"You say that like being your eternal slave wouldn't be my dream come true." He leans back on a thick tree trunk and pulls me up tight against him. "What did I ever do to deserve you, Gabriella Flores?"

I've asked myself the same question before, about him. And maybe that's why we're so good together—we both feel lucky to have each other. When so many things were going wrong in my life, Kai was a glowing beacon of *right*.

After we've exhausted ourselves with kisses, the drive back home is quiet. No talking. No radio. Kai's not even humming a song stuck in his head. This is a first. He doesn't take his eyes off the road, doesn't even glance in my direction. He's so deep in thought I think he's forgotten I'm here.

"Kai?"

"Hmm?"

"You okay?"

"Mm-hmm. You?"

"Yeah." Maybe it was nothing.

He parks the old Subaru Outback he shares with Hunter in the double-wide driveway he shares with me, and then I follow him to his side of the duplex.

The scent of herbs and spices welcomes me with a hug. I navigate the living room floor littered with various toys and small children. Diesel, the Locklears' geriatric malamute, lies among them, watching their every move. His dark eyes flick my way for a second, determine me neither a threat nor worth getting up to greet, then return to the Lego structure that's about to topple. Diesel is huge and keeps constant watch over their family like a guard dog, but I've never once heard him bark, and anyone can quickly win him over with a belly rub. He's a big softy.

One of the identical twin four-year-old girls looks up at me, wisps of a loosened ponytail falling into her face, and waves like I'm a hundred yards away instead of a couple of feet.

"Hi, Gabi!"

"Hi, uhm . . . sweetie." I still can't tell them apart sometimes.

Kai sheds his coat, hat, and shoes, then gives Diesel a quick scrub between the ears and goes to the kitchen to help his mom with dinner. "Need anything?" I say, raising my voice over the giggles of children.

"No, thanks, I got this," he calls back to me.

I busy myself studying the family photographs lined up along the fireplace's mantel. Their father is in most of them, looking happy and content with the children he later abandoned. Kai doesn't usually seem too broken up over his dad's absence, not even bitter over how dramatically it changed his daily routine. I've wanted to ask Kai why he left them, what went wrong. But it never seems like the right time. He's over it. Why would I dampen his positive spirit with bad memories?

Mrs. Locklear steps out from the kitchen. There's a fine sheen of sweat on her forehead, and she's holding a sauce-covered wooden spoon. She catches a drip before it falls, then licks her fingertip. "Gabi, hi," she says. "Excuse the mess." She herds the children into the dining area and sets up a couple of booster seats. "Are you staying for dinner?"

"Do you mind?"

"Of course not." She waves a hand at nothing. "You're practically family."

Family. I'm not even sure what that word means anymore. Everywhere I look, families are broken, pieces of them floating here and there, sometimes thousands of miles apart.

Hunter thumps down the stairs, piggybacking his two-year-old brother. He nods to me in greeting and then starts setting the table. In the three months we've been neighbors, I can count on one hand the number of exchanges we've had. He doesn't go out with me and Kai, so I only see him when I visit their side of the house, or if we both happen to be in the yard at the same time. Not because he's purposely avoiding me, though. He's never rude and doesn't ignore me, but he isn't the type to strike up a conversation or engage in small talk. Hunter and Kai were born from the same mother on the same day, but that's the only thing that makes them twins. They aren't identical, on the outside or the inside. Hunter is taller than Kai and has a thicker build, with copper-tinged skin like their dad, and his brows are always knit together like he has bad news to deliver and can't think of how to word it gently. Kai has laughter playing on his lips and soft eyes flecked with sunshine. Whenever I'm cold or missing home, all I have to do is look into his eyes and I'm back in SoCal, comfortable and warm.

Hunter sets an extra plate for me and pulls up an extra chair. Once we're all seated, Kai right next to me, holding my hand under the table, I notice he's still not as talkative as usual, letting his energetic younger siblings dominate the dinner conversation. He must still be thinking about visiting his dad.

After dinner, Kai and Hunter clean up the table and load the dishwasher. I ask if he needs help again, and again, Kai refuses.

"I may have grown up with a live-in maid," I say, "but I am capable of helping."

"You still have a maid," Kai points out. "You've never washed a dish in your life."

Whatever. "Then I'll enlist one of your brothers or sisters to help—they'd do it if I offered them candy."

"That's bribery," Kai says through a laugh. "You're a bad influence."

"Can't be any worse than their older brother, who thinks it's okay to jump nearly naked into a freezing lake."

Hunter glances at Kai over his shoulder. "You're still doing that?"

"It's tradition!" Kai says.

"It's also stupid." I grab a wet dish towel and snap it at his back.

"Ow!" he yelps, then turns and spears me with a devilish grin. "So that's how you wanna play, huh? All right, then. My turn." He yanks the spray nozzle from the sink faucet, its hose following like a snake, and aims it at me.

I squeal, unsure if I should run or duck, at the same time that Mrs. Locklear enters the room. Her palms fly up. "Don't you dare make a mess in my kitchen!"

Kai doesn't move, still aiming the nozzle at me, as if he's considering how much trouble he's willing to get into for this.

Hunter takes it out of Kai's hand, feeds the hose back into the faucet.

"I could have done that," Kai says, the lines of his jaw hardening.

"I know." Hunter shrugs. "But you didn't." He casually goes back to sorting silverware in the dishwasher cubby. Like nothing happened.

Kai doesn't move.

"Go on," their mother says. "Finish this so Gabi isn't waiting on you."

Kai's face softens and he goes back to cleaning up. I mouth *thank you* to Mrs. Locklear and she gives me a wink.

Later, we laze about on the living room couch, giving Diesel belly rubs with our feet, watching surfing videos on my phone, and stealing kisses when Kai's brothers and sisters aren't looking. A few times I catch him staring at the pictures on the mantel, lost in memories that don't include me. Too soon, Hunter ushers their three youngest siblings upstairs for baths and story time, giving Kai a look that clearly says "come on, we got work to do," while their mom takes care of the other two, who are trying to talk their way out of going to bed. The post-dinner peace of a few moments ago is suddenly a postapocalyptic chaos. I reluctantly say good-bye and head home. A whole ten steps across the driveway.

I find Dad zonked out on the couch and the credits of a movie scrolling up the TV screen. I don't have to wonder if my mother was in it; I only wonder which one of her movies he obsessed over *this* time.

Here we are, the ex-husband and daughter of *the* Marietta Cruz—Oscar winner, sex symbol, property of Home Wrecker

Studios—trying to forget her and the only life we've ever known. We've stepped out of her spotlight—extremely far out of her spotlight. So far that even during the height of Anchorage's tourist season over the summer, there was no finger pointing, no puzzled looks like they were trying to place a familiar face, no cell phones held out to snap a picture. Here, *paparazzi* is a foreign word. These people outside of LA, these normal people in the normal world, didn't give a second glance to the fiftysomething divorcé and his un-noteworthy teenage daughter.

Except Kai. He noticed. And I can't imagine what life in Alaska would be like if he hadn't.

CHAPTER TWO

The front door slams and jolts me awake. A bleary-eyed glance at my cell phone tells me it's nine a.m., which means Dad just left for work and he's feeling grumpy, slamming doors—and now gunning it out of the driveway, engine roaring. As much as I hated seeing him go from hotshot "lawyer to the stars" to counter guy at the post office, at least it gives him a reason to get out of bed Monday through Saturday. He didn't have to take a job in Anchorage. But when we first got here he wanted something to do that didn't remind him of his old life, and even though he later found he hates the job, he's not the kind of person to back out of a commitment.

Nope, that's my mother's forte. At least when it comes to relationships. Which forced us to leave SoCal, even if just for a year, to let the media find someone else's life to publicly shred.

We moved into this neighborhood so people wouldn't know how much money we really have, trying to blend in to average American life, but it didn't take long for anyone looking to realize we're living far below our means. Dad didn't mind downgrading on the house, or his car, or even his job. It was other things he'd gotten used to that he just couldn't give up, like a housekeeper. We're also the only ones on this street who receive premade meals via a delivery service.

And Kai's friends knew from the moment they saw me that something was off. Clothing I thought of as normal everyday wear was coined "fancy." Fortunately, they didn't pry into it too much. When they heard I'm from Southern California, the stigma took over. Apparently everyone there is rich and gorgeous and has a perfect life.

That's like saying everyone in Alaska lives in igloos.

I scramble out of bed and tug on a pair of fuzzy socks, then send Kai a text on the way downstairs to the kitchen.

Good morning.

He immediately replies with a smiley face and a heart, arousing my senses quicker than a jolt of caffeine. Sleepiness evaporates from my mind and body like mountain mist at sunrise. But out of habit I pop a single-serve cup of instant into the coffeemaker. It's Saturday and we have no plans except to be with each other. My favorite kind of day.

After breakfast, I go next door, and Hunter tells me Kai's out back. I find him standing by the river that runs behind the strip of houses on our street, tugging at a fishing pole, a large plastic bucket next to his feet. He's catching their dinner for tonight. He's told me before that people technically aren't allowed to fish here, but everyone does it anyway.

I step up behind Kai and wrap my arms around his solid torso, rest my head between his shoulder blades, inhale the crisp scent of cold mingling with his musk, soak up his warmth. A couple of whitefish splash around in the bucket. Evergreen-covered mountains in the distance surround us like guardians, allowing entrance only to those with the strongest will to survive.

Kai hums a tune I don't recognize, making his chest vibrate. Then he tugs hard on the line, forcing me to back away. After he's reeled in another plump, silvery whitefish and added it to the bucket, I ask, "Did someone teach you how to fish, or is it just something Alaskans are born knowing how to do?"

"My dad taught me," he says.

I had a feeling.

After a long pause, he says, "I think I've got enough fish now. I'm gonna run these into the garage and get them prepped for Mom, then we can go catch a movie or something. Whatever you wanna do." He reels in his empty line.

Clearly, he's not up to talking about his dad. Not surprising, but I hoped he might clue me in a bit more, after telling me last night about his desire to see him. Baby steps it is, then. "Okay, but I get to pick the movie this time."

He leaves the fishing reel on the ground, picks up the

bucket by its handle, and we head across his backyard, toward the house. "What're you in the mood for?"

"Not zombies," I say, thinking of our last movie date. "I'm all zombied out. No more gore for a while."

"How about a rom-com?" he offers, even though he knows that I know he hates those.

"I'm not in the mood for fluff, either."

"Okay . . ." He pauses for a moment, as if trying to read my mind. "I got it. An underdog turns superhero story. There has to be a new Marvel movie playing; there always is."

"Ha, that's perfect!" Leave it to Kai to figure out what I want when I don't even know what I want. I step around the side of the house and onto the driveway, focusing on Kai instead of where I'm walking, and stumble into a soft, portly woman who smells like a whole bush of lilacs got shoved up my nose, branches and all. It's both floral and woodsy. "I'm sorry, excuse me—"

"Aunt Claire?" Kai says, and his face explodes with a grin. He sets down the bucket of fish and tackles her with a hug.

"Kai, look at you!" she squeals. "You've grown at least two inches since last year, eh?"

I back away from their reunion, my presence feeling as welcome as the waiter forced to wear a sombrero and sing "Happy Birthday" to you.

"What are you doing here?" Kai says. "Mom didn't say you were coming to visit."

"She doesn't know, sweet pea. I thought I'd surprise her,

give her a load off for the next few weeks, what with"—
she flicks a glance my way—"you know, this is a rough time of
year."

Kai nods, explaining nothing. "She's doing better, but this
will mean the world to her. Thank you." He gives her another
hug, then remembers I'm standing there. "Aunt Claire, this is
my girlfriend, Gabriella Flores."

"You can call me Gabi," I say.

Her brows shoot toward her thinning hairline. "New girlfriend, eh? Nice to meet you, Gabi, I'm Clarabelle Martin. But
you can call me Claire." She winks and then turns back to Kai.
"How's Hunter doing?"

"Your guess is as good as mine." Kai unloads a couple of
suitcases from the airport taxi idling by the curb as his aunt tips
the driver. "He's inside with everyone else if you want to ask
him yourself."

Claire waddles into the house and Kai moves to follow her,
but then he stops, sets down the suitcases, and pulls me into
his arms.

"What's that for?"

"Aunt Claire being here is a really good thing. It's just put
me in an extra good mood."

I lightly elbow him in the ribs. "Don't *I* put you in a good
mood?"

"Always." He laughs. "But this is different. This was an
unexpected gift."

"Good answer."

While Kai takes care of the suitcases, then guts and fillets his fish, I go back to my side of the house to get ready to go out to the movie and whatever else we end up doing. I've got half my hair wrapped up in hot rollers when my cell phone buzzes with a text from Kai.

Change of plans. Have to run some errands. Movie another time?

I sigh. This isn't the first time his family's needs have interrupted our plans. It's not that I don't agree with him helping them over going on a movie date with me, and I don't mean to be clingy, but he's the only person I have around to do stuff with out here. Okay, I text him, and finish rolling my hair. Just because I'm alone doesn't mean I can't look good.

After dinner, there's a commotion in the driveway. I take a peek out the front window and see Kai packing a bunch of stuff into his Outback in the dark. I put on a coat and slippers and rush outside, immediately pulling up my hood. The wind blows fiercely, sucking away the last bits of warmth left over from summer.

"What are you doing?"

"Just selling some junk," Kai says.

I notice his snowboard in the pile before he closes the back hatch. That isn't junk. "Why would you get rid of your board *now*? It's almost winter."

"I need money."

Well, if that's all it is . . . "You don't have to sell anything. I can give you money. My mom sends me more than I'll ever use."

His jaw hardens. "I don't take charity, Gabi. I'd rather earn it."

"Then you can pay me back. Think of it as a loan. I'll even charge interest—in kisses."

"Tempting." His face softens. "I don't want to owe you for anything, though, okay? I can get another board . . . whenever. It's not a big deal."

He stands right in front of me, but his mind is somewhere far away. He's not thinking straight, forgetting things we've talked about more than once before.

"You were going to teach me how to snowboard, remember? So I don't die of boredom this winter?" I figure snowboarding is the closest I'll get to surfing out here, my favorite hobby back home. I've even been looking forward to it *snowing* just so I can learn.

"Of course I remember," he says.

The wind tears my hood off my head, and my hair whips my cheeks. There go the curls. I can't stop my teeth from chattering.

"Go back inside, Gabi, it's too cold out here." He kisses me, pulls my hood back up, and then gets in the car and backs out of the driveway. Weren't we in the middle of a conversation? I didn't even have a chance to ask what he needs the money for.

Inside, I slam the door hard behind me.

"Everything okay, querida?" Dad says.

"Yes, Papi." Everything is fine, except my boyfriend just took off and I don't know why. But . . . he kissed me before he left. It's the only reason my lips are warm while the rest of me is frigid. You don't kiss someone on the lips if you're mad at them, right? You don't kiss them at all. Okay, I actually have no idea what happened between us. Maybe it had nothing to do with me, but I can't help feeling he's hiding something. Why would he do that? We don't tell each other *everything*, but we also don't keep big secrets from each other. "The wind slammed the door shut," I tell Dad. "It's crazy out there."

I settle on the couch next to him, and he tries to open Netflix, but our wireless is spotty. It refuses to stream tonight. He takes his sleeping pills and calls it a night. I aimlessly flip through channels, for I don't know how long, wondering what has become of my life in such a short period of time. I never used to get bored like this. Channel-flipping on the couch didn't exist on my agenda. There was always some party to be seen at, some beach to get lost in, some movie to go to that some friend of a friend played an extra in. I never had to stay holed up in my house if I didn't want to be there. Whenever I needed an escape from my parents' arguments, I could easily find one. That's what first drew me to surfing—it helped me escape both physically and mentally. The boyfriend who introduced me to it didn't stick around, but the habit did.

My cell phone rings, startling me, and the remote jumps from my hands. But the caller ID is even more of a surprise than the sudden ringtone.

It's Mom's assistant, Amy. Because Mom will never call me again. I don't have regular communication with Amy, either, not like the daily almost-conversations we used to have before my parents' divorce, so her calling now isn't expected. Mom must have added "check on my exiled daughter once every three months" to Amy's to-do list.

I try for a casual tone, like this is a normal part of my nightly routine. "Hey, Amy."

"Gabriella, darling, hello, how are you." It's not a question. That's just how Amy answers the phone, complete with her fake Hollywood-snob accent.

In answer to her questions, I tell her yes, I'm fine, and yes, I've been getting the money. She doesn't ask about Dad, whose depression is only slightly under control. She doesn't ask about school, or whether I've found an acting coach, or if I have a social life. Amy is Mom's assistant because she is extremely efficient. The woman has earned her paycheck tonight.

"Is there anything you'd like me to relay to Ms. Cruz?" she concludes.

"Why didn't she call me herself?" I know the reason, but I don't know if Amy does.

Amy sputters for a moment, then blows out a sharp breath, rattling the speaker against my ear. "She's in a *very important*

33

meeting with her talent manager, Gabriella. She has a *very important* reading coming up for a part that will improve her public image, which she so desperately needs since . . . since . . ." Another forced breath. "Things still haven't settled around here. Last week, they claimed she had gained a hundred pounds. The week before that, she apparently joined a cult. We have to get this target off her back. You understand, don't you?"

"Yes, I understand." I'm not *very important*, like her career. If I were, would I be talking to her assistant right now instead of her—from Alaska?

This shouldn't bother me. It doesn't. *I'm* the one who chose to shut *her* out, because she completely uprooted *my* life to salvage *hers*. I told her exactly how I felt about that before we got on the plane—explicitly told her to never talk to me again—and if she really wanted to fix things between us, or at least apologize, she'd be the one to call me, not her assistant. I'm so angry at her that most of the time, I don't even care if she calls me or not, or if she never apologizes. I'm just glad she's out of my life. I'm glad she doesn't get a say in it anymore. After this mess blows over, after I'm done with school, I'll decide where I go from there, not her.

I'm not following in her footsteps anymore. I will not become a liar and a cheater.

"Sorry, darling. Really, I am. Is there a message you'd like me to relay to her?" Amy asks again.

Yes. "No. Thanks, anyway." *Thanks for nothing.*

CHAPTER THREE

I'm buying my first pair of winter boots online when Dad tells me Kai is downstairs asking if he can see me. We didn't have plans for tonight, though.

"Sure, send him up." I reach for a stick of cinnamon gum, Kai's favorite flavor on me, not sure if I should be excited or worried. He's been quieter and busier than usual, and we haven't gone out together since that day at the lake, more than a week ago. This could be a surprise date or it could be . . . I don't know, just bad somehow. As well as I've gotten to know Kai over the past three months and despite how close we feel, there's still so much I don't know about him. His distance lately could be nothing or a really big something.

Kai enters my room, leaving the door open behind him—one of Dad's few rules for us. His normally bright eyes are dim, deep shadows hanging beneath them. Talking isn't the only thing he hasn't been doing. Sleep doesn't appear to have been on his agenda, either.

Without a word, he scoops me into an embrace. Sleep deprived or not, he's still warm and feels like home. He holds me a little longer than our usual welcome hug, though, like he's just returned from a very long trip away from me. We haven't done anything together the last few days, but we still live right next door to each other.

"Are you okay?" I ask. "You seem . . . tired." Among other things. But we'll start with that.

"I am tired," he says. "I haven't slept much lately."

"Why? Is something wrong?"

"Nothing's *wrong*, it's just . . ." He rubs his hands over his face and blows out a breath. "Going to see my dad . . . leaving you and my family . . . it's gonna be hard. But after talking to you about it, and then Aunt Claire showing up . . . it was like this push from, I don't know, God, the universe . . ." He whispers a curse. "This isn't coming out right. Sorry. Everything about this is hard, but I have to do it. You know?"

"It's okay," I tell him. "When you go, I'll still be here when you get back. How long will you be gone?"

"A few weeks, maybe more. Like I said before, it depends."

"That's nothing in the broad scheme of things!" I say cheerily, trying anything to brighten him up. "And I'll be glad you did it when it's over. You will, too."

He stares at me for a moment, and I can almost hear the gears of his mind clicking in the silence. It isn't like him to not say what he's thinking, but this is an unusual circumstance, with emotions that cut deep. This is the first time I've seen him so low. But he was bound to show me another side of himself eventually. He's seen my darkness already, and he's still with me. It's only fair that I see his, too, so I can show him it's not going to scare me away, either.

"We don't have to talk about it now if you don't want to," I say. "But if you do want to, we can. It's up to you. Okay?"

He nods. "I think it'd be easier if I just . . . if you just . . ." His mouth twists as he looks to the side, and then he digs something out of his jeans pocket. He extends his closed fist toward me, turns it so his curled fingers face the ceiling, and says, "Open it."

A gift? This is a first for us. My lips twitch with the urge to smile before I even see what he's giving me. I wonder if this is what he needed money for the other day and why he was irritated when I suggested he borrow it from me. That would have been like I was buying my own gift. I nearly laugh in relief. It all makes sense now.

A mixture of excitement and uncertainty sets off my nerves like fireworks. I uncurl his fist, hoping he doesn't notice my fingers trembling against his, until his hand is open. A small stone pendant rests in his flat palm, attached to a simple silver chain. I've seen plenty of stones in my lifetime, both in my mother's personal jewelry collection and on sets, everything from brilliantly faceted diamonds to clunky costume jewelry, but never anything like this. It's literally just a gray rock, polished smooth. Not even lacquered. The letters *GF* have been engraved onto it and the grooves painted black.

"My initials?"

"Yeah." Kai flips the stone to show me the letters *KL* engraved and painted black on the other side. Not just my initials; mine and his, together. "It means you and me," he says, then holds the chain open toward my neck. I hold my hair up so he can fasten the clasp in the back. When he's done, the stone rests against my chest, near my heart. It isn't as heavy as I was expecting.

"I know it isn't much to look at." His tone is as tremulous as my fingers were a moment ago. Why would he be nervous? He's the calm and confident one in this relationship. Stressing out and questioning everything is my job. He goes on, "It's just meant to be a symbol of us, together, even when we're apart. Whether I'm on the other side of this wall or the other side of the world, I want you to know I'm thinking of you, of how good I feel whenever I'm with you."

I clutch the stone. It's still warm from Kai's hand. "This is the most perfect gift anyone has ever given me. I love it."

He smiles wide and lets out a breathy laugh. "I have one, too, just like it." He pulls out an identical pendant attached to a chain from underneath his shirt collar, then his brow wrinkles and he swallows hard. His emotions are all over the place. He really needs to get some sleep. "I gotta go now."

"Okay." I push up onto my toes and kiss him more

innocently than I want to, just enough to give him a taste of cinnamon, an invitation to stay with me a little bit longer. We have a couple of hours yet before he would need to help his mom with dinner. But he pulls back, says, "Good-bye, Gabi," his voice strained, and then he's gone.

CHAPTER FOUR

I haven't seen Kai in two days, and he's been here-but-not-really-here for the past two weeks, ever since our chat by the lake and even more so since his aunt Claire arrived. When he gave me the rock necklace I didn't think that gave him liberty to disappear on me without a word. It's not like we're so goo-goo-eyed for each other that we can't go two days without so much as talking—although it is rare, since our houses share a wall—but Jase's Halloween party is tonight, and we told him we were going for sure. I shoot Kai a quick text, hoping the crappy cell service doesn't eat it in transit.

Jase's party yes no?

I add a kissy-face emoji for good measure. And wait. And remove things from Dad's Netflix queue that would fuel his depression. And wait some more. And still nothing. I peek out the front window. Kai and Hunter's rusty Outback is in the driveway, so he's either out with someone else or he walked somewhere. The clock is ticking, and my patience is about as thick as a butterfly's wings.

Where are you? Are you coming?

The signal bars disappear before I can hit send. Fan-flipping-tastic. My boyfriend is AWOL and our costumes for this party don't work individually; we're going as two halves of a whole. If I'm there alone, no one will get it. I'll look stupid. *God, Gabi, like that's even the least of your concerns right now. Find Kai so you can give him hell.*

I check my phone again. The signal's weak, but it's there. I hit send and then let out a little squeal of victory when it says *message delivered* beneath my text.

By the time Dad gets home from work, Kai still hasn't replied to my text. I tried to call and it went straight to voice mail, so I assume his phone is just turned off. I'm dressed, makeup on, hair done, and ready to go. Dad unfastens the top button of his blue USPS shirt—a far cry from the Italian suits he used to wear to the law office he dominated in LA—the exhaustion in his dark eyes so heavy it's tugging his head down. When he clicks on the TV, the local news is doing the forecast. Tomorrow's date is covered in a cute little blizzard icon. With a face, even. That'll be the first time I'll see an actual snow-storm. I'm not sure what to expect.

"Good thing your party's not *tomorrow* night," Dad says, then he squints at me. "What are you supposed to be again?"

I have a feeling I'll be hearing this question a lot. "The TARDIS. Kai is going as Doctor Who." And without him at my side, I just look like a girl in a blue dress that's poorly decorated like a phone booth. A sad, empty phone booth.

"Ah, I see it now," Dad says. "Clever."

Not clever enough, apparently, if I have to explain it. But it's too late to change it now. I plaster on a giant smile, the one I perfected by watching Mom on the red carpet, and go to Kai's side of the house. Mrs. Locklear answers the door, holding the phone against her ear and a bowl of candy in her other hand. She must have thought I was a trick-or-treater. As she gestures for me to come in, I notice the silver chain around her neck, similar to the one Kai gave me. I've seen it on her before, never gave it a second thought, but now I look at it more closely. It dips below the crewneck collar of her shirt, so I can't see if there's a pendant attached. She goes back to her phone conversation, venting to someone about the increase in grocery prices and the decrease in government aid.

The house is spotless, the cleanest, most organized I've ever seen it, and I have to assume Claire is responsible. Even the picture frames on the mantel have been dusted.

Hunter is lying across the couch on his back, one hand dropped over the side, absently petting the top of Diesel's head. His other arm is draped over his face. No kids are around, but I hear laughter and splashing and feet thumping around upstairs.

"Hey, Hunter. Is Kai here?"

"Haven't seen him," he mutters.

"Do you know where he went?"

"Wait a minute." He stops petting the dog, and his other arm slowly drops away, revealing his signature look of utter conflict. "He didn't tell *you* where he was going?"

I try to keep my expression neutral. "I'll ask him at the party. Would you mind giving me a ride there?"

"What party—Oh, right. Halloween." He sits up and gives me a hard look. "What are you going as?"

I grit my teeth, silently cursing Kai for abandoning me. Hunter can't see my full costume beneath my coat, but still. This is already getting old. "The TARDIS. And unfortunately I can't really control time, so if I don't get going soon, I'll be late. And if I'm late," I add in a weak attempt to lighten the mood, "all the pumpkin-spice desserts will be gone. That's really the only reason I'm going."

I'm blessed with a rare Hunter Locklear smile. It makes him look like Kai for once, only emphasizing his absence. He hasn't been himself lately, and now he's missing. Should I be worried? Hunter doesn't seem to be worried. I'll take that as a cue to tell my nerves to shut up. Maybe this is normal for Kai; I just haven't known him long enough to see it happen yet. Hunter puts on a coat and shoes, doesn't bother tying his bootlaces, grabs his keys from a hook on the wall, and then we're off.

I turn on the car radio to fill the silence, so Hunter doesn't think he has to talk to me in our forced close proximity. I don't know if he's just shy around people he doesn't know or if he's simply not a chatty type of person in general, but if he doesn't want to talk, he doesn't have to. He isn't the one who has to explain why he ditched me.

"Thanks," I say when he slows to a stop in front of Jase's house. Orange strobe lights flash in the windows, cotton has been stretched across the porch like spiderwebs, and a few zombie hands reach up from the ground in front of cardboard tombstones with cheesy names like *Diane Rott*, *Ima Ghost*, and *Yule B. Next*. "You're welcome to stay if you want," I tell Hunter. "Hang out. Filch some cupcakes. I won't tell."

Headshake. "Celebrating death really isn't my thing."

When he puts it that way, I feel like I shouldn't be here, either. I just thought I should invite him in after he did something nice for me.

"Do me a favor?" he says.

"Sure."

"Call me when Kai gets here?" He pulls a crumpled napkin out of the center console and scribbles his cell number onto it. "Or if you need to be picked up, okay? Even if it's late."

"Okay." I agree only because calling Dad for a ride isn't an option after he takes his pills with dinner. I take the napkin from Hunter and reach for the door handle—

"Is that a new necklace?" Hunter says.

Instinctively, I grab the stone. "Kai gave it to me a few days ago. It has our initials on it. See?" I let my hand fall away.

"Yeah." His face falls and he's quiet for a moment, just staring at it, before he clears his throat and says, "That was nice of him."

And that was a weird reaction. But whatever. Everything about Hunter is a mystery.

The party is a blur of music and dancing, eating and drinking, explaining my pathetic costume, asking everyone—even the cats—when the last time they talked to Kai was, sitting around and waiting for my Doctor Who to arrive.

But he never does. No one has seen or heard from Kai in over a week, which means I've seen him more recently than they have. That doesn't help.

Some lanky girl wearing devil's horns, a skintight red leather skirt, and a lacy red bustier plants her bony butt next to me. I don't remember seeing her before, but in the last hour more bodies have shown up, forcing me into this corner cushion of the couch. Alone but surrounded by people—just like I was in LA. Though at least here I'm not in my mother's shadow.

The girl shouts something at me. I can barely make out her words over the music.

"What?" I shout back.

She leans in close to my ear and says, "Are you Kai's new girlfriend that everyone is talking about?"

People are talking about me? I answer the other part of her question with a nod.

"Where is he? I was hoping I'd get to see him tonight."

Maybe it's just because I'm already on edge, but something about this horned tart wanting to see my boyfriend sets off alarms of jealousy. "And you are?"

"Kimber Lee. Me and Kai go way back. Like, all the way to sixth grade? He was my first tongue kiss." She unnecessarily adjusts her bustier.

If they were still friends, I would have met her by now. "He's never mentioned a Kimberly before." And I imagine he has good reason.

"No no no. It's Kimber. Lee." Her breath leaves a trail of cheap beer in its wake. She eyes the pendant dipping toward my cleavage, which, unlike hers, actually exists without a push-up bra. "Nice rack," she says.

Wait, did she say rack or rock? She's looking at my necklace, I think, but it's right by my chest. "Uh . . . thanks."

"I'm Satan tonight."

"Clearly." In more ways than one.

"What are you supposed to be?"

"The TARDIS."

She blinks. "Is Kai gonna be here soon?"

This is exactly why I hated parties in SoCal. Everyone is either wasted, fake, or a toxic mix of both. She doesn't want to talk to me. She's using me to get to Kai, the same way people used me to get to my mother. Is it too much to ask for people to be interested in *me*?

There is someone out there who's interested in me for me,

though, someone who wanted to get to know me before he knew who my mother is. Someone who would make this party bearable—if he was here.

"Nice meeting you, Kimberly—"

"It's Kimber." Dramatic pause. "Lee."

"Right. See ya." I hunt for Jase, convinced he knows something about Kai but refuses to tell me, and find him in the kitchen removing his vampire teeth so he can take a swig from the bottle he just cracked open. "It's root beer," he says defensively.

"I didn't ask."

"Then why are you looking at me like that? Oh. Do you want some?"

"No. That stuff rots your teeth. And do you know how many calories are in that thing?"

He eyes me up and down and then grabs another bottle from the fridge. "You could use a few extra calories."

"What's that supposed to mean?"

"It means you're not in SoCal anymore, so lighten up. No one here cares if you're a size two instead of a zero, and it's just a drink."

"I'm a size four—"

"Still tiny." He cracks open the second bottle with too much force. The cap goes flying across the kitchen and lands in a bowl of salsa. "Where's Kai, anyway? It's weird seeing you without him."

And it's weird being around all of his friends without him. No one has talked to me except to ask about Kai.

"Did you guys have a fight or something?"

"No." I don't know. Did we? I think back . . . *No.* The last time I saw him he gave me this necklace. He told me he thinks about me when we're apart, thinks about how good I make him feel. That's not even remotely a fight.

Jase takes a long guzzle of his root beer and lets out an even longer belch.

"That's disgusting."

"That's life. Welcome to the real world, SoCal."

"Stop calling me that!" I spin on my heel and storm out of the kitchen, ready to spit fire. Jase and all his friends and this whole stupid party can go roast in the Devil's armpit. The real Devil, not that boyfriend-stealer passed out on the couch. I lived in the real world before, too. Just because I had a gated house and maids and a nutritionist who warned me about the dangers of drinking soda doesn't mean it wasn't real. The most unreal thing I ever did in my life was moving to freaking Alaska.

I have to call Hunter to pick me up, which feels all kinds of awkward, but what choice has Kai given me? When I call, Hunter doesn't give me a chance to even ask for a ride home. Which is good, because I'm having trouble forming words right now. All I get out is, "Kai isn't here . . ." and he says, "I know, I'm on my way," and hangs up.

He knows?

It's nearing midnight. The outside air is cold as a corpse and dark as my hatred for this godforsaken state. Hunter is way too calm when he leads me to his car, but maybe my confusion and borderline rage are distorting my perception. Anyone not contemplating at least six creative ways of asking Kai what the hell is wrong with him seems calm to me.

"Has he ever done this before?" I say.

"Not exactly this, no. But sometimes he gets tunnel vision on stuff and it . . . distracts him. Makes him forget there are other things happening outside that tunnel. I think I know what's distracting him this time. Did he ever tell you about our dad?"

And we're back to this. But I don't see how it relates. "He's mentioned your dad a few times, usually just to say that he left last November, but lately he's been talking about going to visit him."

Hunter's grip on the steering wheel tightens. "Kai used those words? 'He left' and 'visit him'?"

"Yeah. Your parents are separated, right?"

"Not in the way you're thinking." Hunter sucks in a breath and then lets it out slowly. "Our dad died last November."

"What?" I feel at least sixteen emotions in the span of a half second. I need something to squeeze. The skirt of this pathetic dress will have to do, because if I grab for the pendant Kai gave me, I might accidentally rip it off. "What do you mean he's *dead*?"

Hunter turns his face away from me just long enough to make me feel like a steaming pile of garbage, and then he stares out at the road ahead again. We're a block from home.

"Hunter, I'm sorry, that didn't come out the way I meant it to."

"Not upset at you. It was last November, almost exactly a year ago. Dad went on a trip and died while he was away."

"I'm sorry," I repeat. But I don't think Hunter heard me.

Slowly, my brain starts to process what this means. Everything I knew about their dad is wrong. He didn't abandon them. He died while on some kind of trip. Kai lied. Well, I guess he didn't exactly lie to me, but he didn't tell the whole truth, either. Is everything I know about Kai wrong, too?

"I should have known what he was up to," Hunter mutters. "I was too busy making sure Mom didn't fall apart. He seemed okay, though. Finally. And then when Aunt Claire showed up, he seemed even more okay. I thought we were all finally gonna be okay."

He isn't talking to me anymore, but I can't not hear what he's saying. And the more he talks, the less I understand. I still don't get how this connects to anything that happened tonight, or how Kai thinks he's going to "visit" his father up north this summer. "Can you tell me what's going on? Is Kai in trouble?"

"He might be. He might not be." Hunter parks the car in our shared driveway and kills the engine. "The only thing I know for sure is that he's not coming home anytime soon."

CHAPTER FIVE

I abandon my costume and kick it into the corner of my bedroom, leaving it in a heap. Dad is borderline unconscious, so there's no need for me to temper the volume of my frustration and confusion. By the time I've changed clothes, Hunter has come through the back door and into my kitchen, a folded piece of paper in his hands. I offer him some coffee, but he declines. Fine, more for me. I have a feeling this is going to be a long night.

"Why didn't Kai tell me your dad is dead?" I blurt, and then immediately bite my tongue.

Hunter looks stunned for a moment. "I don't know for sure. But maybe in his mind, he didn't have a reason to."

"I'm sorry, I'm just confused." And more than a little hurt, even if Kai didn't intend to hurt me. I can't help but feel betrayed, the same sourness flooding my mouth as when I found out for sure that Mom was cheating on Dad—and she hadn't been the one to tell me. She never once admitted she was in the wrong, let alone apologized for it.

I shake away the memory. Kai isn't like her. He had to have a good reason for not telling me the whole truth. There's something I'm still not seeing. "Kai mentioned going to see his dad. Your dad. If he's dead, then . . . what was Kai talking about?"

"My guess? He's visiting his grave." Headshake. "*Grave* isn't the right word." While I retrieve my mug from the instant coffeemaker, Hunter unfolds the paper and spreads it out on my kitchen table. It's a map of Alaska. He points to a red dot near the southern coast—Anchorage. "This is where he started."

"Got it."

His fingertip trails a wandering path *up*, *up*, *up*, past the green blob that marks Denali National Park, through the giant expanse of nothing that marks the Alaska Interior, and stops just beyond another red dot. "Fairbanks?" I say. "That's where he went?"

It isn't as far north as you can go in Alaska—Fairbanks is closer to the middle of the state—but it certainly qualifies as "north of here" like Kai said. The more truth I find in his words, the more my trust in him returns, bit by bit. Maybe this was all just a big misunderstanding. I made assumptions based on what I thought he was saying, not what he'd actually said. But I still can't remember the part where he said, or even hinted, that he was leaving now instead of later. Our plan was for next summer—

No, *my* plan was for next summer. Is it possible that Kai never actually agreed to that?

"He's not there yet," Hunter says. "It'll take him at least a week of travel first, maybe more."

It's far but doesn't look *that* far. Not even as far as going from LA to New York, which I've done, and that's only a six-hour flight. "Why would it take him a week?"

"Because he's walking."

I nearly drop my coffee. "The whole way?"

Another nod. How can he be so calm about this?

"When was the last time you saw him?" Hunter asks.

"A couple days ago. Thursday night." When he gave me something to remind me of him when we're apart. I didn't know he meant it like this, though. And I'm the one who told him to go, even tried to make plans to help him prepare. I told him he had to do this, go see his dad, don't worry about leaving any of us behind.

"Me, too," Hunter says, unaware of the guilt fizzing in my veins. "I was hoping you saw him later than that and he was just crashing at a friend's house or something. Two days . . . where would that put him now? Not too far past Anchorage . . ." He starts muttering to himself, studying the map.

"Hunter."

His head snaps up.

"Care to share with the rest of the class?"

"Kai's an idiot," he says.

Okay, he's allowed his opinion on the situation. But that idiot is the only real friend I have in this place. "Why is he doing this?"

"While you were at the party, I ransacked his part of our room. He's going to hate me for it, but I had to know if I should be reporting a missing person or if my brother is just being an idiot."

"And you found evidence in support of the latter." God, I sound like a lawyer. Dad would be proud, if he wasn't stuck in his warped bubble of post-divorce depression.

"I found a map and a bunch of survivalist stuff he printed off the internet, all of it related to the area outside Fairbanks. His fishing and hunting gear are gone from the garage, too."

"I didn't know Kai knew how to hunt."

"We both do. I haven't touched a gun in years, but Kai used to hunt with Dad regularly . . . until . . ." He sighs, shakes his head. "Anyway, some of the stuff he printed was dated as far back as two weeks ago. He's been planning this, right under our noses."

His words suck the air out of my lungs. Two weeks ago, when we talked about his dad by the lake. This is definitely my fault, then. I may not have planted the initial idea in his head, but I insisted he should find a way to make it happen. And his aunt showing up to help gave him the perfect window of opportunity to slip through *now*. Then I unknowingly pushed him out of it.

"He sold his snowboard and a bunch of other stuff around that same time." I set my coffee down too hard; some of it drips down the side of the mug and soaks into the map. "He never told me why he needed the money, but when he gave me this necklace, I assumed that was it. Or at least part of it."

Hunter grimaces, then peers at the initials inscribed on the rock pendant. "Kai didn't buy this. He made it. It's just like the one my mom has, that my dad made for her before he left on his first trip up north. They weren't even married yet. Together always, even when they're apart—that's what Mom said it meant." His Adam's apple works up and down as he swallows. "She used to wear it only when he was away, and she kept it on display on the mantel with his when he was home. She'll *never* stop wearing it now."

"You think this was Kai's way of telling me he was leaving for a while?" I couldn't possibly have known, but still, I feel stupid for not hearing what he said between his words. *Whether I'm on the other side of this wall or the other side of the world* . . . Or, in this case, the other side of Alaska. It seems so clear now. How did I miss it before?

"When he gave this to you, that was the last time you saw him?" Hunter says.

I nod.

"I figured. But I didn't want to worry you with anything before I knew for sure what he was up to." He reaches for my coffee mug and then takes a generous gulp. I'm already dropping another single-serve cup into the coffeemaker when he says, "That's good."

Either he was just being polite before, or he's conceded to

the fact that he can't get through the rest of this discussion without the powers of caffeine. "It's all yours."

"Thanks." He takes another sip, then rips a paper towel from the roll above the sink and dabs at the wet coffee ring circling the triangle on the map that marks Denali—the mountain within the park of the same name. I'm assuming Kai has another map like this one on him. "He doesn't have GPS on his phone. Or any kind of Wi-Fi. It's just a basic one for calls and texts, same as mine. They're cheaper that way."

His phone . . . "Hunter, I texted him a few times before the party and he didn't answer. If he's not that far from Anchorage yet, like you think, then he might still be in cell range. And if he believed I knew he would be gone for a while, then he isn't hiding from me. Why wouldn't he text me back?"

His lips hover over the rim of the mug for a second. "Good question. You wanna try texting him again?" He pulls out his own phone, too, and we both shoot Kai a text. I don't know what Hunter's says, but mine is to the tune of:

Call me right now if you value your life.

I finish half my new cup of coffee before concluding he isn't going to respond. It's late, though. "Maybe he's sleeping now." Another thought hits me—where is he sleeping at night?—and with that, a deeper worry settles in my gut. Is he out in the open, exposed to the cold? Or is he staying with people along the way? Strangers . . .

"Or maybe he doesn't have his phone on him at all." Hunter

refers to the map again. "Dad always took the same path, because there are off-road public shelters along the way—small ones, perfect for hunters and extreme wilderness travelers like Dad. He even built one of them. He also built a cabin in the mountains north of Fairbanks, away from civilization and modern conveniences. If Kai's trying to mimic Dad's journey, on his way to see where he died, that means no modern technology of any kind. That was the point of it—going off the grid. He walks the whole way, he hunts for his food—"

"And he doesn't use a phone," I say. I get it, but it seems crazy. "Why would someone purposely isolate themselves like that?"

"Dad went up there every few years, to get back in touch with the land and reconnect with his soul, or whatever. Not for religious reasons; he just said it made him feel better. Like pushing reset on his brain. That has to be what Kai's doing, too. Once he's out of the city, he'll take the same path through the wild from shelter to shelter until he reaches Dad's last known location—his cabin. He *planned* a survivalist hike, and the anniversary of Dad's death is coming up, and Kai hasn't been handling anything well since he died. It's the only explanation that makes sense."

"What do you mean he hasn't been handling anything well since then? He's the most positive, optimistic, overall happy person I know." Usually.

"That's exactly what I'm talking about, Gabi. He hasn't grieved Dad at all. He's still the same person he was before it happened. Even at the funeral, he never shed a tear. It's like he's stuck in the denial phase—that's stage *one* of grief. It's basically shock. Until he gets past that and lets reality sink in, he won't go through the other stages and heal. I've been through all of them already. So have Mom and my brothers and sisters who are old enough to grasp the situation. This past year has been hell for all of us. Grieving sucks. I wouldn't wish it on my worst enemy. But it's also normal."

"Are you saying Kai *isn't* normal?"

"No, I don't mean that he's mentally unstable or anything like that," he says quickly. "He's not going to do anything reckless, or he would have taken off without making any plans. His viewpoint is just a little messed up. I'm not sure what exactly he's thinking or what he plans to do at Dad's cabin, but whatever his reasoning, it isn't realistic."

"Why didn't you tell me any of this before? I could have helped him. I could have prevented this."

"You could have *tried*," Hunter corrects me, offering a sympathetic look. "I've been trying to get through to him for months, believe me. He wouldn't hear it. But when you came along, you guys just . . . *clicked*. I thought that would help, eventually. I thought he would open up to you—honestly, I thought maybe he already had, since he's been kind of down recently. But I guess I misinterpreted that."

"He started to tell me some things, but I wouldn't say

he opened up. He must have been upset about leaving, not about going."

"Yeah, that makes sense. Now." Hunter runs a hand through his hair. "I don't like that he's taken off on his own, but what if going through with this will help him understand the truth? What if he *needs* this?"

I stare at the map, at the hulking state of Alaska, full of wilderness and wildlife. People have died out there. Kai's own father died out there. He hasn't been thinking straight lately—exacerbated by grief he refuses to acknowledge. Hunter voiced some legitimate what-ifs, but I've got a few of my own. "What if he runs out of food? Or gets lost? We can't just let him go. What if he never comes back?"

Hunter releases a sigh heavier than the moon. "Kai can be an idiot sometimes, but he's also my closest brother. I'm not going to abandon him if he might be in serious danger. He's likely using the shelters, which means he'll be okay. Unless . . ."

I gesture for him to continue, ready to leap across the table and pull the words out of his head if I have to. "Unless what?"

"Unless he gets caught in the storm tomorrow, between shelters. There's several miles between each of them. He isn't completely new to being a survivalist, but he isn't an expert like my dad was, either. If he can't stay warm, he's toast."

The storm. I hadn't given it a second thought until now. I

open the weather app on my phone, and for a second, I can't catch a breath. Then, "It's gotten worse since the forecast this morning. They're predicting twenty-four inches of snow by this time tomorrow." I flash the face of my phone toward Hunter and he mutters a curse. That does it. Kai might not even know this storm is on the way. "We need to find him."

I meet Hunter's gaze, silently daring him to argue one point further on this. There's no sunshine in his eyes like in Kai's, just two dark pools. He says nothing, which is better than telling me I'm wrong, but still no help.

"What do we do? Talk to me, Hunter. Should we tell your mom?"

"No. She's got enough to worry about right now. Let's go find him first, try to talk some sense into him. Maybe he'll listen to you. If he doesn't, then we call the police and, I don't know, get him taken in for truancy or running away from home."

Okay. Am I really going to do this, willingly go farther north and possibly face an oncoming snowstorm? Yes. For Kai, I will. And I won't be alone; I have Hunter with me. He knows how to navigate this area. He knows which path to take. Except: "Kai's got a two-day head start. How can we catch up to him before the storm hits?"

Hunter's mouth quirks up over the edge of his coffee mug. "We don't have to go by foot just because he is."

CHAPTER SIX

"We should be back before tonight, before the snow gets bad." Hunter takes a sip from the thermos of coffee we're sharing, sets it into the Outback's cup holder between us, and then tosses a cell phone at me. "It's Kai's," he says. "The battery was chirping when I got home last night. Found it in his sock drawer and recharged it. Once we catch up to him, he's not going anywhere ever again without it, even if I have to surgically implant the thing into his arm."

I find the stored pictures in his phone and a selfie of Kai and me, taken in August, appears in the line-up. Bright blue sky. Bright white smiles. He looks happy. *We* look happy. My feelings for him have been genuine from the start. But I wonder, now, how much of his happiness was real and how much was just avoidance of darker emotions. Was my moving in next door to him, and my needing someone to remind me of the good things in life, a convenient distraction for him to put off facing reality? If I'd met him before his dad died, would he even be interested in me?

Hunter said Kai is easily distracted—was I simply another distraction before the next one stole his attention?

The sun hasn't quite risen yet; it's just starting to smear orange blush across the horizon. Hunter suggested last night that getting a few hours of sleep before heading out this morning would be safer than venturing into the dark. We're able to travel much faster than Kai, so I agreed, but then I barely slept at all. How could I, when Kai is out in the cold, alone, planning who knows what?

This is the third time in less than a day that I've been in a car with Hunter, the closest I've ever been to him, the most words we've ever exchanged. It's awkward but also not. We know each other, but we're still strangers.

"If we're gone for only a day, that's fine," I say. "My dad won't even notice." Today is Sunday, his only full day off. He usually spends Sundays in bed. Not really sleeping, but not really awake, either. "What about your mom and your aunt? Did they ask where you're going?"

"I said I was going to check on Kai."

"And they didn't ask where he is, or think it's weird that he's gone?"

"Everything is weird with our family right now. We're still trying to figure out how our life works without Dad in it. Mom thinks Kai went to stay with a friend to get away from the stress of home, which he's done before, and Aunt Claire believes her because she doesn't have a reason not to. Even before Dad died, Kai just did whatever he wanted, whenever he wanted, never asked for permission. Once he sets his mind to something, it's as good as done. Case in point . . ." He gestures to the road ahead. "And it's not always in his best interest."

"Like the jumping-in-the-freezing-lake-naked incident of two weeks ago."

A smile plays on his lips. "Did they talk you into doing it, too?"

"No. That's the sort of experience you come out of with fewer brain cells than you had before you went in." Maybe that's what's going on with Kai. His brain is malfunctioning after too many dips in the frigid lake.

I'm trying really hard not to be mad at him for this and to give him the benefit of the doubt. He gave me this necklace—*made* one for me, and an identical one for him—for a reason. But what else am I going to find out about my boyfriend through his brother?

Well, no more. From now on, I'm going to listen to what Kai actually says, not what I think he means. I saw enough evidence from my parents' relationship to know communication either builds you up or breaks you down, pulls you together or pushes you apart. I thought Kai and I were doing okay in that area. Clearly, I was wrong. We can do better.

Outside my window, the humble cityscape scuttles by. The

part of Anchorage we live in is more suburb than big city. There isn't much to see besides houses, junkyards, and evergreens. As Hunter shifts lanes to pass a car, a memory from several years ago springs to mind, with my mother's voice speaking in the heavy Puerto Rican accent she still has even though she's lived in the U.S. since she was twelve. The voice I used to wish was mine so I could be just like her, back when Sundays used to be special. That was our family day. We did nothing but spend time together. And I don't know when exactly, but at some point we stopped. Because Mom got too busy? I don't remember. I was too young. But I do remember one of those Sundays we took a long drive out to San Diego to visit my abuelita on Dad's side, and that was when Mom made up the license plate rhyme game.

I once met a man from Nevada,

Who only would say yadda yadda.

She always had me and Dad laughing with her silly rhymes made up on the spot, just based on the state of the license plate of the cars we passed. It was fun. *She* was fun.

Then she changed, and that changed everything.

My eyelids are gritty bags of wet sand. Stress and lack of sleep have caught up to me. My mother's voice fades with the memory as I close my eyes and let the motion of the car tires against pavement rock me to sleep.

Hunter suddenly swerves a hard right and then an immediate left, tires squealing. My head slams the window and a rainbow of fireworks explodes behind my eyes. My palms instinctively rush in front of me, bracing for impact. It takes another second for me to realize we're still moving and we didn't hit anything. Nothing outside the car, anyway.

"That was close. Are you okay?" Hunter's voice is breathy, like he's been running. "Did you hit your head?"

"Yes, but I'm okay." I will my heart rate to drop below freak-out level and peer out the windshield. The road is clear. It's not even icy. A few snowflakes flutter in the air, but not enough to cause hazardous road conditions. Hunter's gaze keeps flicking to the rearview mirror.

"I'm okay," I repeat. "But what . . ." I turn to look out the back window, and the rest of the question dies on my lips. Something's standing in the middle of the road. A very large, very furry brown something that doesn't seem to care we put ourselves in danger to keep it alive.

"What is that behind us?"

"Moose."

No, that couldn't have been a regular moose. It was in the middle of the freaking road. It was a moose playing chicken. I've seen moose in people's backyards here before, lazily eating their gardens, but never in the streets with a death wish.

"Sorry," Hunter says. "There was a curve in the road and I didn't see the moose until it was right there. Are you sure you're okay? You've got a red mark on your forehead."

I didn't notice it before, but now that my adrenaline is fading, every heartbeat pulses a fresh wave of pain. I gently touch my fingertips to my forehead and feel a knot. "It's swelling."

Hunter pulls the car over. "There's a first aid kit in the back."

Maybe I can play the sympathy card when I see Kai. *See what I went through to get to you? Now get your head together before I give you a matching lump.*

Hunter hands me a bottle of water and some ibuprofen, then shakes up an emergency ice pack. "Hold this against your forehead. I'll drive as carefully as I can, but let me know if you start to feel nauseous, okay?"

"Yeah-kay." My eyelids drift closed and he bats my shoulder. "What are you—"

"Don't sleep."

"Why?"

"I don't know if you have a concussion, and not to be creepy but I need to watch you for symptoms. If you fall asleep before I know for sure, it might not really be sleep. It could be unconsciousness."

More good news. "Okay, I'll try to stay awake."

"If you don't, I'm gonna have to shake you. Only for the next hour, though, until I know for sure you're okay."

"Keep me awake for the next hour, then; I can't do it on my own. I'm exhausted. Talk to me. Tell me about your wild and exciting life growing up in Alaska."

He fires up the engine and eases back onto the road. "There

isn't anything wild and exciting to tell. That moose encounter was the most adventure I've ever had."

I don't believe that for a second. "You said you used to go hunting. Tell me about that."

He twists his mouth and fiddles with the defrost setting. "I'm not much of a talker."

"Then sing."

"I'm even less of a singer," he says dryly.

"How much less?"

"Below zero. Negative infinity."

Me, too. "Then let's play a game. When I was little and we had to sit in the car for a long time, like, if we got stuck in traffic, my mom would play this word game with me . . ."

That was before she was *the* Marietta Cruz, before she became a household name and had an affair. She was just an actress with a dream of hitting it big, married to the man of her dreams, who made enough money as a lawyer to support whatever big dreams she had. And beneath that, she was just my mom. Supermom. Everything I wanted to be when I grew up.

At my silence, Hunter presses. "What was the game?"

"Never mind. It was childish." My forehead aches as it slowly goes numb. "Let's do something else."

But now that Mom is in my head, I can't get her out. Something else she used to say echoes between the throbbing beats of my pulse, something much more recent. *When reporters ask you a question you don't want to answer, or aren't allowed to answer, deflect. Throw the ball into their court. Get them talking about themselves instead of you.*

I don't have the energy to talk, and Hunter doesn't want to, which is his usual, but maybe I can get him to talk anyway, to pass the time and keep me awake. I just have to bring up a topic he's interested in.

So, singing is out. What else do I know about Hunter? Not much. Except: "How did you know that about concussions?"

It's subtle, but I catch it, even as he continues staring ahead at the road. A soft glint in his eye, a tiny sparkle of passion—nowhere near the strength of what I see in Kai when he talks about Alaska, but it's there. It's something. He can give it life if he chooses.

And he does.

Hunter launches into a story about how one of his sisters took a nasty dive off her bike one day and face-planted on the sidewalk. He was twelve and she was three. His parents took her to the hospital, of course, and that was the first time he'd heard the word *concussion*. It scared him because he didn't know what it was, or how she "caught" it by falling off her bike, just that it might kill her. So he looked it up online, and then he got sucked into the unending black hole of internet medical advice. It didn't take long for him to realize that a lot of it conflicted, and it equally frustrated and fascinated him. Not everyone can be right. Not everyone is wrong, either. He decided he was going to become a doctor, so he would know the difference between truth and BS. Now he's six months away from high school graduation and has already started earning credits toward his pre-med degree. It's a lot of schoolwork, on top of everything else he has to take care of at home. "But," he concludes, "nothing worth having comes easy."

So that's why he's so quiet and has no social life. It isn't that he's shy, or he doesn't like talking to me, or he doesn't want to go out with friends; he's just busy and mentally exhausted. He's given it all up to pursue something "worth having." And isn't that the way it is with anything we strongly desire? We believe it is more important than whatever we have to sacrifice.

"Nothing worth having comes easy," I repeat, thinking of Kai and me and this trip. "I like the sound of that."

After a sprint on the highway, we divert onto the back roads. The path their dad took was meant to put distance between him and civilization. Hunter says Kai likely left the roads outside the city. The shelters are off-road, too, which means soon we'll have to abandon the car to reach him. I mean *Hunter* will have to abandon the car to reach him. I'll stay in the nice, warm car and wait, thank you very much.

I don't know where we are specifically—somewhere in the plains north of Anchorage, mountains lining the horizons on either side. It all looks the same. Same mountains, same dilapidated buildings, same trees. Same snow fluttering everywhere but not accumulating. Yet. The piercing headache has dulled to an annoying throb. My brain has given up trying to force me to sleep and remembers that I skipped breakfast. We've been on the road for two hours. "I'm hungry."

"Me, too," Hunter says. "I thought we might have seen Kai by now. Maybe he's farther ahead than I guessed . . ." He rubs the back of his neck. "A quick stop to eat shouldn't set us too far back, though. We're close to the Grinning Bear Lodge now. Their moose steak burgers are the best I've ever had."

Moose steak. Thanks, karma. "You've been out this way before?"

He hesitates, like he just realized he opened a can of worms and can't think of how to close it again, and then he says, "Once. When me and Kai were nine, right before we became big brothers for the first time, my dad took us on a weekend trip, just the three of us. I think he wanted to make sure we didn't get jealous whenever the new baby took his attention away from us or something, wanted to make sure we knew he still loved us." He shrugs one shoulder. "We stopped at the Grinning Bear for lunch on the way out. I remember the food being really good."

"Do you think Kai might have stopped there?"

"Not likely, if he's sticking to Dad's living-off-the-land rules. They don't include paying someone to cook and serve your food."

My chest sinks along with my hope. I'd thought maybe it could be that easy. Stop for lunch and just . . . happen to see him. Or if someone else had seen him, they might have been able to help us find him faster, let us know if we're even close. "Why did he need to sell his stuff for money, then, if not to buy food?"

"Supplies he didn't already have on hand, mostly, and it's always good to have cash just in case. He probably did pack some emergency food, too, in the chance that his hunting attempts were . . . unsuccessful . . ." Hunter's voice gets this faraway tone, like he's remembering something.

If it's about Kai, I want to know. "What kind of a trip was it you went on with your dad out here? A hunting trip?"

"More like a get-out-and-see-nature trip," he says. "Dad went hunting with his buddies a lot, but he didn't want to do anything more than fishing with us until we were twelve or thirteen."

"So did he take you on a hunting trip later?"

"He taught me how to shoot and we went out for practice, but an actual hunting trip? No. He took Kai a few times to some places not far out of Anchorage. I stayed home."

"Why not you, too?"

"I didn't want to go." Another halfhearted shrug. "I don't like killing animals. I'm not against it; I'm not even vegetarian. I just don't want to be the one who pulls the trigger. Kai's never had a problem with it, though. I guess that makes me the bad son." Hunter presses his lips together. He's done, and I'm not going to push him on this one.

The lodge is another twenty minutes away—we were driving on back roads through nothingness and then all of a sudden a town appeared, complete with five whole buildings, including this one—so it's close enough to noon now to eat lunch. And I'm not only starving but, thanks to the coffee, I'm also in dire need of a restroom. A bald guy behind the bar points me in the right direction while Hunter finds us a table. I told him to order right away, so he wouldn't have to wait on me. The less time we spend here, the faster we can get to Kai. Hopefully all three of us will be back in this same restaurant later today, eating dinner together instead of lunch. On our way back home.

The bathroom stall is smaller than a closet. I can barely bend my arms to get my pants down and back up. One of my elbows hits the toilet paper dispenser and my whole arm prickles like I spanked a nerve. The soap doesn't get bubbly, the water is ice cold, and the mirror looks like a prop from a haunted house. The glass is distorted in the middle and cracked around the edges, and—yay!—the paper towel dispenser is empty. My pant legs will have to do.

I've never been in such a rustic place as this before. The overhead plays lyric-free, acoustic guitar versions of songs that hit the Top Forty ten-plus years ago. If I wasn't with Hunter I'd never have known this place exists. The jury is still out on whether that's a good thing or bad. If the food really is as great as he says, that might make up for the . . . atmosphere.

I find Hunter tucked into a corner booth, sipping at a glass of water. Conversations speckled with laughter rise up around us. No one bats an eyelash at me, despite how outrageously out of place I feel here. This is why I generally don't like going to new places, trying new things. I don't know how to act in new environments. I'm a breathing lump of awkward, eyes shifting everywhere at once, taking in as many details as I can without looking like I'm staring. The room is dim, and racks of antlers and various animal skins cover the walls. A faux candle flickers on the table between us. At least the booth cushion is pillowy and comfortable, even if I did have to brush crumbs off it before sitting.

"Nice place," I say.

Hunter smirks. "I know it's not really your style. You'll love the food, though."

"What do you think my style is?" I take a sip of water—and promptly vow to never touch it again. "Do they have bottled water here, you think? This tastes funny to me."

"That," Hunter says, smiling like he caught me in a lie. "That's your style, Gabi."

"What, bottled water?"

"Bottled water. Fancy clothes. Perfect hair and makeup, polished nails. Every part of you screams money."

"And what's wrong with money?"

"Nothing if you got it," he says. "Everything if you don't."

Okay, I'll give him that point. "My family didn't always have money, though. Well, no, that's not entirely accurate. We've always been well off, just not *this* well off."

"Yeah?" He sounds genuinely intrigued. "What changed?"

"My mother." I swallow hard, hoping it'll force down the growing lump in my throat.

Hunter considers that for a moment. "Your mother changed, or her income changed?"

This better be the final question. "Both."

"What does she do—"

The waitress saves me from further interrogation by arriving with our plates. Dad made me promise to tell no one we met in Alaska about Mom. All we need is for the wrong person to overhear and we'll have to move again. Maybe all the way to China. I broke that promise by telling Kai—but not until after we'd been together for a month or so. With how close we became, so quickly, keeping a secret from him felt wrong. It weighed on me heavier and heavier until I had to let it out just to not feel guilty around him. The fact that Hunter knows nothing about my mother proves I made the right choice in trusting Kai. He never said a word, not even to his twin brother, who he shares a bedroom with.

My heart squeezes. I trusted him with my biggest secret, and I don't regret it, but I'm not sure anymore if he has the same level of trust in me. If he did, wouldn't he have told me the truth about his dad? And been clearer about his plans to leave?

A sandwich roughly three times the size of my appetite is presented to me like a divine sacrifice. I'm hungry, yeah, but this is about how much I'd eat in one day, not one meal. The burger is full of juicy meat, melted cheese, caramelized onions, and some kind of sauce is pooling beside it on the plate. My nutritionist in LA would have given me sixteen reasons why even smelling this stuff is harmful, but there are certain "bad" foods I don't mind eating, and greasy sandwiches are one of them. I'm so going to enjoy this now, even if my insides regret it later.

"My name's Vicki and I'll be your server today," the waitress says. "If you're ordering alcohol, you'll have to step to the bar. I'm not old enough to serve it."

"That's okay," I tell her. "We're not old enough to drink it, either."

"Thanks for your honesty. I wouldn't have guessed. You look so . . . mature and sophisticated." She's short and curvy with Southern-girl charm—emphasized by the twang in her bubbly voice—curly red hair, and a turned-up nose dotted with freckles. She's probably around eighteen, but you could mistake her for twelve. "This one already told me his name. And you are?"

"Gabi."

"Well, Gabi, I hope you enjoy your stay." She sets another

plate in front of each of us, these ones smaller and filled with something I don't recognize—purple, whipped and fluffy, but also . . . chunky. A side dish or an appetizer maybe, or an early dessert. "Will you be lodging overnight," Vicki says, "or are you just in for a quick bite?"

"Just here for lunch. We're kind of in a hurry." And it would be awesome if she stopped talking and let us eat now. My stomach is on the verge of a mutinous revolt against my good manners.

"That's too bad. We got some nice rooms, recently renovated. And that storm's gonna get worse before it gets better. Well, anyway, enjoy your lunch!"

"Thanks. This smells amazing." Bet it tastes even better. I'd love to find out. *Go.*

"You're welcome," she says to me while giving Hunter a wink and a dazzling white smile. Then her gaze catches my forehead, and it's like watching someone get news that their dog died. "What happened—are you all right?"

"Moose," I grunt, sweeping my hair across my forehead to cover the mark.

Hunter fills her in on the rest.

"Well, you're lucky you had your own personal medic on hand!" She lets out a trill of laughter, then nudges Hunter on the shoulder like they've been friends since birth.

And the more she talks, the stronger her accent. "You're not from around here, are you?" I say.

"Naw." She waves a hand in the general direction of no one. "I'm a West Virginia transplant. My daddy loves the mountains, but the Appalachians weren't big enough, so one day he just said, 'Hey, we're moving to Alaska,' and here we are! He lives up farther north now, way on the other side of Fairbanks, near the Yukon River, like in some extreme bush-craft community. I stayed here to help Mama, though, after their divorce. She still loved Daddy, but she had to let him go; she couldn't take it anymore. She said, 'If my body were as strong as my heart, maybe I coulda kept on following him, all the way to the moon.' People die up there, it's scary! Not the moon, northern Alaska. Isn't that where that one guy died on the bus? What was his name? The one they made that movie about?"

"I've never seen that one," I say. I didn't ask for her life story, either, but Hunter doesn't seem to mind her rattling on.

"Chris McCandless," he says when she pauses for a breath. "*Into the Wild.* He didn't go as far as Fairbanks, though."

Her face lights up like she just won the lottery. "That's the one!" Somber sigh. "I just don't understand why people do insane stuff like that."

"Me, either," Hunter and I say in unison. We cast a know-ing glance at each other.

"Thank the Lord I didn't inherit my daddy's crazy genes."

"You didn't?" I ask, feigning shock.

Hunter shoots me a look that starts out disapproving but

then falters into conspiratorial. He can't deny she's a little off, even though her quirkiness is adorable.

She's also oblivious to my jab. "Is there anything else I can get for you two?" she asks.

"A bottle of water?" I say.

"We don't sell bottled water. Something wrong with the tap?"

"Uh, it's just a little bland. Can I have a wedge of lemon?"

"Sure thing!" Another explosive grin. She turns away, and Hunter's gaze follows her all the way back to the kitchen.

"So . . . ," I say. "She's cute."

"Yeah. Cute." Hunter gets to work on his sandwich.

After a few bites of my own, during which I'm sure I black out from sheer ecstasy for a few seconds, I say, "Just because we aren't staying doesn't mean you can't flirt a little while we're here, have a little fun . . . get her number . . ."

"That wouldn't be fair to her. I'm not interested."

Oh, oops. I thought he was checking her out as she walked away, but maybe he was looking at something else. "Not interested in her specifically or . . . ?"

"Not in anyone." He swallows another bite. "I've had boyfriends and girlfriends in the past, but not since last year. I'm done playing that game."

"Why, what happened?" I've dated some class-A jerks, the worst of which I broke up with right before leaving LA. That didn't keep me from wanting to meet someone better. If anything, it *strengthened* my determination to find the right guy.

Hunter hesitates, and I open my mouth to tell him it's okay, he doesn't have to say anything, but then he continues, "My dad died, that's what happened. And it was hard for all of us, but it destroyed my mom. She didn't come out of her room for a solid week. Me and Kai literally took care of everything. The family, the funeral . . . everything. After that it was months before she got back into a normal routine. Even now, she's still not the same."

"I'm so sorry, Hunter. I didn't know you were all going through such a difficult time."

He offers a pained smile, as if to say "not your fault" or "it's okay," but it comes out more like "we'll manage." He goes on, "So I promised myself I'd never let anyone who isn't family get that close to me, and I broke it off with Dakota, my last girlfriend, before we got too serious. It hurt, but she's with someone else now . . . We're both over it."

Right.

"No one lives forever," he says. "I don't want someone else to go through what my mom went through when *I* die. No falling in love for me. Ever."

That's the most illogical logic I've ever heard. "How does that benefit *you*? You'll live a lonely life, and you won't save anyone from pain by denying yourself. They'll just find someone else to get attached to and possibly lose."

"True," he says. "But at least I won't be the one who caused their grief in the end."

"So you're doing this just to prevent a guilty conscience?"

He stares at me for a moment. Not harshly, just like he's thinking. Rolling the thought around in his head like you would an especially delicious piece of food in your mouth. Then, "Yeah, I guess I am. And I don't see anything wrong with that. There are worse things a person could do than prevent their own guilt."

"Well, when you put it that way . . ."

He offers me a satisfied grin before digging into his dish of chunky fluff.

"What is that?" I ask.

He swallows. "Something you should try."

It must be made of dog lips or something. "Don't avoid the question."

"All right, I'll tell you what this is, but only after you take a bite. Are you willing to trust me that it won't kill you? That you might even like it?"

"What doesn't kill us makes us stronger, right?" At least, that's what Kelly Clarkson says. And if Hunter can eat it without gagging, it can't be that bad. I scoop out a spoonful and force it into my mouth. It's sweet. The chunky part is definitely some kind of berry. And the rest of it has a consistency similar to . . . "Mousse? I mean the dessert kind."

Headshake. "It's called *akutaq*. Do you like it?"

"I wouldn't say like. But I wouldn't say hate, either." I take one more bite and push the rest of it away. That's more than enough sugar for me. "Okay, I tried it. Now, what's in it?"

"Whipped fat and berries."

He can't be serious. "Like, animal fat?"

"Yeah. And berries."

"But it's *fat*."

"And berries," he repeats, smiling, clearly enjoying my display of culture shock.

"The berries are only there to make it taste good. *Because it's fat*." How is this a real thing people pay to eat? How does he not understand this is gross? "It's flavored. Fat."

"And it's good." He scrapes the last of his out of the dish. "Even you said it wasn't bad."

"That's not the point!"

Hunter's laughter comes out in spurts, like he's trying to hold it in and concentrate on more important bodily functions, like chewing and swallowing and not spewing his *akutaq* all over the table. Although it probably wouldn't look much different in vomit form.

Vicki returns with my lemon wedge.

"Here's your check," she says, and slides a scrap of paper onto the table between us. "Not trying to rush you out of here or nothing, but you said you're in a hurry. And if you've got anyplace far you're going, you'd better get moving before the snow gets any worse."

I pop a glance out the windows on the far end of the dining room. The snow's falling heavier now than it was when we first arrived, almost a half hour ago. For a moment I just stare at it, mesmerized. It's the first time I've seen actual snow showering down from the actual sky—not just tiny random specks of white lazily fluttering on a breeze—and it looks just like the fake stuff from snowmakers on movie sets. But it's real.

Real and *really* beautiful.

Hunter turns in his seat, follows my gaze, but when he turns to face me again, he isn't smiling in awe like I am.

Real, check. Really beautiful, check. Very real problem, triple check.

Kai's out there alone, exposed. We need to find him—now—and get back home as quickly as possible.

"Of course," Vicki goes on, "you're welcome to stay the night if you need to. We have plenty of vacancies right now, but once we get close to sunset, especially with the snowstorm, those rooms will fill up fast."

"Thanks, we'll keep that in mind," Hunter says, reaching for the check. "We might be back later if it gets too bad on the way home." Satisfied, Vicki leaves us to fight over who's paying.

I pull out the credit card my mom set up for me before we left California. No matter how much I use it, she makes sure there is always a zero balance and no limit. "I can pay for this.

And anything else we need while we're out. Gas for the car, food . . ." My gaze travels to the window again. I hope we won't need to spend tonight anywhere but home. But like Hunter said, there *is* a chance. "Lodging," I finish.

"Fine," Hunter concedes, sliding the slip of paper across the table toward me. He shoves his wallet into his back pocket. "I'll save my cash for an emergency. But when this trip is done, I'll pay back half of whatever the total comes to. Just because you have enough to cover it yourself doesn't mean you *have* to. We're in this thing together. We should split it equally."

I consent with a nod. It's more than Kai would have agreed to, allowing me to cover half, let alone cover all of it up front. Wherever Kai got his view on earning money and taking handouts, Hunter either wasn't there with him or simply doesn't agree. My bet's on the latter. So many other things about them have already proven to be different, sometimes so different they are complete opposites. I have to keep reminding myself they had the same parents and grew up in the same house.

We abandon our plates, then head to the front counter near the bar. Vicki meets us at the register. She's been running all the tables by herself, and they've become fuller and busier in the last twenty minutes, and now she's ringing us out, too. I scribble a larger-than-required tip onto my receipt. Not just because I feel for her plight—being dragged out here by her parents, with likely no say in the situation, only to have them split—but because she relies on tips for a means to live, to help her mom, like she said. So I'm giving her something she can actually rely on.

I do feel sympathetic toward her, though. I didn't have a say in moving to Alaska, either, but at least I'm not stuck here for-ever, held hostage by other people's generous or not-so-generous natures and their ability or inability to calculate a percentage. I double-check my math and hand her the receipt, then turn away just as her eyes expectedly widen in disbelief. She doesn't argue it, though, or claim I unknowingly wrote the wrong number. She just says, "Thank you, Gabi," and for a moment I'm the one a bit shocked. Maybe everything about me really does scream money like Hunter said.

I'm two steps farther from the counter and closer to the door when I realize he isn't moving. He's staring at the wall. It's covered with a bunch of old Polaroid photographs, each of them labeled in Sharpie with a date. Some of them also include a quote left by the person in the photo, ranging from silly to inspirational to sarcastic. The ones he's looking at are several years old, but the backgrounds on all of them are the same. They were all taken here, in this restaurant.

"Are you and Kai up there?" I say.

"Yeah." He points to one in the middle, surrounded by so many others with similar coloring, shading, and slightly blurred faces that I would have never picked it out. But there they are, the Locklear twins and their dad standing between them, with the same facial features as they have now but childlike.

Pudgier cheeks. Innocent smiles. Softer eyes. All three of them hold their hands above their foreheads, fingers curled like antlers. They're happy, and once again I'm struck with remorse for assuming they had a deadbeat dad.

"That was another life." Hunter shakes his head, then flips up the hood of his coat. "Let's go find him."

I pull my own hood up, and something on the wall of pictures catches my eye, near the bottom, where the more recent photos have been posted. At first I thought the date was wrong, because who still uses a Polaroid these days, when everyone has a camera on their phone? But there are several from this year, and one of them is another person with their hands above their forehead—the only other person on this wall like that. My brain recognizes that it can't be a coincidence before I've even understood why I leaned in to get a closer look.

And my brain is right. It's Kai. I'd know those eyes anywhere. Below his face, along with a date, Kai's hurried scrawl reads:

The world is too big to ignore how loudly it sings to me.

"Hunter, wait!" I tear the Polaroid off the wall, and the pushpin that was securing it goes flying over my shoulder. Hunter turns away from the exit. I wave the photo in his face, and the usual furrow in his brow deepens to a trench. "Kai *was* here. Just yesterday."

CHAPTER SEVEN

Hunter grabs the photo and whirls on Vicki. "Did you see this guy yesterday? He's my brother. Did you talk to him?"

Vicki nods, and her eyes shift between us a few times. "He didn't stay long, but yeah. I took that picture last night. And no, you can't have it." She fishes a new pushpin out of a drawer beneath the counter and then snatches the photo out of Hunter's hand.

"Last night—" My hand flies to my chest. "Then he can't be too far from here. Can he?" I look to Hunter for an answer, but his eyes are glued on Vicki.

"What else did he say?" Hunter presses. "Tell me *everything* you remember. We're trying to find him."

Vicki stammers for a moment. Her cheery charm has fled, and with good reason. Hunter has gone into full interrogation mode. Instead of answering right away, though, Vicki attaches the photo back to the wall.

"This is really important," Hunter says, his voice so low the words almost sound like a growl instead of a sentence. For someone as levelheaded as he is, the boy can snap in a heartbeat. All it takes is the right trigger, and apparently his twin brother is it. "Kai's headed to the wild outside Fairbanks," he says to Vicki. "You know, where you said people die. If we don't stop him, Kai might die, too. He left home a few days ago, so he might not even know there's a bad storm this close, and if he's not prepared for it, then he'll definitely die."

Every time he says the word *die*, Vicki pinches her sweetheart lips, like she's holding back from an instinctual rain of indignation in response to his veiled accusation. "I didn't know he was in danger. He didn't say what he was doing. We get a lot of people coming and going through here, all ages, all types. He wasn't no different." She pauses in thought. "Except that he seemed really happy," she adds. "Almost too happy. Excitable. Too much energy for someone who was traveling all day. He just stopped by to use the facilities. He didn't eat or drink. Said he'd been here before and liked it, so it wasn't nothing personal, he just didn't have time to spare. Then when he saw the pictures, he asked if I'd take his. I'm not supposed to do that if a customer doesn't buy anything, but he was nice. I liked him."

"I like him, too," I say. "He's my boyfriend."

"Aren't you with this guy?" Vicki jacks a thumb at Hunter.

"Not *with* him, with him—"

"Vicki!" the bartender shouts. "You've got other customers!"

Hunter's shoulders drop on a sigh, and his next words sound more like his usual self. "I know you have to go, but is there anything else he did or said that you think might help us find him quickly? We're trying to get to him before the storm does."

"He didn't say where he was going, but he did say he'd been walking all day. It was just before the dinner rush when he stopped in, but he didn't seem too tired. I offered him a room and he said 'I'm gonna keep going until the sun stops me.' My older brother, Johnny, is like that. He gets so excitable sometimes, disappears for weeks, and we don't know where he's been until he comes back. He always comes back, though, so we stopped fussing over it, and then he sleeps and sleeps for days. Mama thinks he has a chemical imbalance, like bipolar, but Johnny refuses to go to a doctor, says he doesn't want people messing with his brain." She cocks her head. "Is Kai bipolar? Is he off on a manic adventure? He was in and outta here like the wind, Mama would say."

"He just likes the outdoors." My outer calm remains intact, even though my heart is kickboxing my ribs. What if Kai does have some kind of imbalance? I haven't known him long enough to see him cycle through ups and downs. What if these past three months have just been a high for him? All that energy that drew me to him—what if it's about to peak before he dives? What if he believes he's Superman, invincible, and jumps off the edge of a cliff? Or challenges a bear to a duel? Or—

"Vicki!" someone yells from the kitchen. "Orders're up! Before they get cold, will ya?"

"Thanks for your help," Hunter says. He doesn't seem fazed by Vicki's impromptu psych evaluation of Kai, but he's so hard for me to read sometimes, that's no comfort.

"Sure, um . . ." She reaches into the half apron tied at her waist, pulls out a business card, and hands it to Hunter. "That's our number. I'm here every day of the week if, you know, if you need help with anything, or . . . to just let me know you found him?" Her top teeth catch her bottom lip, and she starts to edge away, toward the kitchen. "Nice meeting y'all. Be safe out there. Oh, and don't forget to like our Facebook page!"

Outside, a short, stout woman is hunched over, shoveling a walkway from the door to the parking lot. The snow has already accumulated an inch or so. Not enough to keep us from driving, Hunter says, but more than I've ever seen on the road or on a sidewalk or anywhere. From inside it looked beautiful, but now tendrils of worry creep around my middle, clinging to my ribs like sticky vines. We step around the woman shoveling, and she says, "Come again soon!" in a tone so cheerily similar to Vicki's that it could be her mom.

As I climb into the Outback, Hunter starts the engine. "Do you have GPS on your phone?" he says.

"Yeah." I turn up the heat to full blast. "Why?"

"I want to see if I can find a quicker route to get us close to the next shelter. It's more than twenty miles from here. Kai couldn't have gotten that far from here just since last night, assuming he's being smart and not traveling in the dark. If we take a shortcut, maybe we can get there first, stop him in his tracks instead of chasing him. He's already gone too far."

Fifteen minutes later, the drive has already become monotonous. Snow builds quickly on the road, slowing us down. I keep my focus outside, through my side window, hoping to catch a glimpse of someone hiking across the open plains or through the random sections of trees. But so far, no one.

I lean back and sigh, the thickening white blanket around us suddenly too bright and painful to look at anymore. Vicki's question pounds against my skull. *Is Kai bipolar?*

Of course I've heard of bipolar, enough to know it includes both highs and lows, but I wouldn't know what kind of everyday signs to look for, especially in someone I only just met. My dad has depression, my mother has a diva complex, and one of my exes was a pathological liar. That's the extent of my hands-on knowledge of mental illness.

"You okay?" Hunter says. "How's your head?"

"It isn't *my* head I'm worried about."

He grunts softly through his nose. "This is why you're good for him, you know? You're not like other girls he's dated." He eases off the gas pedal as we go around a curve in the road.

"You're perceptive, Gabi, and you're direct. He needs someone like that. He needs *you*."

"Even though I'm the one who let him slip away?" I counter. "How perceptive am I really, if I didn't figure out that his good-bye meant good-bye? That this necklace wasn't just a gift but a symbol of his absence?"

"I said you're perceptive, not psychic. Not a mind reader. Don't blame yourself for his lack of explanation."

Easier said than done. "Well, you know him better than anyone, I won't argue with that. So tell me—do you think he has . . . something? Like Vicki said about her brother?"

"I'm not studying psychiatry, so this isn't based on anything except the fact that I've lived with him since before we were born—but no. I don't think he has a chemical imbalance. Not like that, anyway. Is he mentally imbalanced lately, though? Yes."

I suck in a breath, and Hunter rushes to explain.

"He and Dad were really close, closer than any of us, except Dad and Mom. And when Dad died . . . the way it happened . . . we never got to see him—I mean his body—so the whole thing was hard to believe. We were told what happened and that there was no chance he survived, and we understood it, the reasons were logical, but it took a while for all of us to accept that he was never coming home, so it didn't strike me as odd that Kai didn't cry at the funeral. Other people were crying and *he* was comforting *them*. Helping Mom became our top priority, and it didn't really hit us until long after condolences stopped coming. It hit me, anyway. Then I was so overwhelmed by my own grief that I didn't realize Kai still hadn't changed his behavior six months after the fact. It was an especially harsh winter, but it wasn't until spring that Kai started . . . reacting to Dad's absence. Like, I don't know, maybe he thought Dad hadn't come back because the bad weather prevented him, and when the weather turned, he realized the truth. He sank into a depression, but I thought he was finally dealing with it, so I let him be.

"But then he got so low it worried me all over again. He kept taking care of everyone, every day, but he stopped taking care of himself. He wouldn't shower or change his clothes for days. He stopped going out with his friends. He almost didn't pass junior year."

My chest constricts and the back of my eyes sting, picturing Kai in that state . . .

Snowflakes come down harder, and the already gray sky has darkened. Hunter flicks on his headlights and turns the windshield wipers up a notch. "I tried talking to Mom about it," he continues, "but she said Kai just needed more time to process. That everyone grieves in their own way and on their own schedule. It wasn't long after that when you moved in next door, and . . ."

I swallow hard, silently willing him to finish. The five on the far right of the car's digital clock flips to six before my patience runs out. "Was that a good thing?" My voice has the strength of a mouse.

Hunter lets out a breathy laugh. "It was a very good thing. He became himself again. Kai's crazy about you—but he isn't *crazy*."

I want to believe that's true.

"Don't take this the wrong way," Hunter says, "but your moving here was a relief to me. With you keeping him occupied and happy again, Kai was one less person I had to worry about. What happened to Dad really messed him up. They were close," he repeats.

I'd thought *we* were close, too. "Then why didn't he ever tell me about him?"

"I don't know." Hunter's jaw tightens. "Are you sure you want to find out?"

"Yes." The truth can't be any worse than the frustration of wondering.

Know that I'm thinking of you, Kai said when he gave me the rock necklace, *and how I feel whenever I'm with you.*

I'm thinking of him, too, but all the good I felt when we were together, all the warmth in our connection, is chilled with uncertainty now.

A yawn stretches my mouth, throat, lips, and lungs so wide I let out a squeak. Exhaustion and a full belly are working hard to shut me down. The snow is practically impossible to see through, but Hunter doesn't show any indication he thinks we should stop driving.

"You can sleep now, if you need to," he says. "You're out of the woods."

Out of the woods . . . As I lose the fight to stay awake, I see an image in my head of Kai in the woods, snowdrifts building around his stiff, frozen corpse.

Hunter shakes me awake what feels like only seconds later, but the clock tells me I just lost over an hour of my life to dreamless sleep. "We have a problem," he says.

"What?" I bolt upright and rub my eyes. There's nothing but white. Everywhere. Despite the chilling view around us, the inside of the car is musky and warm. I cling to that comfort like a child would its mother. "Where are we?"

"That's the problem," Hunter says. "I think I missed a turn somewhere. I have to stay focused on driving, though. Can you check the GPS? Your phone is dark. I think it went into sleep mode with you." He huffs a laugh, but it sounds forced, like he's trying to keep me from worrying, and there's a tense underlying edge to his voice.

I pick up my phone and swipe the unlock pattern across the screen. Nothing happens. I try holding in the power button. Still nothing.

Which means the battery's dead.

Which means no GPS.

Which means, if Hunter doesn't know where we are, then I definitely don't know where we are, and we're officially lost.

"So where are we?" he says.

"Somewhere in outer space." I hold up my phone, its solid black face toward him. "The battery died."

"No."

"Yes."

"How?"

"It wasn't fully charged before we left, but I thought it had enough juice to get through a day, so I didn't bring the charger. I don't use the GPS that much, though." More like never, because that would mean I'm going somewhere I've never been, without someone to accompany me, and that would require more adventurous spirit than I possess. "It uses up more battery life."

We pass some dilapidated barbed-wire fencing that encloses a snowy pasture with tracks crisscrossing over it. A small herd of cattle mill about inside, literally the only living things in sight besides trees. We have officially entered The Middle of Nowhere, Alaska.

In a last-ditch effort to salvage control of the situation, I scramble toward the backseat and find the map of Alaska that Hunter showed me last night. But it doesn't tell me which mountain that is ahead of us or which mountain that is behind us, or where that . . . scary dirt road leads to . . . Not going there.

"We need a more detailed road map," I say. "This one only shows the major cities and major highways. Of which there are, like, maybe two in the whole state?"

"Okay." He sucks in a deep breath and lets it out slowly. Steadily. "I'll just keep driving until we pass a house or a lodge or something, and we can ask for directions." He flashes a smile at me, but it's shaky. "We'll be fine. Everything will be fine."

Nothing about this is fine, including my lack of patience for it. Hunter's outward calm is unfortunately not contagious. I let loose a string of expletives, some of them English and some of them Spanish. The acidic tone of my voice sounds like Mom, which makes me want to cuss even more. For most of my life I wanted to be just like her, and now I'm afraid that I'm becoming just like her.

Eventually we do find a lodge, but we also find we've made zero progress.

Hunter unbuckles his seat belt. "Are you *kidding* me?"

"At least we know where we are now." Which pales as a bright side to the situation.

I hop down out of the Outback and we walk to the entrance of the same place we left two hours ago. The Grinning Bear. We were so turned around, we did a complete circle, probably more than once. And it's too dangerous to head back out, even if we did have the GPS. Visibility is nil.

Blustering flurries rage on with a vengeance, swirling miniature tornadoes, and when we enter the building, our hair is more white than black. My eyelashes tickle as flakes melt on them. We stomp snow off our boots, marching in place.

"Well, hi there!" a girl with a familiar twang says.

Hunter snaps his head up and stops brushing his arms. "Vicki. Hey. You're still here. That's . . . that's great. This whole day is just *great*."

Her cheeky grin drips innocence. "What's the matter, did y'all forget something?"

CHAPTER EIGHT

Vicki swings open the room door and hands me a brass key hooked to a ring with a dead rabbit's foot. The number 211 has been shaved into it. "Stay as long you need to. This room ain't accounted for."

"Thanks, but we don't plan on staying." I drop the rabbit's foot key on the nightstand and plug my cell phone into the charger she's letting me borrow. "This shouldn't take more than an hour to recharge." An hour of us going nowhere while Kai moves farther and farther away. A lot of good having a car did us.

Hunter kicks off his boots, sheds his coat, and turns on the TV. The news has taken over regular programming to report on the blizzard. It's already a whiteout outside, but according to the radar, the worst is coming overnight. "Look," Hunter says, pointing between blobs of blue on the screen. "There's a break here. If we leave as soon as it lightens up, we might be able to catch up to him before the next wave hits—the bigger one—and bring him back here for the night."

"Not if the roads aren't plowed," Vicki says. "With how fast it's coming down, they won't be able to keep up. Y'all might as well just stay until morning when it's been cleared."

"We can't. Kai's alone out there." I sit on the queen-sized bed. There's an openmouthed bear's head on the wall above it—hello, nightmares. "What if he gets stuck somewhere, exposed, or gets lost like we did? We can't just leave him to freeze to death overnight."

"Vicki has a point, though," Hunter says. "Driving's out, and walking won't make us any faster than he is." Headshake. "We need a snowmachine."

"Snowmachine? Doesn't that *make* snow?"

"Not from around here, are you?" Vicki says through a grin, using my earlier words to her against me.

So I mimic her earlier response. "No, I'm a California transplant."

Vicki's eyes light up, but before she can riddle me with questions, Hunter explains. "A snowmachine is like a car for the snow, with skis on the bottom, so you can ride on top of the snow instead of trying to muscle through it."

"They call them snowmobiles in West Virginia," Vicki chimes in. She fluffs a pillow, a bit too obviously trying to find reasons to stay here and chat. "Some people around here call them snowmachines. I never heard that term before we moved to Alaska, either."

She's still talking when I step to the window and pull back a curtain. Everything is covered. Rooftops, roads, vehicles, trees. Like God took a paintbrush and whitewashed the world. Someone heavily bundled up treks across the road to the general store on the other side, marring the landscape's purity—and somehow not sinking too far with each step. Snowshoes?

If that person is prepared enough to have snowshoes on hand, then maybe—

"Vicki," I say, turning, at the same time that Hunter asks her, "Don't you have to get back to work?"

"Naw, I'm off the rest of the day." She goes to the bathroom but leaves the door open. I think she's checking supplies. Shower curtain rings rattle against a metal rod.

"Vicki, I—"

"Then shouldn't you be getting home?" Hunter raises his voice so she'll hear him. "Or are you stuck here, too?"

"Not stuck here," she says, entering the main room. Seeing nothing else to address, she flops down on the bed. "I live here, in an apartment with my mama. She and Daddy used to run this place together, before they split." Vicki looks down for a moment and her mouth twists. I want to tell her I get it, and that it's a relief to meet someone who gets it, but we don't have time for my issues right now.

"Vicki," I repeat instead, taking advantage of her silence. "Do you have a snowmobile we can borrow? I can pay you for it."

"I'm sure you can," she says. "But we need them here. And besides, you would need two, not just one. They each only hold two people. Once you pick up Kai, you'll have three people."

"Well . . ." Crap. "Is there somewhere we can rent them?"

"Yeah, across town." Vicki's expression dims. "How bad were the roads when you came in?"

"We barely made it back here; we're not going out again until it lightens up," Hunter says. "But even if we could get there, Gabi, you don't know how to drive a snowmachine, and we need two. So we need two *drivers* until we get to Kai." He turns his face toward Vicki, pleading with his eyes. And his mouth. "If we got back here by tonight, could we . . . ? Could you . . . come with us?"

"I—I don't know," she says. "I want to help y'all, but I'll have to ask Mama. Taking two would leave her with nothing. On a day like this . . ." She worries her lip. "I don't know."

I hate to pull the "I'm filthy rich" card, but: "All I can offer her in return is money. My credit card info is already in your system. Tell her she can charge whatever she wants, whatever she thinks is fair."

Vicki nods. "Okay, I'll ask her as soon as she's done with housekeeping. Shouldn't be more than a half hour or so, and you can't go anywhere before then anyway."

"Thank you." I squeeze her into a hug. "You're the best." I

can't help but gloat a little over this small victory, silently taunting what's on the other side of the window. Alaska tried to scare me off with a storm, and lost.

"I'm going to be in debt to you forever," Hunter says, shoulders slumping.

"This is nothing compared to the debt you're going to rack up in college."

"Thanks for the reality check."

"Anytime." I settle onto the bed and cocoon myself inside the plaid comforter. "What do you want to do now?" I'd rather not just sit here and watch the weather, waiting for it to get better before it gets worse, wondering if Kai is okay when there's nothing I can do about it. "Vicki, do you have any games we could play? Cards? Anything?"

"No," she says, "but I have movies! Just got a new one the other day that I haven't watched yet. *Man of Mercury.*"

Something catches in my throat, and I let out a small, choked sound, but neither of them seems to notice.

Vicki goes on, "At first I thought it was a sci-fi movie, but it's actually a chick flick. Do you mind chick flicks, Hunter? You don't seem like the kind of guy who would mind romantic stuff."

He ignores the question. "Is that the one with Tom Morgan and . . . What's her name? Mary something?"

"Marietta Cruz," Vicki fills in for him. "That woman is one hot mama, let me tell you. If my rack looks half as good as hers by the time I'm her age, I'll count myself lucky."

Hunter refuses to reply to her comment or make eye contact, going as far as looking around at every rack in the room—every set of antlers, real or fake, even the coatrack—except Vicki's.

I throw the blanket off me, suddenly hot. "I didn't realize that movie was out on DVD already."

"New release this month," Vicki says. "I heard it was good. Have you seen it?"

"Yeah, I . . ." Was *in* it, a bit part in one scene. And so was my mom, as the lead, aka the hot mama with an amazing rack. There's a sex scene in it, too, with the guy she left my dad for— the guy she chose over our family. The reason she sent us as far away as possible without leaving the country or crossing the ocean. I'd sooner jump in a frozen lake naked than watch this movie, and I've recently concluded that is *never* happening. "I saw it at the theater." At its LA premiere, to be exact. "It's cliché, and boring, and the acting is painful to watch. Marietta's worst role yet. I used to be a fan, but now I'm just kind of embarrassed for her."

None of those is a lie. The movie *was* her worst yet, and I *am* kind of embarrassed for her subpar performance in it, but that might have had something to do with her personal life being utter chaos while she was filming. What should have been one of the best times of my life—my first speaking role in a major motion picture, even if it was just as a waitress taking the heroine's order and refilling her mug—turned into an experience I just want to forget. Seeing Mom and the guy who she was cheating with on Dad giving each other lovey-dovey eyes over coffee made me regret ever auditioning for the role in the first place.

It also made me stumble over my lines. Repeatedly. And every screw-up took us "back to one"—the director's cue for everyone to go back to their first mark and start the scene over.

"Sorry, oh—Crap."

"Back to one."

"Chai latte with a dimple—I mean a dollop—"

"Gabriella, *focus*—"

"Back to one."

"Oops—"

"Ow!"

"Back to one."

Back to one ... Back to one ... Back to one ... Until everyone moved in sync and every word came out flawless, every syllable of inflection perfectly intoned. Sometimes I wish I could go "back to one" in my life. The truth is I'm not a very good actress. Performing doesn't come naturally for me—it isn't rooted in my heart like it is in Mom's—but I kept trying to make it work because it was the only connection she and I ever had. Now I wish I had severed that connection a long time ago.

I'm not naïve. I knew what she was doing with Tom even before Dad told me about the divorce. He didn't tell me why; he knew he didn't have to. And I didn't expect Mom to sugarcoat things for me. I just wanted her to talk to me about it, come clean, admit what I already knew. I *wanted* her to be honest. I wanted her to say to me, just once, "I'm sorry. I messed up. I'm only human." I understand human imperfection—I don't understand my mother. She didn't say any of those things. She didn't even act like anything had changed.

So, before I got on the plane, I had to let her know how wrong she was, how much she changed *everything*, and once the flood started, I couldn't stop it. Dad had to pull me through security while I was still screaming at her. People were staring and shaking their heads. They probably thought I was a bratty teenager throwing a tantrum. If Mom hadn't been completely incognito that day, though, we would have made headlines, and people would have understood why I was so upset. Her image took a huge hit after the scandal went public. People never side with the cheater.

Vicki looks to Hunter for a dissenting vote, but he only shrugs. Of course he does. "I'm not really in the mood for a movie, but there's nothing else to do here."

"If you're bored," Vicki says, "you can go downstairs and play darts by the bar. Half-price drinks and appetizers if you score a perfect game!"

"I'm not old enough to drink," he reminds her.

"But you're old enough to eat," she counters.

"This is true." He tugs on his boots without lacing them. "I'll be back in an hour."

"Hunter, we just had lunch," I say.

"That was closer to a brunch, and it was two hours ago. Aren't you hungry?"

"No."

"You sure you don't want anything?" The corners of his mouth twitch. "Not even *akutaq*?"

"Funny." I level my gaze at him, silently daring him to take another jab.

He releases the laugh he was holding back and then heads out. I guess I need to work on my death stare.

"See ya!" Vicki chirps as he closes the door behind him, leaving us alone.

To do what, I don't know. Talk?

"He's kind of an enigma, isn't he?" Vicki says, then quickly changes topics. "So, what brought you to Alaska?"

Talking it is, then. "My parents."

"Your daddy a mountain man, too?"

"No." I stifle a laugh, imagining Dad with a scraggly beard, wearing flannel, or doing *anything* outdoorsy. "He's a lawyer. But my parents got divorced and . . ." I pause, choosing my words carefully so they aren't lies but also don't reveal all the details. "He wanted to start a new life. I did, too. So I came with him, left my mom in California, and . . . Where better to start over than Alaska?"

Vicki swallows. Says nothing.

I have to fill this awkward silence. "Sometimes I think I'm being childish for hating it as much as I do. I mean hating that they split, not hating Alaska. It was obviously the right choice for them. They were so miserable . . . they fought all the time . . . for years. Why should I want them to stay together and be miserable?"

That's the first time I've given voice to those feelings, and I'm simultaneously anxious to hear her validate them and scared she'll judge me. Like the odd mix of fear and excitement you feel going up the first hill of a roller coaster—the kind that sometimes results in puking on your own face.

"I was twelve when my dad left." Her voice has lost all its bubbly, girlish charm, and she suddenly sounds and looks much older to me. "I can't believe it's been six years already. Because it still hurts now like it did then. If anyone is being childish, it's me, stuck in the past, hung up on feelings that should have faded a long time ago."

The relief I hoped for dashes out of reach. "So it doesn't get any better with time?"

"Maybe it will for you," she says. "You said your parents were miserable together. Mine weren't. They were happy, I know they were. Their divorce blindsided me and my brothers. I don't think they wanted to separate. I think they each thought they were doing the other a favor by letting them go. Daddy had a dream that Mama didn't share. She let him go so he would be happy, and he left her behind so she would be happy. But they aren't as happy now, apart, as they were when they were together. And I don't know why they can't see that. I don't know why they can't . . ."

"Find a way to make it work?"

"Yeah." Her voice goes soft and delicate, fragile, and we decide it's enough talk of things that can't be fixed. I wish I could say she's right about my situation, that my knowing they were miserable together is justification enough to realize their divorce was a good thing. But the problem is they're still miserable. Or at least Dad is. Leaving each other didn't resolve anything.

I don't think their getting back together is the answer, though—that wouldn't help anything now. I think they should have never let it go this far. They were happy once, a long time ago. They shouldn't have forgotten that. They should have tried harder to *stay* together in the first place.

Hunter has returned to our room, my phone is charged, and the snow is starting to let up, but the roads are a mess. There's clearly no way we're driving a car. It's a snowmobile or nothing. All we're waiting for is word from Vicki on whether her mom will agree to our deal. I'm antsy, ready to get moving.

"Maybe you should call your dad," Hunter says. "You might not get another chance for a while. I was able to get a hold of my mom with the landline to let her know we're spending the night somewhere so she doesn't worry."

"I tried while you were downstairs. Several times. He's not answering. Since the divorce, it's been really hard to get through to him, you know? Even when I'm talking to his face."

Hunter nods. "I felt the same way with my dad. For a long time. Then I stopped trying to get him to pay attention to me—the real me, not the me he wanted to see. And now I . . . wish I hadn't. If he were still around, I'd keep trying." Swallow. Grimace. "Keep trying, Gabi. Just keep trying."

CHAPTER NINE

The money worked. Because it usually does.

We leave for the shelter around three p.m., which only gives us about three hours until sunset. Hunter isn't sure if that will be enough time to find Kai and get back to the lodge—especially since we're going off-road now, so we have to rely on a trail map Vicki provided that shows the location of the shelters in this area—but there's a *chance* it might be enough time, and staying put gives us a 100 percent chance of *not* finding him. So here I am, taking my first ride on a snowmobile.

I can't really enjoy it, though. Completely encased in my heavy coat and a pair of snowpants I borrowed from Vicki, somehow I'm both sweating and freezing. Wearing this helmet, my head is a watermelon, heavy and oversized, and I don't have any peripheral vision. Plus Hunter's back is blocking everything ahead of me. Turning my head to watch the trees zoom by on either side of us just makes me dizzy, so I rest my clunky head between Hunter's broad shoulders and close my eyes. Every bump and turn catches me off guard. I thought I had developed excellent balance from surfing, but if I didn't have a death grip on Hunter I'd have been eating snow a mile ago. The vehicle's movements are rough and jostling. There's no fluidity, no easing into a natural rhythm like I do with waves.

But the good thing about not being able to follow the roads anymore is that we don't have to follow the roads anymore. The trail, marked by small signs, takes us where cars and trucks can't go. We'll get to Kai faster this way. No traffic. No stoplights. No speed limit. No rules.

"You doing okay?" Hunter shouts over his shoulder. The words come out muffled from behind his helmet, but his tone makes the meaning clear enough. I stretch my arm forward to give him a thumbs-up and he guns it. I cinch my arms around him tighter. My belly flips with excitement. The landscape has opened up, there aren't quite as many trees, and the behemoth mountains remain a comfortably safe distance away on the western and eastern horizons. I dare a peek around Hunter's shoulder, pushing up onto the balls of my feet to get a better view. An unending field of sparkling white lies ahead of us, inviting us to spread our wings and fly. There's no one around to tell us what to do, what to say or think or feel. The frozen tip of the earth is our playground.

Maybe Alaska wasn't trying to scare me away after all.

Maybe this is Alaska's gift to me. Freedom. The pressures weighing me down don't exist out here. I'm not the broken child of divorced parents, or the lost girlfriend of a lost boy, or an aspiring actress who can't act her way out of a paper bag. I'm just a girl with the whole world at her feet, trying to decide where to make her first mark. It can be anywhere. I can be anything.

We speed along for an hour before Hunter slows us down. Ahead, Vicki comes to a stop by a wooden structure that's little more than a shed. *Please let this be as far as we have to go.* I pull off my helmet, gasp at the cold rush of air against my sweltering skin. "Is this it?" My heartbeat quickens with hope. "Is he here?"

"This is it," Vicki says. "My brothers and I stop by here all the time when we go hunting. Not sure if Kai's here, though."

Hunter parks, removes his helmet, and steps off the snowmobile. The temperature gauge on the control panel reads twenty-nine degrees. "No tracks in or out. If there were any before, the snow covered them."

Without Hunter's warm body right up against me, the cold quickly seizes me. The insides of my nostrils are freezing over, and breathing through my mouth makes my teeth ache.

My dismount isn't as graceful as Hunter's was, my legs stiff, protesting every movement.

Vicki does a 180, eyes still cast on the ground. The

snow isn't quite as deep here as it was at the lodge, but it's still cumbersome to walk through. Her gaze drifts upward and out, toward the way we came from. "Let's check inside," she says. "Kai might be in there if he was waiting out the storm."

"Only one way to find out," Hunter says. He wrestles with the door for a minute and then it pops open with a *crack!* Vicki and I hustle in behind him.

But Kai isn't here.

Why did I think it would be that easy? The previous hope in my chest shifts into worry, keeping my heartbeat quick. If he's not here, then where is he?

The shelter's interior is furnished with a single bed. No sheets or pillows, but a couple of blankets are folded on top. A small hearth connected to a chimney sits opposite the bed, filled with ashes. It isn't warm enough in here for there to have been a fire recently. If Kai was here at all, he didn't cook anything. I'm not sure if that's a good thing or bad. Hunter said Kai would have packed some food for emergencies. I just hope he has enough.

Hunter analyzes everything in the room, turning slowly. Then he gets up close to the wall right next to the hearth. With the tip of his pocketknife he works something out from between the wood slats. A note?

I step up beside him as he unfolds and then silently reads the paper. He hands it to me.

I recognize Kai's handwriting—today's date and a new message:

Everyone you meet in life is either a blessing or a lesson.

"What does this mean?" I ask Hunter. "And the one he wrote on his picture?" *The world is too big to ignore how loudly it sings to me.* "Am I missing something? Are they connected?"

"Not really," he says. "Except that they're both things our dad used to say."

I flip the paper over, but nothing is written on the back. No names listed as either a blessing or a lesson, no explanation. I refold the paper and consider tossing it into the cold ashes but jam it back into its hiding place instead. "There's nothing else to see here."

Vicki heads for the door, but Hunter turns away from us, focusing on the wall. He touches it gently, reverently, then pulls out his pocketknife again and etches something into the wood slat. Stepping closer, I see two sets of initials beside the glint of his blade. The *ML* has been there a while, darkened and worn with age, but the *KL* is clean and sharp, bright wood pulp freshly exposed. He adds *HL* to the group, for Hunter Locklear. No matter what happens after this—today, tomorrow, whenever, wherever—he, his twin, and their dad will always be together.

We continue on in the direction of the next shelter, which is thankfully not as far from here as the first one was from the lodge. We might still be able to beat the sunset, only two hours away now. Kai's note had today's date on it, but his tracks have been covered with new snow. He must have left that shelter before the storm got bad, but he can only go so fast by foot, even at an energetic pace, so he can't be much farther. It's possible he was caught between shelters during the blizzard's first wave, like we'd originally feared. It's also possible he made it to the next shelter. We won't know until we find more evidence of . . . anything.

Finding him and making sure he's okay is my first concern. But if we find him and he's okay, plenty of other concerns are waiting in line to be given voice. *Why didn't you just talk to me?* We never had a problem talking before. Is it too much to ask to have a boyfriend who explains himself clearly before he leaves on a long, dangerous trip like this? But I can't change the past, and I can't control what Kai does or doesn't do, or what he says or doesn't say. I'm not sure what I'm going to say, either. I've considered every reaction I might have, and I decide on doing nothing. I want to see what he does first, want to hear his reasoning for taking off like he did, want to see what he thinks of me coming after him, and I'd rather he not be swayed by my words one way or the other.

Too soon, the snowmobiles stop again, leaving my body buzzing. Vicki and Hunter remove their helmets.

I take off my helmet, too, and gulp in a few crystal breaths of fresh air. Looking around, I notice two things right away. One, the sky is getting dark again, both from thickening cloud cover and the sun getting lower. It's not even dinnertime yet. When I first moved here, in July, daylight stretched into the night hours. The Alaskan sun is a tease.

And two, there are no shelters in sight. "Why did we stop?"

"I thought I saw something . . ." Vicki removes her fleece cap and fluffs out her hair, scratches her scalp. Bright red curls fly in the wind, then she secures them under her hat again. She heads toward a copse of trees, and Hunter follows. I hang back, waiting to hear what they find first. If Kai is there, I don't want to see him unless he's warm and breathing, eager to take me into his arms.

"Gabi, come here!" Vicki shouts. She sounds more excited than horrified, thank goodness.

I trot up to them. They're standing by a person-sized hole in the snow—but it's empty. A bunch of feathery evergreen branches lie around it. "What is that?"

Hunter says, "Someone was taking shelter from the snow . . . in the snow."

"How ironic."

"It's the next best thing when you don't have a building," he explains. "I remember my dad said he had to do that a few times. You dig a hole in the snow and it works like insulation with your body heat, keeps you warm. Then you cover the opening with branches. If this was Kai, at least we know he's being smart."

"But we *don't* know for sure this was Kai."

"There are some tracks we can follow now, though." Hunter gestures ahead of us. A single set of footprints leads off from the hole, heading the same direction we were going. "Whoever this was waited out the first wave of the storm and then left, probably thinking it's over now."

"And it isn't," Vicki says. "But if we follow these tracks, we don't know if we'll find the right person. And even if we do find Kai, will we have enough time to get back to the lodge before the next wave hits? Before it gets dark?"

"Maybe not, but what's the alternative?" I press. "I know you need to get back home, Vicki, and I really, *really* appreciate you helping us with this, but if we head back now, we have nothing, no answers, and we'll be leaving Kai to face the worst part of the storm tonight. We have to keep going."

"I know." She grins. "I just wanted to make sure *you* were sure."

"Okay, how about this? We follow the tracks, and when we get to the next shelter, we go no farther, whether we've got Kai with us or not. If by that point we can safely return to the lodge, then we will. If we can't, we stay at the shelter overnight and figure out what to do from there." A far cry from ideal, but it's better than getting caught in a blizzard in the dark. "Sound like a plan?"

"Yeah," Hunter says, and Vicki nods.

"All right." I turn back toward the snowmobiles. "Let's go, before it gets any later."

X • X • X

117

The tracks follow the marked trail, leading us to the next shelter, this one close to a wide, tumbling river. We slow to a stop. Gray water rushes past us at a ferocious speed, eager to get somewhere else. I don't blame it. I'd rather be anywhere but here—wherever "here" even is I don't know anymore, but the dark side of the moon is probably warmer than this. Mountain ridges monopolize the horizon now, and I assume we're near Denali National Park, somewhere close to the middle of the path marked on Kai's map that Hunter found yesterday. I thought I saw a snowplow on a road somewhere, but it was far in the distance.

Hunter goes to the shelter first. Vicki's right on his heels, and so am I—if Kai isn't here, either, I don't know what we'll do. Go home? Let him go? Get someone else to find him?

Then what?

As we near the shed, I see another set of footprints, coming in from a different direction, that mingles and blends with the first. One follows the riverbank while the other ventures into the trees.

Hunter pushes the door open and all three of us let out frustrated sighs. "Nothing extra's in here but firewood," he says. "So someone was here, but they're gone now."

I mutter a curse, try to think. The sky isn't dark yet but it will be soon, and flurries have started up again. "Two sets of tracks. Do we risk following the wrong ones, or just . . . what do we do?"

"I don't know." Hunter studies the ground again. "If either of these tracks is Kai's, it's possible he could be getting food, and will return to this shelter. He could be hunting in the woods or he could be downriver, fishing. I hope it's that. He needs to eat, and he's better at fishing than shooting—" He catches himself. "Don't tell Kai I said that. I was just thinking out loud. It's kind of a point of pride with him, to be able to hunt as well as Dad did."

Vicki steps into one of the footprints. Her boot fills half of it. She steps into the next one, and the next one, stretching her legs unnaturally wide for her gait in between each imprint. She's like a little girl playing dress-up with her mom's heeled shoes, off-balance but having too much fun to let that stop her. She plants both feet, legs spread wide, and turns her head to face us. "Does Kai walk like that?"

"Like a drunk?"

"Hang on," Hunter says. He watches Vicki as she hops over to the other set of tracks and repeats her previous action. The boot prints are nearly the same size, but this time her movements aren't quite so erratic. "Or like that?" she says.

"She's a genius." Hunter lets out a puff of laughter and quickly snuffs it out, but he's still smiling as he trots up to Vicki, then turns back to me. "Watch me, okay? Imagine I'm Kai."

"Have you both lost your minds?"

"Just watch," they say in unison.

Awesome, they're teaming up against me.

Hunter steps into the tracks the same as Vicki did, except not at all the same as Vicki did, because he has a naturally longer stride. It just looks like he's walking, his back toward me, along the bank of the raging river. It's not his walk, though. It's like I'm watching a stranger. How is this helping?

He hops to the other set of tracks and heads for a dense patch of trees behind the shelter. He shifts rhythm, but it's still not like his heavy, clomping gait. It's fluid and light-footed. Like Kai. If Hunter could be compared to a Clydesdale, then Kai would be a Thoroughbred.

Imagine I'm Kai . . . I see him now, walking off into the trees, ready to face his next adventure. He's in those woods somewhere.

"Hunter, that's it!" I run up to him. "Come on, he's right there. Let's go!"

But all trace of his prior enthusiasm has fled. He's back to his usual serious calm. "He most likely went out to hunt. We should wait for him to come back."

"What? Why? He can't be that far off." After we came all this way, he wants me to sit on my heels? What if Kai isn't going to come back to this shelter, and escapes us again? I tug Hunter's arm and he shrugs my hand off, like he's flinching from an insect.

"He's *shooting* at things, Gabi; we can't just walk in there. And those 'things' are wild animals, and that forest is their home, and they didn't invite us in. Bears, wolves, moose—"

"What's a moose gonna do?"

"Oh, moose can get nasty if they think you're a threat," Vicki chimes in, nodding. "Even nastier than that bump on your head."

"That was from the car, not the moose."

"Moose have killed people." She stiffens, suddenly defensive. Of a moose. "They're not as slow and stupid as they look."

Hunter ignores us both and heads for the snowmobiles, his decision final. "It's safer to stay here, under a roof. I'll get a fire going. Kai's smart; he'll be back. But if he doesn't show up, or if we're wrong and it wasn't him, we'll have to spend the night here." He looks up at the sky, then right at me. "We won't have enough time to get back to the lodge before dark, even if the snow holds off until late. It took us almost two hours to get here, so we're only a little more than an hour from sunset now."

"Okay, but he's right. *There.*"

Hunter ignores me and says, "Vicki, you got any water in these?"

She bounds toward him and opens the small back compartment of a snowmobile, then pulls out a bottle of water. It's frozen solid.

Just put it in my hand; my fury will melt it. "After all we've done and how far we've come, you're going to *sit* here—"

A crack of thunder ripples through the air. I flinch and look up, instinctively searching for rain clouds. But there aren't any. It's *snowing.*

"That was a gunshot." Hunter glares at the trees as if they'd fired the shot at *him.*

If that really was Kai and he's already killed something, then he should come back now. Vicki and I exchange a look of relief. This excursion might be over soon.

Then we hear a scream.

CHAPTER TEN

The voice slicing the air is definitely Kai's. It's almost exactly how he sounded when he swung on a rope over the lake, throaty and robust, full of life.

Or maybe begging for it.

Is he in danger? My gut twists into a mess of knots.

Hunter takes off like a rocket toward the trees. I didn't know he could move that fast.

"Wait!" I shout, but he keeps going. After he just argued all the reasons why we needed to stay out of there.

The forest isn't dense, but the trees are close enough together that I've already lost sight of him. The trunks are only half covered with snow, as if the snow came in sideways, creating a dizzying pattern of dark and white. Vicki trails him quickly like a wolf chasing prey, leaving me behind. Alone. Unsure whether I should go or stay. This is my time to be brave. Kai might need me. But how can I help him against . . . whatever made him shout like that—*after* he fired his gun? This isn't a jump in the lake. I can't just show up with a dry blanket and expect a wild animal to stop its attack. Hunter and Vicki can handle it. They know what to do. I don't.

"Kai!" Hunter's voice echoes back to me.

His panicked tone forces me into action. No, I can't just stand here and do nothing. If Kai is hurt, I'll never forgive myself. I take off running across the open stretch between me and the woods. My legs scream murder from the sudden exertion of pumping them through snow, at a pace I haven't used since I was last on the beach, happily jogging toward the surf. *Move move move.* I'm breathing icy needles.

The forest darkens the sky even more. But the snow isn't as deep here, making it easier to move, and before I know it I've run farther than I meant to. "Hunter! Vicki! Kai . . . ?" I stop and listen for a reply. My heart kicks madly as I spin in a full circle, but all I see is trees and snow. Which way did they go? And . . . mierda, which way did I come from? My gaze instinctively drops to the ground, searching for footprints, but there's more brush here than snow. The evergreens must have caught most of it in their boughs higher up.

Movement above catches my eye, and I look up just in time to see a bird of some kind, with a gray wingspan that seems as wide as I am tall, soar right over me. Snow flutters down from the branch it was perched on. It saw me before I knew it was there—and took off, thank God, but what else is in here watching me that I can't see?

"Over here!" Vicki yells. I turn toward her voice and find her in her black snowsuit jumping in place, waving her little arms over her head. Beside her, Hunter stands tall and broad and stoic as the tree trunks, waiting for me to catch up, but his eyes are wild, scanning the area.

I trot up to them. "Where is he—Did you see anyone at all? There aren't any tracks."

"I can see that," Hunter says through gritted teeth. Maybe he isn't really annoyed with me, just with the situation, but his reaction stings a little.

"Now what?" I say.

Hunter shushes me like he would one of his younger siblings. "Listen," he whispers.

Something rustles nearby, or at least it seems like it's nearby, but I don't see anything moving. It's so soft at first I think it must be an animal, and part of me—strike that, *most* of me—fights the urge to turn tail and run.

Then I see a person walking toward us, still quite a distance away, maybe fifty yards. The closer they get, the more their pace slows and their brows knit, like they think they're seeing a mirage in the desert..

"Hunter?"

That voice . . . dripping over me like warm maple syrup, even in this chill. It's *him*. He's okay!

"I should've known," Hunter says, not loud enough for Kai to hear but still light with relief. "He was just yelling because he was excited he killed something."

"Ain't nothin' wrong with that," Vicki says, then shouts, "Hey, Kai! Remember me?"

"Vicki? What the—" Kai stops short, as if his confusion hit a wall, and his eyes lock with mine. For a second I'm not sure if he recognizes me—wearing these puffy snowpants, my hair tied back and tucked under a fleece cap—but then he gives me a familiar, disarming smile. It's full of sunshine and sandy beaches, as inviting as alcapurrias fresh out of the deep fryer, the kind my mom used to make on special occasions—before she hired a personal chef for all occasions, special or not. "Gabi," he says, my name sounding more like laughter than a word. No one else's smile does things to me like Kai's does, even at a distance. My heart leaps toward those bright teeth and soft lips. Toward him.

But the rest of me is frozen in place. I'm not sure why. I want to move, to run, to shout "Hallefreakinglujah, we found you!" Instead I just stare and drink him in. He holds a rifle in one hand and a dead rabbit by its hind legs in his other. A large rucksack is strapped onto his back, and he's bundled up, making him look bulkier than usual, but his face seems thinner, his jawline sharper. It's been only three days since I last saw him. They were three days of worry, frustration, and confusion for me. But three days of *what* for him?

"Is that really you?" He walks briskly toward me.

That soaring hope in his voice is the push I needed. My feet sprout wings and fly me straight into his arms, planting me hard against his chest, between a dead rabbit and a loaded gun. I don't care—he's here, in my arms. My previous determination to say nothing, do nothing, until he gave me something more to go on than his shock at seeing me, was dead on arrival. I worried about him so much that the relief of finding him is almost painful. My heart's going to burst.

"What are you all doing out here?" he says.

I pull back enough to meet his eyes, soaking up the sun within them but not letting myself melt into him. Not yet, because: "We're here to ask you the same question."

Hunter and Vicki stayed in the forest to collect firewood for the night, leaving Kai and me alone by the shelter with a dead rabbit between us. The high I was on a few minutes ago from finding Kai has faded, and the snowflakes are getting heavy again, fat and fluffy.

I can't believe I'm out here, miles from civilization and cell service, with an oncoming blizzard. But I am—because of Kai, and this journey he's on. I don't know why I thought it was a good idea to go after him. It seems silly now. He's obviously fine.

Did I really think he'd be helpless out here? The Alaskan outdoors is his life.

"We found your hidey-hole a ways back," I say, unsure of

how to get this conversation started. "That couldn't have been easy. Are you okay?"

"I'm okay." His tone is relieved, like he's glad I'm not going straight to the what-the-hell-were-you-thinking questions. "It works pretty well, but a shelter is safer." He glances at the snowmobiles, then shakes his head. "I still can't believe you're here. Are *you* okay?"

"Better now that we've found you." I return his smile, and for a moment it's like we're back home and none of this ever happened. But only for a moment. "We're going to have to stay the night here, Kai. I mean me and Hunter and Vicki. We don't have enough time to get back to the lodge before dark, and the storm that passed earlier was just one part of a bigger system. According to the radar, this is going to get a lot worse. We might as well wait it out and leave in the morning, when it's safer."

"Yeah," he says, nodding. "I was afraid of that. I'm not going to get as far as the next shelter before it gets dark, either. How close is the next wave?"

"Now? I'm not sure. We left the lodge a couple hours ago, and it was getting close then. This is probably the start of it." I raise a palm and catch some snowflakes on it. Each one is so innocent and tiny, incapable of any damage on its own. But how quickly they can band together and smother anything in their path. "Are you staying here for the night, too?"

"It'll set me back a bit, but yeah."

Good. We'll have plenty of time to talk, and maybe by morning he'll change his mind and come back with us.

"Night travel is dangerous enough without a blizzard on top of it," he says. "And since you're here, I'm not going to eat and run." He tries another smile on me, but this one is uncertain, and the one I offer back feels sluggish, the corners of my mouth hesitant to rise. His gaze drops away from me and then he pulls a knife with a bright blue handle off his belt.

I guessed preparing a rabbit would be disgusting, but I still wasn't ready for this. He starts by peeling the skin away from its body, like he's sliding off a sweater, and then pulls it down the rear legs as easily as removing socks, revealing shiny pink muscle. I turn away, face the river, but the metallic scent of blood is still in the air. And so are the sounds.

Bones crack and snap, once, twice. My whole body tenses, my imagination filling in what I can't see. Those little rabbit feet being plucked away and tossed aside. The poor thing had just been going about its daily life, and then *bam*. Gone. Stripped bare to be roasted in our campfire. Is our survival really more important than the life of that creature?

I get Hunter's aversion to his namesake act. I couldn't pull the trigger, either. But if Kai hadn't today, we'd be scrounging for roots or berries or something, and hoping they weren't poisonous. Unless Kai has a field guide. God, I hope he has some kind of field guide in his pack. And a bar of chocolate.

There's nothing a bar of chocolate can't fix, Mom used to say. Before all things sugar became off-limits for us. I can't remember the last time I craved it. Maybe that's why her life got so messed up—she stopped eating miracle chocolate.

"Sorry you're stuck out here," Kai says. "I know this isn't your thing." His tone is neither condescending nor judgmental. Just matter-of-fact.

That's probably why he didn't invite me to come along on this trip with him. Dead animals, frigid temperatures, venturing into the unknown—I've never given him the impression those are things I enjoy.

I still don't understand, though. Even if he wanted to be alone . . . "Why didn't you tell me you were leaving?"

A pause, then he says, "I almost didn't leave at all. Walking away from our house, away from my family, away from you . . . that was the most difficult thing I've ever done." He blows out a sigh. "I tried to tell you, though. I know it didn't come out perfectly, but I thought I'd gotten the important stuff across; you seemed to understand my meaning. Guess I was wrong. And I'm really sorry you misunderstood—no, that came out wrong, too." Another sigh and a curse under his breath. "This isn't your fault. I'm sorry *I* wasn't clear. And I can't imagine what you think of me right now, if you thought I just . . . disappeared for no reason. I am *so, so* sorry. Are you mad?"

"Wouldn't you be?" At first I was just relieved. As soon as I knew he was okay, all those negative and insecure things I felt seemed insignificant. But now my initial frustration is creeping back in, along with a new worry. I know things about him now that I didn't before. About his dad being dead, and his struggle to process it. And he never said anything about it, so I believed his dad abandoned them on purpose. The same way I believed he was just saying good-bye for the day, not good-bye for a month. Or however long this trip is going to last.

"Yeah, I would be mad," he says. "I'm sorry."

"For what, exactly?"

"Gabi, please look at me."

"I'll turn around when you're done playing butcher."

"Okay." He goes back to brutalizing the rabbit. "I'm sorry I didn't explain myself better. At the time, I didn't think everything through." He lets out sigh number three. I'm surprised he's not getting light-headed. "I know that now, but it's not like I could just turn back, have a chat with you, and head out again. Once I'm out here, I'm out here until it's done."

"Until what's done?"

"Until I find out the truth."

"About what? Your dad?" I don't wait for his answer. "Why didn't you ever tell me what happened to him? Why did I have to find out from your brother?"

All the sounds disappear behind me. I don't even hear him breathing anymore.

Then he mutters, "Hunter probably told you his version of the story."

"That's not the point. I've kept nothing from you. Not even the secret about who my mom is, the one that could force me to move again if it gets out."

"I haven't said a word to anyone about that."

"You haven't said a lot of things," I snap, then clamp my mouth shut before I let slip something I'll regret. We are not my parents. We will not turn every disagreement, every misunderstanding, every conversation of any kind into a fight, like they did. "We've known each other for more than three months. You had plenty of opportunities to tell me yourself."

"Three months of bliss," he says. "That was kind of the problem. The solution *and* the problem. And this is why I never talked to you about it. It's not that I wanted to hide anything from you, Gabi. It wasn't that at all. My head just hasn't been right since—" He chokes on his next word. "I didn't like the person I became. I got better when I met you, though. Being with you gave me a reason to get out and be me again. But that didn't distract me from dealing with it completely, and I didn't want to burden you with my problems. You're dealing with enough of your own." He pauses for a breath, then says, "Hang on, I'll be right back."

He walks off, leaving me with nothing but the sight and

sound of rushing water as a companion. What he's told me so far lines up with what Hunter said, so at least I know he's being honest.

The snow falls thick as a curtain around me. I'm ready to huddle around a fire and eat and try to forget this day long enough to get some sleep. When Kai returns he walks past me, up to the river, and rinses his hands. Dries them quickly. Those hands have held mine too many times to count. Caressed me. Comforted me. Cherished me. Since day one, he's been protecting and nurturing me, inside and out, helping me navigate this foreign world that's completely natural to him.

His intentions are too good for his own good. By not "burdening" me with his issues, he created a rift between us—both literal and otherwise. I wonder how much distance and how many secrets would have piled up if I hadn't come after him and demanded an explanation. Would they have become a mountain? So that all we could see were the issues standing between us rather than each other?

Kai stands and turns to face me, eyeing me cautiously. I'm not sure where we go from here, either, but did I really expect things to be perfect with us forever? We had a conflict—more like a misunderstanding—and he apologized. There are still some things we need to discuss, sort out, and settle, and I can only take one step at a time. This is a really big first step, but like he said, the first step is the hardest.

So, one tentative step at a time, I close the physical gap

between us. Every step closer is a promise—*I'm willing to try. Let's figure this out, together.*

"Kai . . . I'm here now. Talk to me, as clearly as you can." I take off one of my gloves and touch his cheek. He's a furnace, even in this cold, and I melt under his heat. A familiar tingling sensation zings through me, straight to my core. I don't just want to move on. I want *him*. But first, I need to know: "Why are you doing this?"

He leans his cheek against my palm and holds my other hand between his. "I need to know what really happened to my dad, and the only way to do that is to ask him myself."

What?

My head spins as I try to make sense of his words. "You're trying to find your dad?" I ask slowly. "I mean, so you can actually see him and . . . talk to him?"

"Yes, that's what I've been saying all along." He twists his mouth. "I'm sure Hunter told you he's dead."

I hesitate. "Isn't he?"

"Everyone seems to think so." His voice softens like butter on a hot plate. "But they have no proof. There were no witnesses. He was presumed dead. That's not the same as found dead."

"No, I guess it isn't." I want to support him, but Hunter told me they had a funeral, and their mom, their *whole family*, thinks he's dead. Everyone grieved him—except Kai.

Hunter also said they didn't see a body. No one ever found

his corpse, and no one actually saw him die. Even Hunter said he didn't believe their dad was really dead for a while.

As crazy as it sounds, it would explain why Kai never told me about his father's death—because he doesn't believe it happened. Understanding his line of thinking and believing it's the truth are two different things. But the hope blooming on Kai's face right now, that he might get to see his dad again . . . I won't be the one to shatter that. He's had enough people trying to do that already.

He has to find proof one way or the other. It's the only way to resolve this; I get that. But he doesn't have to do it alone.

"I'm with you on this," I say. "I believe the proof is out there, farther north, wherever your dad supposedly died." My mind races with the possibilities and grabs the first thing that will put me back in the driver's seat of the situation. "I'll look into hiring an investigator for you, who will either find him or find out why he hasn't returned—"

"No." He turns and walks away from me.

I'm right on his heels. Well, as close as I can be in the deep snow and with him moving like it isn't even there. "Why are you so against me helping you with this?"

"Because it's my problem, not yours."

"Your problems *are* my problems. That's how the whole relationship thing works. And this in particular? Is also your family's problem. It's not all on you."

"Everyone else has moved on," he says. "I'm the only one

who believes he's still out there. I have to prove it to them myself."

Trying to talk him out of this journey isn't going to work. It's clear he's going to continue, no matter what I say. And he has that right, no matter how much I don't like it. But still, I have to ask: "If he's alive, then why didn't he come back?"

"I don't know." His tone wavers and he stops to face me squarely. "That's what I'm trying to find out."

"What *do* you know?" I can't help him without more details. "Can you at least tell me what happened to him? Or supposedly happened?"

"Avalanche took out his cabin," he says, shoulders slumping. "That I know is true. They had evidence the cabin that was destroyed was his. But what they can't prove is their claim that he was buried under it. He might have gotten swept away and injured or disoriented or . . ." He shakes his head slowly, as if doing so will help him think up another option. "Something."

"I—" My throat catches. "I'm sorry. That's awful."

He offers a pained smile. "It's not your fault."

A rifle shot thunders behind us, then ricochets off the mountains, followed by a high-pitched squeal of victory. "You gave your gun to Vicki?" I say, wiping away the snowflakes that keep landing on my lashes.

He gives me a nearly imperceptible shrug, like *so what?* "One hare isn't going to feed all four of us. We needed to talk, Hunter refuses to shoot, and Vicki knows what she's doing."

"How? She's a waitress."

"A waitress who spent half her life in the Appalachian Mountains and the other half in rural Alaska. And her dad is a professional hunter with zero gender bias. She's the only daughter among four sons, and she can outshoot every one of them."

"How did you know all that? She said you weren't at the lodge very long. I didn't think you talked to her about anything."

Kai laughs, and despite the gravity of everything we've just discussed, my heart does a somersault at the sound of it. "I wasn't the one doing the talking. Have you met her? She can tell you her whole life story in under five minutes."

True.

I open my mouth to resume our conversation, but Vicki trots out of the woods, holding up her kill by its hind legs. "Look at the size of this one!" Hunter appears a moment later, arms loaded with branches. The hatchet he borrowed from Kai's pack hangs from his waist.

"I'm gonna get the fire going inside," he says, then disappears into the shed.

Vicki is already skinning her rabbit next to Kai's on the snow. "I always have trouble pulling the heart out," she says to Kai. "Give me a hand?"

Kai says, "No problem," and I avert my eyes from the carnage. "I'm gonna go inside while you do that," I say. "Can we finish talking later?"

"Yeah." Kai squeezes my hand. "There's an extra blanket rolled up in my pack, if you need it. We'll be in as soon as we're done with this."

"Okay." I enter the shelter and shut the door behind me. It takes a moment for my eyes to adjust to the dark after being blinded by white outside. This shelter is a little bigger than the last one, but it's still going to be cramped with all four of us sleeping in here tonight. And there's only one bed—strike that, there's only one *mattress on the floor*. Hunter is squatting by the hearth, blowing on the tiny flames just coming to life in the kindling. "It'll be nice and toasty in here in no time," he says.

I sit on the edge of the mattress and crisscross my legs. The pile of logs and branches in the corner doesn't look up to the job we need it to do. "Is that enough wood to last all night?"

"I'll get more after we eat. Trust me, I don't want to sleep in the cold any more than you do." He blows another long, steady breath, and the flames grow. Smoke shimmies up the chimney. "You and Kai good now?"

"Yeah, I think so. It was just a misunderstanding. And now that I know more about what he's doing, there's something I need to talk to you about."

He glances over his shoulder at me, brows bunching together. "That sounds bad."

"Only if you were planning on Kai going home in the morning."

He turns his whole body this time. "Wasn't that the plan, to try to convince him to turn around?"

"Yes," I say. "But Kai refuses. And I'm not sure forcing him back home is the right answer."

"Why?"

"Hunter . . ." How do I say this? Bluntly, I guess. "He thinks your dad is still alive."

He doesn't seem surprised by this, but that seems to be his default setting. I relay what Kai told me as well as I can remember it, and Hunter takes it all in silently.

"Gabi," he says when I'm done, "I know you care about him and want to support him—I do, too—but we have to do what's best for Kai, and that might not be what *he* thinks is best. We have to get him home. Get him help. Let a professional handle his issues."

"But we're already out here . . . Where are we now, anyway?"

Hunter tears through Kai's pack until he finds a map, then he spreads it out on the floor and points at a large area labeled *Alaska Interior* just under a curving ridge of mountains labeled *Alaska Range*. Somehow, Kai has to get through that. Or maybe over that? An airplane would be so much easier and faster, but I don't know if he'd agree to use one. Not far to the northwest is Denali National Park. And south is where we came from, Anchorage, with about as much distance left to go to get to Fairbanks, where the land flattens out before bunching into another group of mountains northeast of the city—the White Mountains—which Hunter says is Kai's final destination.

"He's come this far, and he's fine. Why not just let him keep going to see if he's right?"

"Because he's wrong." Hunter refolds the map and tucks it into the pack.

"I know that's very likely. But *what if he's right?*"

Hunter's stoic expression cracks. "We had a funeral, Gabi."

"You had a funeral with no body."

He runs a hand through his hair. "It's been a year."

I sigh. I don't know exactly what he's feeling, but I do understand this isn't easy for him. I keep my next words gentle. "What if he's still alive—"

"Don't," he snaps, and his tone pitches. "Don't feed that kind of hope in Kai. Or me."

The sudden anger in his eyes nearly shatters my determination. "I'm sorry, but it's too late. Kai already has that hope in spades. And I didn't give it to him—I don't even fully believe it myself. But we have to consider all the options."

Hunter presses his lips together and turns away from me, shaking his head.

"All he wants is proof, and he's not going to stop until he finds it. You said so yourself: Once he gets an idea in his head, he gets tunnel vision. We can find a way to force him to turn around and go home, but that won't fix anything. And I know

140

the chances are muy slim, but doesn't he deserve—doesn't your whole family deserve—to know if he's right?"

He spins to face me again, but the vitriol has left him. Weakened him. "And what if he's wrong? What if he gets there and finds *proof* that he's wrong? There's a chance of that, too."

"A good chance of that, I know. But you said when the reality of your dad's death hit you, it hit you hard. If that happens to Kai—and you're so sure that it will—don't you think we should be there for him?"

His shoulders drop on a sigh bigger than the mountains.

Whether Kai's right or wrong, neither outcome is good. Either he's right, his dad is alive and something bad has been preventing him from coming home. Or he's wrong, and he'll be crushed under his own grief. Either way, he'll know the truth, whatever that truth is, and he'll have to deal with it after that. And who better than us—his twin brother and his girlfriend—to be there with him when either of those happens? Anything less than our full support would be a cruel abandonment, knowing he's going to get hurt.

"I don't like this, but you're right," Hunter says. "We have to go with him."

I start to smile, then realize what he said. *We* have to go with him. I realize too late that I said it, too. I started worrying about Kai more than anything else, and the plan—my own thoughts—got away from me. But it's only right, I suppose. Hunter and I have been in this together since we discovered

Kai was gone. So we should continue on together, finish it together.

This isn't the same as driving a few hours to pick him up, though. This is . . . I don't even know what it involves, that's the problem. But before I can ask Hunter what I just argued myself into, the shelter door opens.

CHAPTER ELEVEN

Kai and Vicki walk in, carrying their pieces of cut-up meat, and quickly shut the door behind them. In just those few seconds, enough snow blew in to lightly coat half the floor. "It's really bad out there," Vicki says. "I hope y'all have some good stories to pass the time, because we're not going anywhere for a while . . . and I left my darts at the lodge." She winks at Hunter, then sets her pile near the hearth and starts rummaging through Kai's pack for cooking utensils.

Hunter is still standing next to me by the mattress, the final words of our conversation likely ringing through his head as they are through mine. *We have to go with him.*

How?

Kai sets his lump of slimy rabbit parts next to Vicki's and adds more kindling to the fire. The flames lick higher, and the bigger logs are starting to catch.

"I was going to do that," Hunter says.

"But you didn't," Kai shoots back.

Hunter skulks across the room and nudges Kai out of the way so he can take over. "I got this," Hunter says. "Take care of the food."

Vicki eyes them for a moment, then pulls a handful of salt and pepper packets out of a side pocket of Kai's rucksack, trying to act like nothing is out of the ordinary when the air feels like it's crackling. Just like that night in their kitchen a couple of weeks ago. Something is definitely up between Kai and Hunter. I've often seen them helping out in their house side by side, but it's rare that I see them working *together*.

It's getting warm in here, finally, warm enough to take off my coat and these cumbersome snowpants. I unzip for miles and shed my bulky second skin. Hunter and Kai do the same, and Vicki removes her full snowsuit. If it gets too cold overnight, I suppose our coats could pass for extra blankets. This isn't ideal, but it also isn't horrible. We're protected from the elements.

Everyone is quiet now. Kai sits next to me on the mattress and runs his palm up and down my back, like he can sense I'm nervous about something. Vicki adds the raw meat to her heated skillet and the sizzle makes me flinch.

"You okay?" Kai says.

"Yeah, I . . . just, um . . . I mean *we* . . . We need to talk to you about something."

Hunter casts a worried look at me, and Kai notices the exchange before Hunter turns back to the fire.

"Okay, you guys are scaring me." Kai's tone is teasing. His natural instinct is to be optimistic and give us the benefit of the doubt, but I think there's some truth to his words. "What's going on?"

Maybe it would be better if I just spat this out. "We want to go with you. The rest of the way from here. Both of us. Me and Hunter. If . . . that's okay?"

The fire crackles and pops in the silence that follows, and the surprisingly mouthwatering scent of rabbit is suddenly overpowering. My stomach is about to declare mutiny if it doesn't get fed soon. I'm not used to going this long between meals.

"It means a lot to me that you're offering," Kai says, bringing my attention back to where it belongs, "but I don't need help."

"I know you don't need help. We *want* to help. Right, Hunter?"

"Yep." Hunter keeps his eyes on the fire, poking the logs around with a stick. Somehow that makes the fire bigger. "You think we came all this way just to say hi?"

"No. I thought you came all this way to tell me to go home."

"We did," I admit. "Originally."

Hunter tosses a look over his shoulder at me like, *Why would you tell him that?*

Because I can't not be totally honest. Not after I saw *dis*honesty destroy my family.

"We also wanted to make sure you were all right," I add, "and we wouldn't feel right about letting you go by yourself."

"Why? I'm fine."

"You're fine *now*," Hunter says, not turning away from the fire. "What about later? The hardest part is still ahead of you—the mountains."

"So you *do* know where I'm going," Kai says to Hunter's back. "I knew you'd figure it out, but I assumed you wouldn't come because I didn't think you'd agree with it."

"Yeah. I know where you're going, and I know why." Hunter finally turns to face him. "And you're right, I don't agree with it."

"But you want to come along?" Kai says.

"That's what I just said, isn't it?" Hunter busies himself trying to find something in Kai's pack. "You got any plates in here?"

"Why?"

"So we can eat," Hunter says. "We're all hungry."

Kai blows out a breath. "You know that's not what I meant." He joins Hunter on the floor, unzips a side compartment of his rucksack, and pulls out a couple of plastic plates. "We'll have to share. And this is how it'll be the whole trip, if you two come along. More people means more work. More food to gather. More chances of something going wrong." He shakes his head. "This is a bad idea. I've still got a long way to go and only enough supplies for one person."

"We'll pass towns on the way, right?" I say.

Kai nods.

"Then we can get more supplies." Maybe this *isn't* such a bad idea. We're in Alaska, not on the moon. Hunter and Kai both know how to survive out here, and I can buy whatever we need. I push up off the mattress, kneel beside Kai, and take his hand. "We don't think you're helpless without us. But now that we're all together, do you really want us to leave? Would you really rather be alone?"

"No," he concedes. "But what I'm doing isn't a stroll on the beach."

"Okay." I square my shoulders, ready to take this on. "What is it, then?"

"An extreme hike," Hunter cuts in. "It's what we encountered today, except colder, windier, and the hardest cardio workout you'll ever have." He shrugs. "As long as we have food and shelter and fire, and stay away from predators, we'll be fine."

"Doesn't sound too bad," I say. But I know he's downplaying it. He has to be. Ten minutes ago, he was totally against this. He had me fooled before I got to know him; that casual-shrug act of his is worthy of an Oscar. "What about . . . bathing?"

Kai shakes his head. "We spot clean with a rag."

"I can't wash my hair?"

"Wet hair at these temperatures is too risky," Hunter says.

"Especially with how much you have. That's just asking to get hypothermia."

I keep my face neutral, but inside I'm dying a little. I have long, thick hair. It's never not been washed and conditioned regularly, and even then, it can be a chore to manage sometimes.

"Hunter," Kai says, "I need you to be very, very clear."

He smirks. "Like you were before you left?"

"I guess I deserve that." Kai blows out a breath. "Just tell me you're okay with this, with seeing Dad again after believing he's been dead."

Vicki lets out a little gasp. I forgot she doesn't know what's really going on here.

"I'm okay with that," Hunter says, but his face is hard. "I know we didn't get along very well, but what kind of person would I be if I didn't want him to be alive? Did you ever think that maybe I want to find him, too?"

"No, I . . . Sorry. I didn't think that at all. I'm okay with you coming—I am. I just didn't think you'd want to."

"Well, maybe you should have asked." Hunter goes back to the fire. If he said all that just so Kai would let him go along, the boy really could have a career in Hollywood. If he was speaking from the heart, though, Hunter is just as messed up as Kai is over all of this.

Kai nods, then turns to me. "What about you, Gabi? Are you sure?"

"This is important to you, so it's important to me, too. Like I said, I'm with you on this, one hundred percent." And I'm not my mother. I won't back down from a commitment just because circumstances changed and things got harder to deal with.

He smiles, briefly. "The Fairbanks area is still a long way off, and this might not be the only bad weather that hits, and once we get into the mountains . . ." He sighs. "If we weren't walking the whole way there first, it actually wouldn't be that bad. We wouldn't be completely spent by the time we got to the hard inclines."

I dare to hope—does he mean we don't *have* to walk, that he'd be willing to go another way? "Isn't that the point of the journey, though, going by foot? To connect with the land or whatever? Wouldn't a car or a plane be against the 'no modern conveniences' rule?"

Kai shoots a hard look at Hunter.

Don't get mad at him, I want to say. *He told me because you didn't.* But I hold my tongue this time. We need to stay on point, come up with a plan. Not be at one another's throats.

Vicki breaks the short silence. "I'm not sayin' you two aren't, like, living my ideal version of a relationship with how supportive y'all are of each other, but . . . are you crazy? I don't mean certifiable crazy, I just mean—what in blazes are you thinking?"

Hunter doesn't turn away from the fire and doesn't make a sound, but his shoulders shake like he's suppressing a laugh.

Vicki goes on, oblivious. "Fairbanks is a whole lotta

walking from here. Through snow, and where there isn't snow, there's sure to be mud. Like, serious mud. The kind that will suck your boots right off."

"Dad went by foot," Kai says, "but I'm not doing this to cleanse my mind, like he always did. Well, actually, I *was* doing that, at first. And it's been nice walking in his footsteps the last few days—literally—but then I remembered it isn't really my main goal. Right now I just want to find him, and his last known location was at his cabin. If I could take a car or a plane to get up there faster, I would. But I don't have a car, and I can't afford to charter a plane." He avoids eye contact with me after saying that last part. He knows I'll pay for it if given the chance, and for some reason, that's a cardinal sin.

"Oh, well, if you need a plane, I can help you with that," Vicki says. She pokes a piece of meat with a fork and juice runs onto the skillet, sizzling and smoking.

I hadn't thought of how she'd factor into all this. Here we are making plans without her, and she's the one who helped us get this far in the first place. She can help. Of course she can. She already has.

"I don't remember passing any airports," I say.

"Not that kind of plane." Vicki laughs. "Sorry. I'm not laughing at you. I just keep forgetting you're still new to this place. I meant a bush plane. They're small, so they can go places bigger planes can't. I know a pilot, Jack Randy, who lives not far from here. He'll take you anywhere for the right price."

"Money isn't an issue."

"Yes, it is," Kai says.

"Only because you don't have any," Hunter cuts in. "Gabi has plenty, and if she wants to take a bush plane, it'll cost her the same whether we go along for the ride or not. So we might as well go along for the ride."

Kai practically snorts out steam. But he doesn't refute Hunter's logic.

"Okay," I say, glancing back and forth between them. "So we're good, then? Vicki takes us to the pilot, he takes us to the mountains by Fairbanks, and Vicki—Oh, shoot. Vicki, how are you going to get both of your snowmobiles back home? You need another driver."

She pulls the skillet away from the fire and starts dividing the meat up evenly onto two plates. "My brother Jimmy can swing by Jack's to pick it up with his truck. No biggie."

"I thought his name was Johnny."

"I have more than one brother. No sisters, though. I always wondered what it would be like to have a sister." She holds a plate out to Kai and Hunter, then gestures for me to come share one with her. "Sorry if it's a little bland. I didn't have much to work with."

We dig into the meat all at once, not bothering to let it cool first, and I notice Kai is just as ravenous as the rest of us. "When was the last time you ate?" I ask.

"Last night," he says, like eating once a day is no big deal.

"I didn't get any kills this morning, and didn't get a chance to hunt again until the storm broke. Last resort, I was going to go fishing, but I've had nothing but fish since I left. I wanted something different today. Fish is good, but it doesn't really fill you up, you know?"

Hunter swallows the bite he just took and then scoots away from Kai, adds another log to the fire.

"You done?" Kai says.

"Yeah, I had a big lunch. You can have the rest."

Hunter may have eaten a big lunch, but he's also a big guy, the largest person here. He needs this food just as much as we do. Stubbornness seems to be part of the Locklear code, though, and I believe Hunter would sooner starve himself than let his brother go hungry.

So, this trip with them together should be interesting.

The next bite burns my mouth. It's delicious, though, and worth the blister. The best wild rabbit I've ever had. Okay, the only wild rabbit I've ever had, but still.

"Vicki, you should be working in the kitchen of the Grinning Bear," Kai says, "not the dining room. This is amazing."

"Naw, I didn't do nothin' special. Just a pinch of salt and a dash of love."

She's entirely too modest.

The wind howls outside, like a lone wolf searching for its pack, rattling the walls of the shelter. I huddle closer to the fire and Kai pulls a rolled blanket out of his rucksack. He opens it up, wraps it around my shoulders. "I'm going to get some more wood, before it gets dark."

Hunter grabs the hatchet. "I'm going with you."

"You don't have to."

"We can carry twice as much back if I do."

Kai eyes him for a moment and then opens the door. A blast of cold air and snow hurries inside. "Be careful," I say.

"We're not going far." They both hustle out the door, slamming it shut behind them.

When the boys come back, Vicki and I are practically comatose. Wrapped in our plush blanket and with our bellies full, we didn't stand a chance against the built-up exhaustion of the day. We pulled the mattress closer to the fire and had to squish together for us both to fit on it. This is the warmest, most relaxed I've felt since we left the lodge. Kai brushes a chilled thumb across my cheek, stirring me awake.

"I still can't believe you're here," he says. "I just needed to touch you, make sure you're really real."

"I'm really real." My lips stretch with a sleepy smile.

He and Hunter drop their armloads of sticks and logs into the corner, and Vicki sits up. Kai adds more logs to the fire, then strips off his coat and boots. Hunter does the same. And then they both huddle in on either side of us, Kai next to me and Hunter next to Vicki. We have to all sleep together to stay warm, and I don't mind, but I wonder if Hunter does. He made it clear that getting close to someone, physically or otherwise, is nowhere on his agenda. Tonight, though, he doesn't have a choice.

I lean against Kai and goose bumps prickle me everywhere. He's cold from outside. This is the first time I've ever had to warm *him* up, and I like that he needs me. Even just for this one small thing, in this one small moment.

Vicki strikes up a one-sided conversation with Hunter, to which he gives her nods and "mm-hms" the few times she pauses. The air is much more relaxed now than it was before. We can't go anywhere until the storm passes, and with our new plan in place, there's nothing left to debate. I turn to face Kai so my back is toward Vicki, letting her words fall into the background.

I pull the rock necklace out from under my collar and rub my thumb over our etched initials. "I haven't taken it off since you gave it to me."

"I still got mine on, too," he says, smiling. "That's how it works. My dad always wore his whenever he left. My mom still wears hers."

"I noticed." The necklace is doing its job. It's been a constant reminder of him.

"You know what I missed the most while we were apart?" he asks. "Talking to you."

"Then talk to me now. What have you been doing the last three days? Did you see anything interesting?"

"Yeah. Every time I saw something cool, I wanted tell you about it . . . Where do I even start?" He tells me about birds and other creatures, how awesome it is to see and hear them up close, and about sleeping under the stars one night, how small it made his day-to-day problems seem. He tells me about being the most exhausted he's ever been, but at the same time feeling the best he's ever felt. Every step is both tiring and energizing. And stopping at the lodge was harder than he'd thought it would be, because he saw that picture of him and his dad and Hunter when they were so happy together, but it reminded him that not all his memories are bad, and that's what he needs to focus on, the good.

"I've been thinking about you, too," he says. "Always. You're constantly there, floating in my mind. That first night away from you I thought my chest would explode. Missing you caused physical pain. And I kept reaching for my phone, but it wasn't there. I almost turned around and went home."

Wow. I hadn't even realized he was gone at that point. "Why didn't you?"

"Being out here, doing what my dad enjoyed doing—it's almost like he's with me again, you know? With me the way we used to be, before . . . It hurts, but it's also a relief. And that probably makes no sense, but it pushed me to keep going."

Before I can respond, his lips find mine, and it takes all my willpower not to get lost in the kiss, urge him to continue all night, forget we're not alone. *This* is what *I* missed most since he left, this feeling of utter contentment between us, of wanting only what's best for each other. In his arms, lips locked in a molten embrace, I feel like I can do anything, be anything, like this whole trip will be a cakewalk, because being with him is worth whatever hardship I might face. Like we can face anything together and come out victorious in the end.

Even the wilds of Alaska.

CHAPTER TWELVE

I wake up shivering. Kai is gone, and Vicki is curled up against Hunter. They're both breathing deep and steady, keeping each other warm—the fire has been reduced to ash—but only Vicki's eyes are closed. Hunter catches my gaze and puts a finger to his lips. *Shh.* I nod, but I have to pee. Where am I supposed to pee? Maybe that's where Kai went, outside, to nature's bathroom.

I put on my boots, coat, hat, gloves, and snowpants as quietly as I can and then open the door. Snow as high as my knees has been pushed aside to allow access in and out of the shelter. The morning sun is just starting to rise, and where the light touches, everything sparkles. The storm is long gone, and it left a work of art behind. Cold sucks the air out of my lungs and heat out of the rest of me, reminding me that I don't have the luxury of getting mesmerized by the picturesque view.

Taylor Swift suddenly breaks the silence, the beat and lyrics of her newest hit single even more out of place here than I am.

Shock lasts only a second before I realize what I'm actually hearing. My phone is ringing!

How am I even getting a signal? It takes me three rings to get my hand into the zippered pocket of my snowpants and pull the phone out. And it's Dad's cell on the line—which means it could be an emergency, or he just thought of something he needed to tell me on the way to work. Or . . . maybe he's noticed I'm not there? I have to think for a second to remember what day it is and how long I've been gone. Seems like weeks, but it's only been since yesterday morning.

One more ring and the call will get sent to voice mail. I tap the green dot to pick up. "Hello?"

"Gabi—" His voice crackles, pieces of it breaking off and scattering between here and Anchorage. I can't make sense of what he's saying. The bits I do catch sound alien and garbled.

"Papi?"

Nothing.

Still, I try. "If you can hear me, I'm okay. I'll be home soon. Okay? *I'll be home soon.*"

Silence.

I check the screen: no signal. Dad won't think anything of a dropped call. Alaska drops our calls, and our internet signal, on a regular basis. He won't worry. He *isn't* worried.

I shove the phone back into my pocket and follow Kai's tracks, stepping into his deep footsteps as quickly as I can without toppling, and find him zipping up his pants behind a tree.

He turns and smiles, releasing a flock of butterflies in my gut. "Good morning."

"It is for you; you don't have to hold it anymore." I smile anyway, despite my frustration, because I can't not when I see him. "I can't just pull down my pants and squat in the woods. I'll literally freeze my butt off."

"Right. We should go to this Jack guy's house first thing. Can you hold it until then?"

"Yeah, I think so." I run my tongue over my teeth and try to swallow the pasty feeling inside my mouth. "What are the chances Jack has a spare toothbrush?"

"We don't need toothbrushes out here." Kai scoops up a handful of snow and then rubs it over his teeth, swishes it around, and spits. "There. Clean."

I copy what he did, only because I don't have another choice. The shock of cold stings as the snow hits my gums. It doesn't leave me feeling minty fresh, but it does help a little.

Kai turns me gently by the shoulders until I'm facing the tangerine sunrise spilling over and between the mountain peaks, then he comes up close behind me and wraps his arms around my middle. The landscape is so pure I don't feel worthy of laying eyes on it, like I accidentally peeked behind a holy curtain meant only for angels to pull back.

This is Alaska, dangerously beautiful, luring people into death traps like a Siren's song.

"Remember this," he says. "Remember how it takes your

breath away—remember that *this* is how I felt the first time I saw you, and how I've felt every day since then, whenever I'm with you. This is my version of heaven, Gabi, and so are you."

Kai's rucksack is firmly secured to the back of our snowmobile. After a breakfast consisting solely of the protein bars Kai packed for an emergency, there's thankfully nothing left to do but go. Vicki says it'll take us about a half hour to get to Jack's house from here, another hour or so before the plane is prepped and we're in the air, and then at least a couple of hours of flying. I'm looking forward to that, just sitting there with nothing to do, while the dangers are far below us.

Hunter returns from the woods after relieving himself. This is the only situation I've ever been in where I've wished I were a boy.

"Finally." Vicki shoots an exasperated look at Hunter, who was indisposed for all of twenty seconds. "Can we go now? Before me and Gabi burst?"

"Okay, hang on," Kai says. "Let's take a selfie together." He's been taking pictures of the scenery with my phone for the past ten minutes. He also took one of me standing by the river with the mountains behind me and the blue sky above me, white snow glistening all around. Then he added a caption: *Sun shines upon those strong enough to part the clouds.*

Another one of his dad's sayings. I hope he *is* still alive, so

I can meet him. He seems like the type of person I would like, full of optimism and life. He seems a lot like Kai.

He holds the phone out in front of us, then taps the camera shutter icon, capturing three bright smiles and one wrinkled brow. I notice something large and dark lumber into the background, near the river. By the time I turn and see that it's a brown bear, Kai is already ushering me toward the snowmobiles. "Looks like somebody's squeezing in one more meal before hibernation," he says. "Perfect time to go. Don't make any noise, just get on. Maybe it won't notice us."

There's a stretch of open land between us, but still, I've never been this close to a bear that wasn't enclosed in a zoo, close enough to hear its paws crunching the snow. My brain is suddenly struck with indecision: fear or awe? That thing can kill me if it wants to.

Kai straddles the snowmobile in front of me, and I get situated behind him but keep my eyes on the bear. It dunks its snout into the river and the sound of a splash hits my ears crisp and clear, as if I were standing right beside it. Both snowmobiles' engines start with a growl and then settle into a low rumble. The bear's head pops up and turns to face us. No hiding from it now. A bright coral fish hangs in its mouth, tail flopping with the final twitches of its life.

Maybe it's my imagination, but I think the bear is looking right at me. Right *into* me. My heart thumps hard in my chest, my head, my ears, my throat; I feel it everywhere. But this thing I'm feeling isn't "scared." I don't know what it is. Exposed, maybe. Vulnerable. Or . . . trust? I'm putting my absolute trust in this creature not to charge and attack me. That has to be it—trust in its purest form—and the realization calms me. Tension falls away like I'm shedding a heavy coat. For the first time ever I let go of my control of a situation without feeling *out* of control.

Total serenity. From a bear.

It lazily turns its head back to the river, and soon we're riding off, every second giving us more and more distance from a possible threat. The moment is gone, but the impact of it stays with me all the way to Jack Randy's house.

Even if I had been paying attention to how we got here instead of contemplating whether the brown bear is my spirit animal, I couldn't find this place again if I had to. Jack has taken great care in keeping himself hidden away. The little log-and-stone house is nestled among the evergreens, like not even one tree was razed to make room for the structure, and lies far from any signs of civilization. The forest opens up behind the house into a vast flat land. Piles of random junk cover the yard. Everything from a tire-free truck propped up on cinder blocks to stacks of plastic buckets to rusted pieces and parts of I-can't-even-guess-what are scattered and stacked in no particular order.

The front door opens slowly, hinges screaming like they're in pain, and I see the end of what I assume is a shotgun pointed at us before the person holding it comes into view. He's thin, pale, and wiry, wearing a sleeveless T-shirt, soot-smudged jeans, and intent to harm. Curly tufts of blond hair stick out from under his backward baseball cap. Shotgun aside, I could knock him over with a whisper, but the tendons of his arms are wound tight, ready to spring into action. One wrong move and I don't doubt he'll pull that trigger.

Vicki removes her helmet and hops off the snowmobile from her position behind Hunter, but he thrusts an arm out to hold her back.

"It's okay, he won't shoot me." She weaves a path through the junkyard, walks right up to Jack, and pushes the tip of his shotgun down until it's pointed at the ground. "We need a fly to Fairbanks."

Jack's stern expression falters. His lips twitch like he might laugh. "Well, I guess hell must have actually frozen over. Isn't that what you said the last time you dumped me—less than a month ago?" He adds a twang to his voice and heightens the pitch, mimicking her. "'The day I come back to you for any-thing, Jack-hole, is the day hell freezes over.'"

"This is Alaska," Vicki says. "Doesn't take long for any-thing to freeze here."

"Including my plane's engine. And the airstrip. You know I don't fly in winter, and you never go that far north, not even for your daddy. Why're you headed there now?"

"How about you let us in so we can talk about it before *we* freeze? Or are you just going to keep standing there in your stupid cutoff shirt and your stupid backward hat, looking at us all stupid like that?"

This guy must be a real snake if he makes innocent, cheerful Vicki let loose a string of stupids. That's the harshest word I've ever heard come out of her mouth, and she just fired three of them at him—bing, bang, *boom*—with barely a breath between them.

Jack eyes her up and down. A wicked grin slithers from cheek to cheek. "Missed you, too, babe."

Kai hasn't let go of my hand since I stepped out of the bathroom. Jack's house is surprisingly tidy and simple and smells like freshly chopped wood. A fireplace crackles in the main room, making it so hot in here we have to remove our coats and snowpants. Books line the shelves on either side of the mantel, but I have a hard time imagining Jack indulging in nightly pleasure reads. I'd sooner believe he uses the pages for kindling.

There are only two chairs, one a rocker and the other a lounger with sunken cushions barely held together by threads, and the guys insisted Vicki and I take them. Even with me sitting and Kai standing, he keeps a firm grip on my hand. Being around Jack has awakened some primal protective instinct within him that's too strong to fight. Not that I really need protecting; I could send Jack to the floor with one well-placed kick. But some primal instinct within *me* likes that Kai is playing bodyguard.

"Nice boots, princess," Jack says to me with a smirk. "Where'd you get those, overpricedoutfitters.com?"

I unlace them and pull them off my feet, one at a time. Kai helps me nudge my chair closer, so I can prop my feet up on the hearth. They prickle as heat wraps around them, bakes my toes. "What's wrong with my boots?"

"Nothing. Not one thing. They're perfect. The best money could buy, I bet."

"Save it," Vicki says. "We're not here to listen to you whine about the economy."

Jack shoots her a side-eye, then clears his throat. "So let me get this straight. You three need a ride to one of the dry cabins outside of Fairbanks."

"Dry cabins?" I say. "What are those?"

"That means they have no plumbing," Kai says. "But don't worry. They usually have an outhouse close by." He hands Jack a slip of paper. "Get us as close to those coordinates as you can. And as soon as possible. Like, right now." Then he turns to me. "If we're away too long, your dad will start to worry."

I pull out my phone to see if Dad tried calling again, but there's no signal here, either. Kai goes on, "If we don't find my dad within a day or two, we'll hike into the nearest town and get you a ride back home. Okay?"

"Yeah." I shove the phone back into my pocket. "What about you and Hunter?"

"Depends on what we *do* find."

Jack points at Vicki. "And you're doing what, then?"

"Going home," Vicki says, at the same time Hunter says, "Not your concern. Can you take us, or should we go find someone else? There's only so much daylight, it's a long ride, and we still have to hike up the mountain from wherever you drop us off. We'd rather not have to do that in the dark."

Jack levels his gaze on Hunter. Which actually requires him to lift his chin a bit. And when Hunter doesn't cow under his pitiful attempt at staring him down, Jack turns to me and Kai. "That'll be a thousand bucks. Half now, half when we get there."

Kai tightens his grip on my hand. "You'd better be serving caviar for that price—"

"No problem." I reach for my credit card.

"Cash only," Jack clarifies.

"Oh." Hm. Okay, that *is* a problem. "Hunter, you said you have cash, right?"

"Not that much, are you kidding?" he says. "I got maybe thirty bucks."

"Kai? Vicki?"

Headshakes all around.

Except Jack, who just grins. "Well, it looks like you're grounded. Unless you can offer something worth the same. Or . . . some*one*." His grin slides from me to Vicki. "Whaddaya say, Vicks? Just like old times?"

"You can't take her as payment, you vile swine," I snap. No, he's lower than swine for suggesting such a thing. He's swine dung. He looks up at swine from the mud and wishes he were that clean.

"Don't get your panties in a bunch, princess, I didn't mean nothing inappropriate. Tell 'er, babe. Tell 'er how we used to fly together."

Vicki presses her lips together. I'm starting to realize just how much of a sacrifice she's making for us—first the snowmobiles and having to spend the night in a shed, now taking us to the home of her less-than-pleasant ex because he's the only person she knows with a plane. "Yeah," she says, "I used to be his copilot, helped him run summer air tours over Denali, back when we used to be together. Emphasis on *used to*."

"All I'm asking for is a ride with you," Jack says. "So it isn't so lonely on the way back? I just want someone to talk to."

Sure he does. "Forget it, Vicki," I say. "You don't need to put up with him. I'd sooner walk."

"No, I'll do it," she says, then cuts Jack a glare. "But I'm doing it for them, not for you. So don't get any ideas."

"Or what?" He practically laughs the words.

"Or my boyfriend will beat the tar out of you," she blurts.

Jack's grin doesn't budge, but the humor leaves his face. "You got a boyfriend? Who?"

"Yeah, he's, um . . . He's . . . ." She tosses a glance at Hunter.

Raises a finger toward him. "Right there," she finishes, her tone ending high like a question rather than a statement.

Oh, mierda. Like we need any more complications on this trip.

Hunter's face remains oddly neutral, except for the usual wrinkle in his brow. That could mean he's upset. Or it could mean he didn't even catch what she said. You never know with him. And a little white lie might be considered harmless to most people, but Vicki doesn't know how adamantly Hunter doesn't want to be in a relationship, likely even to the extent of not agreeing to a fake one.

If it were me, I wouldn't. Small lies lead to bigger lies lead to hurting people you love.

"Really, babe?" Jack says, ignoring the fact that Hunter really could beat the tar—and probably a few organs—out of him if he had reason to. "You're with Hulk?"

That did it. I can almost hear the gears shifting behind Hunter's eyes, his protective instincts kicking in like Kai's did over me. He crosses the room to Vicki's chair and stands behind it like a sentinel. "That's none of your business. And how about you stop calling her babe."

Not a question, a command. He might as well have just said, "Back off. She's mine." Jack stares at the tops of his shoes and mutters something about getting the engine warmed up, then makes a hurried exit.

Firelight dances in Vicki's eyes, and a distinctly pink hue

has blossomed on her freckled cheeks. She's lucky Hunter is actually a big softy under that hard-to-read exterior.

Try as he might to deny it, he does care what happens to her. Maybe that's the real reason he put the brakes on his social life, and used his extra schoolwork and taking care of his family as an excuse. Kai found a way to get out, regularly. But Hunter . . . Hunter didn't want to. Spending time with someone leads to getting to know them, and getting to know someone leads to caring about them, and caring about someone can lead to loving them, and loving someone allows them to love you in return—the exact thing he wants to avoid.

"We left you two alone for five minutes this morning," Kai says, grinning. "That was fast."

I smack his arm.

But his brother ignores him. "Vicki, this doesn't mean we're—"

"I know," she says, and a tiny smile twitches the corners of her mouth. But whether she's glad she's in a fake relationship with Hunter or that doing so got Jack off her back—maybe both?—isn't clear.

While Jack is out preparing the plane, and Kai and Hunter are out making sure Jack doesn't change his mind, Vicki and I are left with a moment of peace by the fire.

"I can't believe Hunter went along with that," she says.

"He's a good guy. Kai is, too. It must be genetic."

She shakes her head as if confused. "What are y'all doing up by Fairbanks that's so important, anyway? I thought you were trying to stop Kai. Now you're going with him."

She's helped us so much, she deserves to know everything. And with Kai and Hunter and Jack outside, this might be my only chance to explain it to her without interruption or someone telling me she doesn't have to know. Keeping secrets never does anyone any good, though. I've learned that from my mother's mishaps with the media. People find out the truth eventually. You might as well be the one to tell it to them and at least salvage your credibility.

I relay as much as I know, in a way that I hope makes sense. Hunter and the whole Locklear family think their dad is dead. Kai thinks their dad is alive. One of them is right, and one of them is wrong. Both of them are emotionally screwed no matter what the outcome. She listens without a word, occasionally nodding. And in Vicki's world, I'm not sure what her silence means. Maybe it's this place making her pensive rather than chatty, just being here, remembering her past relationship with Jack, whatever it was. From what I've seen of him so far, it couldn't have been that great of a time in her life.

Blessing or lesson—not hard to guess what Jack was for Vicki. But at least she got away from him. Now she can find someone better. I just hope she doesn't believe that "someone" could be Hunter. He's a road to nowhere—but it's not my place to tell her that. It's his.

The shrill ring of a telephone interrupts my thoughts.

"There's a phone here!" I shriek. "Why didn't you tell me there's a phone here?"

Vicki yelps at my outburst, and then again as I jump out of my chair. "You don't have to answer it."

Still in my socks, I pad across the wood floor like a dolphin using echolocation. It rings and I move. Pause. Ring. Move. Pause. Ring. Move. Until I've stepped into a tiny room housing a bed so large it leaves no space for any other furniture but a nightstand, and on that nightstand is a corded rotary phone, something I've seen only in old movies. It's stopped ringing. No answering machine picks up. This is my chance to call Dad before crossing the great Alaska Interior and I've no clue how to use this dinosaur contraption.

I hold the clunky receiver against my ear and try to remember how I saw actors dial a phone like this. Finger in the hole. Spin it . . . which way? It doesn't move in the direction of the number order, which makes no sense at all, but even more infuriating is that spinning it the other way does nothing, either.

There's still a dial tone. What am I doing wrong?

"Help!" I yell to Vicki.

She's a ferret racing into the room. "What what what— What happened? Are you okay?"

"Do you know how to dial this? I need to call my dad."

Vicki rolls her eyes. "Is that all? Pig on a stick, Gabi, I thought you saw a rat."

"Are there really rats here?"

"You've seen the yard?" She jacks a thumb toward the front of the house. "All kinds of critters take shelter in that mess. Might be a whole family of Sasquatch in there!"

She has to be kidding. Please let her be kidding.

"But Jack don't mind," she goes on. "He loves animals, rats and all. He's a jerk-face otherwise, but he'd never even swat a fly. That gun he's got? For human trespassers only."

"How comforting."

I give my dad's work number to Vicki and she spins the numbers in—clockwise—hitting the metal stopper hard with each one. That was my mistake. I didn't turn the wheel far enough. In the vintage films, people are always in a hurry or angry when they dial a phone. I thought they were just being overdramatic, spinning each number with the force of a punch. But it's actually necessary. How did people use these for years and years on a daily basis without getting calluses? And what if you had long nails? Impossible.

The post office picks up and I barely get out "Alex Flores, please" before I'm put on hold. Vicki gestures at herself and then at the doorway. *Thank you*, I mouth to her, and she walks out. A few decades of Muzak pass.

Then, "Hello?"

"Papi, it's me." Finally. And he's loud and clear—God bless landlines.

"No personal calls!" someone shouts on his end. "Is that an emergency?"

"Is this an emergency?" Dad asks.

"No, but . . . I didn't catch what you said when you called earlier. The connection was bad and you got cut off."

There's some shuffling on the line and he says something that I can't decipher, his voice low. Then, to me, "Your mother called me while I was on my way to work—first thing on a Monday morning—just to accuse me of being a bad parent. She said I'm letting you run wild."

"Why would she do that?"

"I don't know, querida. Why does she do anything she does?"

That's the million-dollar question. Or, in her case, *multi*million.

He sighs, heavy breath rattling the phone. "She was talking so fast I couldn't keep up. Something about an alert on the credit card she gave you. Odd charges or something. I told her to put a freeze on it if she was worried about theft. Do you still have your card?"

"Yeah, I . . . still have it . . ." And I'm an idiot. That's the first time I've ever used my card outside of Anchorage or for something other than an online purchase. No wonder Mom freaked. She isn't worried about theft like Dad thinks—she knows I'm not where I'm supposed to be. And at a lodge, of all places? With charges for two lunches, a room payment, and an exorbitant fee for the snowmobiles likely marked "other" or "miscellaneous." Fantastic. I can just imagine what she thinks I'm doing there.

Stay out of trouble, Gabriella. Those were her last words to me at the airport before I unleashed my fury onto her. Not "good-bye." Not "I love you" or "I'll miss you." *Stay out of trouble*, as if I was the one to blame for all of this. Like I was the one who forced us into exile.

She's the one who needs to stay out of trouble, not me. But she was so worried I might do something to draw attention to myself, that someone would recognize me and connect it back to her, that she *didn't even say good-bye.* Good freaking riddance.

"Then I don't know what she was going on about," Dad says. "And when I asked her to slow down and explain, she hung up on me. Can you believe that?"

No, actually, I can't. If she wanted to give Dad an earful, she'd make sure he got it. There were plenty of times I heard her screaming at him long after he'd slammed a door shut or driven off. She'd stand at the front door, yelling at a pair of taillights. Our neighbors loved us.

Nothing Mom does anymore surprises me, though. Maybe hanging up on Dad is just part of who she is now, I don't know. And I don't care.

"What are you still doing back here?" that same gruff voice snaps at him. He's gone from a scolding wife to a scolding boss. Moving to Alaska got him nowhere.

He smooth-talks his supervisor into giving him two more minutes using his charismatic lawyer voice, then says to me, "I got a call from your homeschool teacher a little bit ago, too. She said you didn't sign into class this morning. Are you feeling okay?"

Part of me wants him to piece it together that I'm gone, panic and worry, become unreasonable, do *something*. But when I think about it logically, it's not that unusual that Dad hasn't noticed my absence yet. He leaves for work before I'm out of bed, and more often than not, I'm out somewhere with Kai when he gets home. His sleeping pills have knocked him out by the time I come home again. I'm entirely self-sufficient in the hours between. This phone call is the most we've talked in weeks.

"I had a headache." It's not a lie. I did have a headache after slamming it into a car window. That happened yesterday, but it did happen. "It's better now."

"That's good," he says. "I have to go. I'll see you at dinner."

"No, wait. I'm"—*don't lie*—"going out with Kai. I'm not sure when we'll be back."

"Okay. Have fun."

Fun. Right. We say our good-byes, but I can't get myself to pull the phone away from my ear until I hear the dial tone again. He's gone. And he doesn't know I'm gone.

Mom knows, but what can she do about it, so far away? Except call Dad again, after she's cooled down. By then I'll be somewhere in the mountains north of Fairbanks, where neither one of them will find me even if they tried.

But I still want them to try. Just because they've given up on each other doesn't mean they should give up on me.

During the twenty-minute walk to the airstrip behind Jack's house, we discuss the plan. Jack's going to have to find a place for us to land as close to the coordinates of the Locklear cabin as possible—which might end up being not very close at all. Jack has never flown to that area before, but Vicki assures us it's not a problem. Despite her not having much faith in him as a human being, she has complete faith in his piloting skills. Flying is his life, and has been since he was a kid.

I wonder if that was part of the problem when they were together. A passion like that can consume your time and mental focus so much that it drives other things—and people—out. Like Mom and her acting career. It started small, with bit roles and commercials, things that didn't interrupt our life too much. I remember going with her to some of the auditions because she couldn't find a babysitter, although I was too young to remember much more than that it happened. The details are fuzzy. I do remember she always took me out for ice cream afterward. Then some big shot "discovered" her and put her in a leading role of a blockbuster film, and after that, *everyone* wanted a piece of her.

And I still wanted her, too. But more and more of her went to other people instead, until there were only crumbs of her existence left for me. Passing her in the hall on my way to the kitchen. A text to say happy birthday while she was on location in Italy. So when she made room in her busy schedule to talk to me face to face, one on one, I knew it was bad news.

"You're going to live in Alaska for a while," she'd said.

It was more lecture than discussion. No asking me how I felt about it. No remorse, for anything.

When we reach the plane, Kai helps me climb inside the tiny cabin. Hunter hunches over to keep his head from hitting the ceiling, even after he sits, and stares out the window on his side. Jack is up front in the pilot's seat, which is only a few feet from where I'm sitting. I've been on plenty of planes before, but nothing this small. I could stand on the nose and spit on the tail. Although I'd rather spit on Jack.

Vicki climbs into the copilot's seat up front and gives me a cheesy grin coupled with two thumbs up. She and Jack start flipping switches and turning knobs, speaking to each other in aviation terms that might as well be gibberish to me. Hunter leans and reaches across me and helps Kai into the cabin, then Kai sits across from me, facing me, his back to the pilots. Our knees are touching. How is this safe? Hunter props one foot up onto the empty seat across from him and stretches the other leg toward the cockpit, the picture of calm. Once we're all settled and buckled in, Kai pulls the cabin door down and it clicks shut.

"This is a first for me," Kai says.

"Me, too." I reach over and take his hand. "I've flown before, but not like this."

"I haven't flown ever. Hunter has. But I prefer to stay on

the ground." His knee bounces and he tosses furtive glances out the window. We haven't even started moving yet.

"I'm sorry I messed up your big plan," I say.

"You didn't mess anything up. This is good. It's good to try new things." He tries a smile, but it's tenuous, and his voice trembles. But he's *trying*. He's not giving up or demanding we find another way or insisting I go home because I threw a wrench into his journey. This is Kai, eternally optimistic, even when he's doing something that obviously scares the snot out of him. "Remember what Dad used to say, Hunter? About trying new things?"

Hunter shrugs and keeps staring out the window.

"Wherever you go," Kai says, "let your heart lead your feet."

Nice sentiment, but: "What does that have to do with trying new things?"

"Because if you really want to try something, and you have a really good reason for wanting it, your heart will make you do it no matter how much your brain tells you not to."

Hunter doesn't respond, so I give Kai a smile and say, "I like that."

The engine roars to life and the propeller spins outside the front window. Kai squeezes my hand hard and grips the edge of his seat with his other, the rest of his body completely rigid. As we move forward, which is actually backward for Kai, slowly at first and then faster and faster, Hunter reaches across the cabin, pulls Kai's death grip off his seat, and holds his hand.

He doesn't let go until long after we've shot into the air and Kai has visibly relaxed. I know it'll only be a couple of hours, but it seems like we've been flying for days already. The drone of the engine has dulled my ears into thinking the constant buzz is normal. But when I try to talk, I can barely hear my own voice, let alone Kai's. We tire of shouting at each other after a while and opt for staring out the window, like Hunter's been doing on his side.

It's beautiful, with all those mountains, rivers, and trees, and what isn't snow-covered is a lovely shade of muddy green. From above, it doesn't seem real, like we're just analyzing a painting in a museum. The earth is a living work of art. We even see a herd of something running across a plain. Kai says it's caribou. But then we fly into a dense fog that blocks the view. I lean back in my seat. Neither Jack nor Vicki seems concerned about the lessened visibility. I assume their instrument panel is helping them "see." Hunter starts snoring, leaning against his window, and Kai is nodding off. They must be exuding sleeping gas because suddenly I'm fuzzy and warm and can't fight the urge to nap along with them.

I give in and close my eyes. Everything feels right and at peace. We're together again. Soon we'll get to the cabin and hopefully find the truth, whatever it is.

I've just started slipping into a dream when the whole plane jumps, jolting me upright, eyes wide and alert.

"Y'all okay back there?" Vicki shouts.

"We're okay!" Kai and I shout in unison.

Hunter rubs his eyes and looks around. "What happened?"

"It's probably just turbulence," I say.

Jack and Vicki frantically work the control panel, each of them claiming the other is at fault for whatever happened. Oh God, are they having a fight? Now?

"No!" Vicki smacks his hand away from a big red switch.

He shoves her off and flips the switch. "We have to land!"

"But *we. Can't. See!*"

"I know my plane. Are you saying you know my plane better than I know my plane? This is *my* plane and—"

We bank hard to the left. Kai grabs both of my hands. His first time in the air and *this* happens. I don't even know what *this* is. I'm afraid to look out the side window, but looking straight ahead is no better.

The plane bucks again and shudders. Kai and I both grab our seats to keep steady, and Hunter's head thumps against the ceiling.

Definitely not turbulence. It felt like we hit something—or something hit *us*. "What's going on?" I yell over the noise. "Are we going to die?"

"We are not going to—" Hunter starts, but Vicki cuts him off with a hoarse shout over her shoulder at us.

"We're okay! We just have to land and check for damage! We're okay—okay?"

Her voice is a thousand miles away.

Hunter takes one of my hands from Kai and holds one of Kai's with the other, so we're all connected now.

Vicki can claim we're okay all she wants, but all I hear is *we're going to die.*

I'm going to die.

I look at Kai, look right into his sunshine eyes fraught with worry, those eyes that always make me feel safe and warm.

But I don't see him. I see my mother.

Long before I met Kai or came to Alaska, long before I chewed her out at the airport, even before all the nonsense with the paparazzi and my parents' divorce, it was just Mom. It was always Mom. She was my everything.

She was the one who instilled confidence in me. *She* was the one who knew how to make me feel good about myself, encouraged me to go into acting because she said I had the trifecta—beauty, talent, and brains. *She* was the one who always made me laugh—if I was ever in a bad mood around her, it didn't last.

Things are so different now . . . the past might as well have been all a dream. Would she be relieved if I died? Just one less thing for her to worry about ruining her image?

We hit the ground, skidding, sliding, screaming, and for the first time in a long time, all thoughts about my mother disappear. All thoughts about *everything* . . . disappear.

CHAPTER THIRTEEN

The plane settles, and a heavy silence dumps over us. It's too quiet. No one is even breathing, but then a second later, we all let out our breath at once, a tidal wave of relief.

Vicki spins to face us in the back. "Is everyone okay?"

"We're *alive!*" I say. "So that's a yes. We're okay."

Kai squeezes my hand and starts laughing—a little too hard, given what just happened. But even when it seems out of place, his laughter is contagious. Despite my heart still racing, my face relaxes with a smile. "We can check 'scary emergency landing' off our bucket list now, Gabi," he says. "What's next?"

"I don't remember . . . It was either 'eating a live scorpion' or 'dropping a live scorpion down your pants.' But both of those seem tame after this, don't you think? We need something more dangerous."

Jack flips me off through his rearview mirror. I ignore it, chalk up his response to the stress of the situation, but if Kai had seen it, I doubt he would've let it slide.

"What happened?" Hunter says, unbuckling his seat belt. "Where are we?"

Vicki rattles off the latitude, longitude, and altitude, like that means anything.

"Not close enough," Kai says, sobering quickly. "That's at least a full day of walking."

Okay, I guess the numbers meant nothing just to me. But if we're only a day's walk away, that means we're much closer than we were before. These mountains we're in were the final destination on the map. Now all we have to do is get to the cabin. "How long before you can get us back in the air?"

"Sorry, princess," Jack says. "This baby's going nowhere until I can take a look under her skirt and see what the damage is. We've got plenty of daylight left, so either we stay here, in the plane, and hope I can get it running again. Or we start walking and hope we find another cabin."

"Unbelievable." Hunter shoots a glare that could wilt steel at the back of Jack's head.

Oblivious to Hunter's death stare—which is way better than mine—Jack starts going on about how Vicki miscalculated this or that, we swiped a mountain in the fog and blew out something or other, this is why we don't fly in winter, blah-whine-blah. I'm done listening to his finger-pointing, which helps us zero, and look out the window. We're in a huge open field of white, although the snow doesn't seem deep, not like what it was at the shelter. A thick bundle of trees stands proud in the distance, the snow and cold not affecting them at all. Why can't I be a tree? Life would be so much easier as a tree.

Hunter pushes between me and Kai and muscles the door open. Frigid air smacks my cheeks. It's much colder here than where we came from. The air has teeth. My whole body shudders.

"Better to stay inside." Hunter flops back onto his seat. The plane rattles and shifts with his movement, more than it should just from him sitting down. He's a big guy and this is a small plane, but . . . I don't know. Maybe I imagined it.

"Did you guys feel that?" I say.

"Jack . . . ?" Vicki draws out his name. She leans forward and looks hard out the front window, past the propeller. "I don't think you landed us in a clearing. Well, it is a clearing, but not the kind of clearing you thought it was when you said, 'We're in luck, there's a clearing over there!'"

He opens his door and hops down, out of the plane. "What are you rambling on a—Whoa."

The plane shifts again and we all freeze. In the quiet, I hear something crunching. Outside the cabin door, the ground is distorted and cracked.

Not the ground. That's ice. Snow-covered ice. We're on a lake! And it isn't completely frozen yet.

"Trees," I say, my ragged thoughts unable to form full sentences. "Trees need dirt. Get to the trees." I'm not talking to anyone other than myself, but Hunter responds, "Okay. The trees aren't that far. We just have to get out of the plane really carefully, and then run for it."

"You mean like Jack's already doing?" Kai says.

My face snaps toward the door's opening and, sure enough, Jack is halfway to the trees, feet kicking up tufts of snow behind him.

"That weasel!" Vicki shouts. "This is *his* plane. The captain goes down with the ship, Jack-hole!"

Jack doesn't turn or slow down until he's reached the trees, then he waves his arms at us like, *Why are you still out there? Move!*

"Okay." Hunter lets out a long, slow, steady breath. "Okay. We can do this."

If I had an ounce of his confidence, however forced—

"Vicki, you go first. You're the smallest; your movement might not affect anything. Get out. Slowly. As soon as you're clear, run."

"I'm not gonna leave y'all like that—"

"Yes, you are," Hunter says, gently but firmly. "It's okay. We'll be right behind you."

She smashes her lips together, a whirlpool of worry swirling in her eyes, then nods and starts her agonizingly slow crawl across the pilot seats to the door Jack left open. Nothing moves. Everything but Vicki is on pause. I don't even think my heart is beating right now. She drops out the door and takes a few tentative steps, then flat-out runs, following the line of Jack's footprints through the snow, slipping sideways a couple of times, but she doesn't fall.

Hunter lets out a quick breath. Two people down, three to go.

"My stuff," Kai says. "I can't leave it here. What if the whole plane goes down?"

"Then you can get new stuff," I say.

"With what money? Yours?"

"Yes! Why is that always a problem for you?"

"It wouldn't be a problem if you'd stop offering it whenever I need something. Like money can solve everything."

"I'm sorry, Kai. I didn't realize my wanting to help you was such a burden."

"Gabi . . ." He sighs. "That's not what I meant."

"Then why won't you let me take care of it for you?"

"Give a man a fish, you feed him for a day—"

"Are you really going to start spouting quotes right now?" Hunter snaps. "Get off your transcendental horse. Gabi's right. The pack isn't worth it."

"Yes, it is. Some of that stuff is Dad's. It's not replaceable." The look he gives Hunter is painfully reminiscent of Caesar's after Brutus stabbed him. Kai gets up from his seat, crouching under the low ceiling. My breath hitches, but nothing happens. "Don't move. Either of you. My bag is right there." He points behind my seat. "I'm just gonna grab it and . . ."

His fingers find a strap and pull. The rucksack is as wide as he is and half as long. I could fit inside it if I hugged my knees. And if it wasn't already packed full. Kai threads an arm under one of the shoulder straps and creeps toward the exit. The plane takes a big awkward dip and we all brace ourselves against the walls and ceiling. The door opening is pointed more at the ice now than the horizon, and the bottom lip is *below* the ice. Water starts to seep into the cabin.

I pull my feet up. With Kai and his friends at the lake a few weeks ago, I imagined what it would be like to plunge my whole body into cold water. I'd rather not find out today if my imagination was accurate.

"Okay, new plan," I say. "On the count of three, we all make a mad dash for it. I'll lead, then Kai right behind me, then Hunter. One two three, all together. Okay?"

They nod. But nothing about this is okay.

"One," Hunter says.

I stand up, and water rushes over my boots. Thank God for overpriced waterproofing and insulation. Kai sidesteps to give me more space to move. The cabin creaks and moans, like a bear woken from a cozy nap, ready to shred whatever disturbed it.

"Two . . ."

Vicki's shouts drift to me from across the ice. I focus on Vicki, her arms waving, her body bouncing up and down. That's my target. Just get to Vicki.

"Three!"

From the lip of the opening, I leap over broken ice, but my maneuver is neither graceful nor athletic, and I land on all fours. Faster than I thought possible, Kai is right beside me, pulling me upright by the elbow. I stagger to my feet. The ice beneath me is solid. Now we just have to—

"Run!" Hunter yells.

Where is he? I dare a glance over my shoulder but don't see him—or half the plane. It's going down nose first, the back end tipped up like the sinking *Titanic*. Oh God . . . Is he still in there?

Kai tugs me along. Too fast. I can't keep up. Behind us an angry splash urges my legs to pump harder. My feet slide this way and that; my knees twist and threaten to snap. It's like trying to surf on a board that's been greased. My next step, I wipe out completely, losing my grip on Kai's hand and slamming my butt onto the hard ice.

It cracks and gives a little beneath me.

A line of footprints roughs up the snow ahead of me. We all ran on the same line, all those feet pounding this weak spot before I got to it. My butt was the last straw. The ice couldn't take any more.

Kai's momentum kept him going after our hands separated. He stops and spins, notices I'm down, then immediately starts back toward me, hand extended to help me up. But his attention shifts, his eyes darting back and forth. "Where's Hunter?"

"Wait, stop!" I flash a palm toward him. "The ice is breaking. It won't hold both of us."

He freezes in place, eyes back on me. "Okay, Gabi, don't try to stand or even crawl," he says with a forced calm, each word tensed and vibrating like a plucked guitar string. "You need to roll over to me."

"Roll?" My teeth chatter hard, catching my bottom lip, and I taste blood. As I turn and face Kai, a red droplet hits the snow and freezes into a tiny marble. Where the snow has been brushed away, the ice is spiderwebbed with thin fractures. Below it, something swims by. So many things are able to thrive in this environment—why can't I? Why have my fingers gone so numb that they hurt? Why is my heart beating in over-drive, pumping blood everywhere, yet I feel none of its warmth? It isn't fair.

The fish swims by again, then disappears from view. How deep is this water? I'm already too cold. My muscles are locking up. If I fall in . . .

Warm thoughts. Warm thoughts. Warm thoughts. California. Sunshine. Beaches. Desert. Jalapeños. Heartburn. I'll take *anything* even remotely lukewarm over this.

"I can't do this. Kai—" My throat closes up, anticipating the worst. "I can't do this."

"Don't give up," he says. Now his attention is focused intently on me and nothing else, never taking his eyes off me, not even to check on his brother, who still hasn't passed us. "I'm not giving up on you. Don't you give up on you. I'm right here. All you have to do is get to me. Just imagine you're rolling down a grassy hill. You can do it. You've done harder things before, Gabi, this is nothing."

This is nothing? I'd take a total wipeout on my surfboard over this, a million times over and over and over. But that isn't the card I've been dealt, and I've got nothing up my sleeve to cheat my way out of this. Kai's right—money can't solve everything. "Okay, I—I'm coming."

I do as Kai said and roll toward him like I used to roll down grassy hills as a child, expecting to fall through the earth any second, but I don't. And I don't breathe again until his arms are around me, helping me stand.

"Are you okay?" he says, squeezing me. All I can do is nod, fast and furious. I can't stop shaking. My whole body is buzzing with adrenaline.

"Hunter!" Vicki and Jack yell in unison. "Get Hunter!"

Kai's face snaps away from me and he curses low and hard. I turn to follow his gaze. The first thing I see is the giant hole in the ice left by the plane, but it's not just water. Chunks of thick broken ice bob on the surface and two arms flail up between them, grasping for anything stable but finding nothing. Hunter manages to get his elbows up on a solid edge and pushes—only to fall back under the water when the ice gives beneath him.

Kai wrestles with his pack for a second and it falls off his shoulders, then he digs out a rope. "Get off the ice, Gabi. And get help." He pushes his pack closer to the shore, away from the cracked ice. "We have to get him warm and dry as quickly as possible. Go!" He doesn't wait for me to take action before he's heading back toward his brother.

Go where? I don't even know where we are! But Hunter could die if I don't find someone to help us, give us a ride to somewhere, at least. I run to the shore, practically flying. I can't feel half my face. But God, that has to be nothing compared to what Hunter is feeling right now. Or not feeling.

Just before I reach the trees, Jack runs past me, back out onto the ice.

"Jack, wait, it's too dangerous!" Vicki screams, but he keeps going.

I tell myself not to look out onto the ice, afraid of what I might see, but my eyes don't listen. Kai and Jack, standing at a distance from the wreckage, tug on the rope they've somehow gotten looped around Hunter's chest. He doesn't push himself up this time. He hangs there, limply, but together Kai and Jack manage to drag him out. Once he's clear of the broken edge, I heave a sigh of relief, but he doesn't move.

He isn't moving.

"We have to get help, Vicki." I fumble through my pocket and grasp my cell phone, then tap out 9-1-1. No signal. No nothing. It was worth a try, but now I'm tempted to throw this useless thing into the hole in the ice. "Where can we get help?"

"I don't know . . ." Vicki scans the area quickly, does a complete circle, then hustles ahead of me, some invisible hand pushing her along with ease. "This way! I see something!"

The farther we go uphill, the farther I fall behind. Shock and anxiety have turned my legs to jelly, wobbling out of control. But still, I keep sight of Vicki's bright red curls and keep running.

"Vicki, wait up," I say, but she doesn't hear me. I'm losing steam. No, the steam is long gone. I don't even have enough to run on fumes. A weight presses down on my chest; every breath is a struggle, prickling with chills. There are ice floes in my blood, crystallizing my veins.

"We're almost there!" Vicki's shout ripples back to me, light-years away. She's a speeding comet even in this cold. Nothing ever slows her down.

I see a small cabin ahead—I think?—and Vicki is running up to the door, but my vision is strained. It's too bright out here, with the sun glaring off the snow, and an odd thought crosses my mind—I should have worn sunglasses. Here in the frozen north, I need my shades as much as I needed them in Southern California.

When I catch up to Vicki I can see the cabin is real, not just some arctic version of a mirage. I nearly collapse with relief, but then I realize it might be empty. And locked. Vicki pounds on the cabin door, and we both scream various versions of, "Is anyone home? We need help!" But no one answers.

"Now what—"

Vicki kicks open the door. "That's what," she says, rushing inside.

"This is someone's house—we can't just break in!"

"Yes, we can, and we did. Unless you're okay with Hunter freezing to death?" She darts around the rooms. I hang back in the doorway and look around. It's empty. There's a small hearth and some basic furniture, like a wooden table and two chairs in the main room, but it doesn't appear lived in. Everything is dark and dingy. Musty.

"There's a bed in here, with blankets, and some wood." Vicki exits one of the adjacent rooms. "Either the owners don't stay here regularly or this is a public cabin for mountaineers. Whichever it is, this will work. Now we just need to get a fire going."

"Right." Fire mage isn't on my résumé, though. "You do the fire. I'll go back and get the guys, show them where to go."

Vicki waves me off as she opens cupboards and drawers. "Matches, matches, come on, where are you?"

I follow our tracks through the snow, back to the lake. Kai and Jack are crouched next to Hunter, close to the trees. There's a blanket under him, with a rope securing one end of it around his feet, and a thick line through the snow-covered ice leads to him. They dragged him, which explains why they're both so out of breath. Hunter's not dead like I feared, or even unconscious, but he's definitely not well. His breaths are ragged, he's almost hyperventilating, and he's sickly pale, like the blood drained out of him. And I think he's trying to talk, but it's nonsense, words jumbling together through his chattering teeth. How are we going to help him out here?

Panic bubbles up from my gut and threatens to seize control. I swallow it down. I can do this; I can help by making a plan. *I'm* in control.

"We found an empty cabin, not far up the mountain," I tell Kai. "Vicki's working on warming it up. Can you get him there? I'll lead the way."

"Yes. That's the best news I've ever gotten in my whole life." He looks to Jack. "I'll take one corner; you take the other. Ready?"

Jack nods, chest heaving from the work they've already done. That was across flat land, though. Now they're going uphill.

Hunter sputters, "W-walk . . . I—I can w—"

"No," Kai says firmly. "Save your energy. Stop talking. Concentrate on not dying." He picks up his rucksack and puts it on my back. "I can't carry him and this."

My balance wavers for a moment while he tightens the straps. What's he got in there, cinder blocks? Once it's secure, I lead the way as best I can. Kai's and Jack's grunts behind me blend with the rush of blood in my ears. My lungs burn, refusing to expand, and my heart throws a tantrum. I'm desperate for air, for heat, for this to all be a dream. I'm not made for this kind of physical exertion in this kind of weather. Survival of the fittest is going to remove me from the gene pool.

Somehow, after a century of hiking, I reach the cabin and open the door for them. They drag Hunter inside. His shoulders just barely clear the doorway. "In here!" Vicki shouts, and they make a hard left into the adjacent room.

I close the main door and then find them heaving Hunter onto a bed that's a few inches too short. His feet hang over the end. Then Kai starts stripping him. Coat, boots, shirt, pants, another shirt. *Slop, slap*, everything hits the floor in a wet heap. When he's down to his underwear and Kai tugs at that, too, I turn away to watch Vicki on the other side of the room.

She has the beginnings of a fire going in a small wood burner. The tiny metal chimney shoots straight up and through a hole in the ceiling. She fans the flames and they glow bright red for a few seconds.

Kai leans against the wall, his face flushed and glistening with sweat. I turn to see Hunter bundled up in blankets from neck to toe. Vicki abandons the fire, finds a towel in Kai's pack, and uses it to rub the ice out of Hunter's hair.

Jack visibly bristles, watching his ex-girlfriend take care of the guy he thinks is her new boyfriend. Then he turns his ice-blue gaze onto me. "What's the plan now? We have no means of transportation and no way to contact anyone for help. Coulda used the radio in my plane *if I still had a plane.*"

"I'm sorry about your plane," I say. Because I can't answer

his question; I don't have a plan. What *do* we do now? "There's nothing we could have done to save it."

"Not good enough."

"Hey," Kai interjects, "Gabi isn't the one who landed us on a lake. Losing the plane is your fault."

"And it's your fault we went to the Bermuda Triangle of Alaska in the first place."

"Fighting won't get your plane back," I say. "Stop worrying about what you can't change." I'm the queen of telling people not to do things I excel at doing—where is my crown?

"That plane is my life," Jack snaps.

"It's just a thing," I say, trying to sound reasonable. "Things are replaceable. I'll buy you a new one." Which means I'll have to get my mother involved and somehow convince her to add tens of thousands of dollars—a hundred thousand? How much is a plane?—to my monthly allowance, and the chances of that happening are slim to none, but Jack doesn't need to know that and I don't have room in my head to think about it now, anyway. I'll figure it out later.

"Kai," Hunter says weakly. "Dad . . . Is-s-s he here?"

He must be delirious.

Kai rushes to his side so fast that Vicki practically jumps out of the way. "No, this isn't his place," he tells his brother. "We're at a different cabin. The owners aren't here. But don't worry about that now, okay? Just get warm."

"I c-c-can't."

"Yes, you can, you're a human furnace. That's what Dad used to call you, remember? He said you were born to live outside." Kai's voice is crumbling. "The cold never bothered you."

Vicki pokes at the fire, twisting her mouth. "We can't go anywhere until he's better. So I guess we're spending the night here."

"And then what?" Jack says. "You and I were going to drop them off anyway, Vicks. We don't have to stay. There's gotta be a town around here somewhere. If we leave now, we might find one before dark."

"Good idea. Go. I'm not leaving Hunter like this."

"And I'm not leaving without *you*."

"It's not your job to worry about me anymore," Vicki huffs.

"I don't need your permission to worry about you. And I don't care if you hate me for it—you can't hate me any more than you already do. I am *not* leaving you stranded here. But I'm not going to stand here and let you grump at me, either." Jack moves toward the doorway and I step in front of it, palms out toward him.

"Wait," I say. "Don't leave the room before we know what we're all doing. We don't know yet if we're close to any towns or doctors, and there's nothing more *we* can do to help Hunter right now, so let's take care of our immediate needs first." I instinctively look to Kai for direction. "What should we do?"

He offers no suggestions, still focused on Hunter. I'm not even sure he heard me, and he's two feet away. Hunter is still shaking but has given up trying to communicate. I wonder how much he'll even remember of what's happening now.

I guess I'll figure it out, then. What do we need to survive? Shelter, check. Heat, check. Although we'll need more wood soon—*lots* more if we want to heat the other rooms, too. What else . . . ? Water. Kai has a canteen in his rucksack, but that won't be enough for all of us, even for just one day.

My shoulders drop with a sigh while my gaze drops to the floor, which is sprinkled with wet spots. Small puddles have formed everywhere our boots tracked the snow inside.

Snow. We can melt the snow for water. *Yes.*

What's left, then? Food. Kai can hunt, but it doesn't seem like he's going to leave Hunter's side until he's better. Vicki can hunt, too, but can she get enough for all of us on her own?

I look up at Jack. "How well can you hunt?"

"Not at all," he says.

Right, Vicki said his shotgun's just for human trespassers. "All right, you're in charge of getting wood to keep the fires going. We can't let it get cold in here." I'm not a doctor or even a med student like Hunter, but that much I know. The cold is trying to kill him. The only way to fight that is with heat. And the fire that's warming him up now will go out soon if we don't keep feeding it. Thankfully, Jack doesn't argue.

"Vicki, you're in charge of food," I say, and she nods. "And Kai . . ." Is acting really worrisome right now. "Kai's going to take care of Hunter."

"What are you in charge of, then, princess?" Jack says. I misinterpreted his silence before. He was seething at me. "Because no way are you going to sit around here barking orders at everyone and not lift a finger of your own."

That snaps Kai out of his trance. He turns his head slowly and locks a glare onto Jack. *Watch it.*

Jack shakes his head and mutters, "Nothing like being a fifth wheel on a broken wagon." He grabs the hatchet from Kai's pack. "If anyone needs me, I'll be freezing my butt off chopping wood. Don't say I didn't pull my own weight when this is over. I pulled mine *and* his." He points at Hunter, then storms out of the room and, moments later, out the front door, slamming it behind him.

One of the bigger logs in the wood burner catches in the draft, bathing everything in a warm glow. My chest loosens, and even Hunter's ragged breaths seem calmer now. He's getting better, slowly.

And we have a plan. We're going to be fine. "Okay, while Jack's out doing that, let's—"

"You're right, Gabi," Kai says. "Even if we found someone . . . by the time we did that and brought them here . . . the worst of it will be over already. All we can do now is wait and hope Hunter pulls through." He tugs off his gloves, tosses them beside his pack, and exits to the main room. Vicki goes back to Hunter's side, and I follow Kai. "This isn't worth it," he says, pressing the heels of his palms against his eyes and then onto the tabletop for one breath . . . two . . .

Suddenly he kicks one of the chairs, sending it careening away from the table, and stomps off.

CHAPTER FOURTEEN

"Kai?" I close the door behind me and approach him hesitantly, like if I get too close he might vanish into thin air. We're in another bedroom, as small and suffocating as the other one, with a narrow bed, an empty wood burner, and a single-paned window completely frosted over.

He turns to face me, and his jaw pulses. Whether he's holding back anger, frustration, or fear, though, I can't tell. "I can't lose him, too," he says.

Fear it is, then. "You're not going to lose him."

"No. I said that wrong." He sits on the edge of the bed and drops his head in his hands. "Hunter's *already* gone. He's been gone for a long time, and I don't know why. You didn't know us then, how things were before."

I may not be able to survive Alaska on my own, I may not be able to tend the fire or provide the food, but this I can do. I can be here for Kai when he needs it most. When things were at their worst between my parents, how often did I want someone to just listen to me vent? *Let him speak*, my heart whispers to my brain. I sit next to him on the bed. "I'm here now. I'm listening. You can tell me more about what happened, if you want to."

His head pops up and his gaze catches mine. He looks shaken for a moment, then everything drains out of him and he's just an empty shell, eyes cold, so devoid of their natural sparkle that they seem black. He's putting as much emotional distance as possible between himself and the past. I wish I could do the same.

"We used to be close—we did everything together, Hunter and Dad and me. Going out with Dad was one of our favorite things. When we were really young, we'd go camping in the backyard. Then as we got older, Dad taught us how to fish, how to chop wood and start a fire, how to hunt, what to do if you fall through ice." For a second his brow tightens, but he relaxes it again before it can change his whole expression. "Hunter did it all. And we had fun. But then he just . . . stopped. Everything. He never told me why. I mean, he said it was because he didn't want to shoot animals anymore, and I respected his view on that, but why stop *everything*? You saw how he was with the fire yesterday. And tracking. He's a natural at that kind of stuff. He always has been. That's why I don't understand how he could just shut it off, without warning, as easily as flipping a light switch."

He takes in a breath and lets it out slowly. "Before we

were born, even before Mom and Dad were married, he built a cabin somewhere around here. Probably similar to the one we're in right now. Dad said there're a lot of dry cabins in this area, but none too close to each other. People come out here to be isolated."

Which means we really are alone out here. Perfect.

"Anyway," Kai goes on, seeming less agitated now than he was a minute ago. Hopefully he can see that talking about this is helping. "I don't know for sure what Dad's cabin looked like or how big it was. I never came up here with him. He always said I was too young. I'd ask every year if I could go with him, and every time, he said no. 'Just enjoy being a kid for now,' he'd tell me. 'You have the rest of your life to be an adult and do adult things, like exploring the world.'

"Then, last year, when I was sixteen, he finally asked me to join him. By that time, Hunter hadn't done anything with us for a few years—he barely even talked to Dad anymore—so Dad didn't bother asking him. It would have been more than a month of just the two of us. I really wanted to go, to make the hike, to learn as much as I could from him, to finally see the 'Great White North' he'd been telling me stories about my whole life. But I said no." His lip quivers and his tone trembles. "One of my last memories of my father is the crushed look on his face, him asking me why, and I couldn't tell him the truth. I lied and said I had something going on that was more important. But the truth was, I . . . I did it for . . ."

"Hunter," I say. If there's only one thing I've learned on this trip, it's that Kai and Hunter love each other more than anything or anyone, apparently even more than their dad.

"Yeah. Hunter—" His tongue trips and he swallows. "He's, I don't know, jealous, I think, of how close me and Dad are, even though it was his choice to stop doing things with us. It still didn't seem right to go off with Dad and leave Hunter behind. He's my closest brother; I know there's something he's not telling me. But he doesn't know why I said no, and how much that upset Dad, and I can't tell him. He's messed up enough already by Dad disappearing, and believing he's dead. How can I tell Hunter the last thing I did with Dad was hurt his feelings because I wanted to spare *his* feelings?"

His logic in this is as twisted as Hunter's reasoning for not wanting to pursue a romantic relationship. But even so, I get why he felt he did what was best, for his brother's sake. Both of them are too selfless, but that doesn't make them wrong. They're also not right. And here I am stuck in the middle, stretched taut between them, without a clue how to help either of them. Just like when my parents would fight, and when they were trying to decide "what's best for me" after the divorce. They told me things they should have said to each other instead.

"I knew Dad favored me," Kai goes on, "because I liked to do the things he did. I didn't agree with it or encourage it—I said no to the trip I'd wanted to go on my whole life so that Hunter wouldn't feel bad. But I thought I'd have more time, like I could put off the trip, just go when Hunter was in college and too busy with his adult life to notice what I did or didn't do with Dad. I didn't know he wouldn't come back this time. I just . . . thought I'd have more time."

Isn't that what we all think? We expect bad things to happen to other people, not to us. So when something strikes out of the blue, we always think, *I thought I'd have more time.* If anyone told me a year ago that my parents would be divorced now, I would have thought, *So soon?* even though I knew it was coming. I'd mistakenly assumed they'd wait until I was in college, away from the situation. *I thought I'd have more time.* To do what, I don't know. Fix what was already broken beyond repair? Hindsight has a way of making you feel like a moron.

"You couldn't possibly have known—" I start.

"But I *did* know it was possible," he counters. "We all knew it was possible, every time Dad left." His gaze darts to my rock necklace, and I remember what Hunter said about how their mom wore hers whenever their dad was away, and now she'll never take it off. "We knew there was a chance he wouldn't come back. I'm not stupid, Gabi, I know there's a chance he really is dead like everyone else thinks. It's just not something I can get myself to believe without proof. Do you . . . Do you think that's crazy?"

"No," I say, and for the first time I really believe it. "If it were my mom or dad, I'd want proof, too." The realization smacks me hard, leaving a stinging handprint of truth. Yes, even if it were my mother, with all the hurt she's caused, with all the anger I hold toward her, I'd still hope she was alive.

"Whenever he was gone I pictured him getting attacked by wild animals or something like that, you know, going down fighting. He's a strong guy, big like Hunter, but I know he's not invincible. There's still a chance, too, that something like that has happened in the past year . . ." He squeezes my hand and I squeeze back, keeping us tethered. "What supposedly took him was an avalanche. The cabin he'd built to protect himself from the elements didn't hold up against them. I know that much is true. The fact that his cabin was destroyed is meant to be proof of his death . . . but for me that isn't enough."

I shudder, wondering if the same thing could happen to the cabin we're in now. This is the tiniest house I've ever been in.

"The force of the avalanche knocked out half the structure," Kai says, "and they think it swept him away, burying him somewhere underneath rubble and heavy snow. Diesel was with him on that trip, like he always was on every trip. He ran to the closest town. He was barking and barking and barking, so they knew something was wrong, and they used his tags to identify his owner. Then he led them to the wreckage and kept on barking while they searched. He barked so much it destroyed his vocal cords. He can't make more than a squeak now."

"Is that town near here?" I wish he'd told me this sooner. Maybe we aren't so isolated after all.

"Dad said it's a little more than a day's walk down the mountain from his place, so it could be less than that from here, depending on where it is—but I'm not sure where it is exactly. And it's too small to be on any of my maps. If Diesel left right away to get help, Dad would have only been stuck for a day or so. We don't know when he left, though."

He's not done with his story yet, so I let him go on. We can spare a few minutes before looking for the town, if it'll help him clear his head.

"In the end it didn't matter," he says. "They couldn't find Dad. The rescue crew dug as much as they could until it became too unstable and too dangerous to keep digging, and too much time had passed for him to have survived anyway. If Diesel hadn't signaled anyone, it would have been a lot longer before we knew anything happened. But we still don't know *what* happened. Maybe he got out. Maybe he wasn't inside—Diesel wasn't, and he's always right with him, so maybe they just got separated, and Diesel lost his scent and assumed he was stuck in the rubble, I don't know. Dad could have been knocked down the mountain, and by the time he got back, everything and everyone was gone, even his dog."

That's a stretch, but not impossible. Even so: "How do you plan on finding out what really happened? If the cabin is gone, and your family hasn't heard from him in a year . . ."

Kai meets my gaze. "I have a theory on that. I don't think he'd abandon our family on purpose. That's just not the kind of person he is, and he and Mom were happy. Their relationship wasn't perfect, though; he can be really stubborn. But the only time he and Mom ever argued was when he knew he was wrong about something and still refused to back down."

I raise a brow. Definitely a genetic trait.

He goes on, oblivious to my analysis. "He wouldn't have just left his cabin in ruins. He worked too hard on it; it meant too much to him. I think, assuming he survived, that he made his way back and rebuilt it. It would have taken a long time, even in ideal conditions, so . . ."

"And there's no way for him to get word to your family while he's here? What about the town?"

"Probably too small to have a post office . . ." His expression shifts and he looks to the side, like he's thinking.

"But they have to have phones," I say. "Something." My mind has shifted again from Kai's dad in the past to us, here and now. "We need to find the town. I can use my GPS."

"What?" He looks right at me, confusion tensing his brow. "Why? You think he's there?"

"No. Sorry. Not for your dad. For us. A doctor for Hunter. A ride home for Jack and Vicki. And you and I will need to restock supplies before we head out again, won't we?"

His eyes have sharpened in a way that unsettles me. "Someone there can take us back home. Or at least give us a ride to the airport in Fairbanks—"

"Home?" He obviously stopped listening after I said "ride home"—but I meant that for someone else, not us. "Why turn around when we're this close?"

"Because my brother almost *died*, Gabi."

"Hunter won't be coming with us. We'll find someone to take care of him, *then* we'll go."

"That's not the point. This isn't worth risking anyone's life again, not yours or mine. I'll find another way to figure this out, another time . . ."

He doesn't have an answer, though. Deep down he still wants to do this; I know he does. He's just scared, and he has reason to be. And I'm scared, too, but: "If what happened to your dad happened to someone in my family—or to *anyone* I cared about—finding the truth would make it worth the risk to me."

His expression softens and twists, changes from determined to conflicted.

There's a hard knock on the door right before it opens. Vicki is holding Kai's rifle, and a stern glint has replaced the usual cheery glimmer in her eye. "Hunter seems okay for now," she says. "We need to eat, and I have some serious steam to blow off. Let's go kill something."

CHAPTER FIFTEEN

As Kai and Vicki leave for their hunt, I realize I'm starving. Not hungry—that feeling came and went hours ago, when we were in the plane and skipped lunch. This is a wretched kind of hunger, the kind where your stomach feels like it's cannibalizing itself. In the past twenty-four hours I've eaten nothing but a little bit of rabbit meat and a protein bar. I would even eat *akutaq* right now, a whole bucket of it.

Fortunately, it doesn't take them terribly long to find food—longer than I'd have to wait at a restaurant on a Saturday night, though. Then waiting for it to be prepped is agonizing. Hunter isn't delirious anymore, but he's not up for conversation. I have nothing to distract me from the clawing need in my gut, and later, the smell of the cooking makes it even worse.

I survive, though. I'm beginning to understand just how far my body can be pushed.

By the time we've finished eating, there isn't enough daylight left to venture anywhere safely, so we all agree to make a plan now about finding a town that we'll put into place tomorrow. Hunter should be okay for the night; he looks closer to normal. He isn't talking much, though, or eating, but he was able to get up on his own. He's been sitting in front of the fire in the bedroom, huddled in a blanket, for hours, moving only when another log needs to be added.

Jack gathered a lot of wood, but with three fires going, one in each room, we're running low already. We can't stay here more than one or two nights; we don't have enough supplies for five people. Jack, Kai, Vicki, and I are sitting at the table in the main room, somber faces all around, like we're at a council meeting that will decide whether someone will hang. I pull up the GPS on my phone—still no cell signal, because that would be asking for too much—and punch in Fairbanks, then wait for the satellite to lock onto our location and show me a map.

If I knew the name of the town that was close, it would be much more helpful. But no one ever told Kai or Hunter what it was. At the time, it didn't seem important. There were more urgent things to take care of, like a funeral with no body.

Using the GPS will drain my phone's battery, so I pull it up just long enough to see how far we are from Fairbanks and what kind of path it suggests we take to get there. When it pops up on the screen, I set my phone in the center of the table so everyone can see, then I zoom in . . . and in . . . and in . . . until a tiny dot labeled *Ukiuk* appears. I tap it and mark it as our destination, then zoom out again. Ukiuk is about the same distance from Fairbanks as it is from the red dot marking our starting location. It's the closest thing to us resembling civilization, but who knows what it can actually offer.

"That has to be the town my dad mentioned," Kai says. "Looks like it's a bit of a hike from here. We'll need to make sure we have enough food packed before we go."

I sit up straighter. "You mean before we go to your dad's cabin."

"No," Kai says. "I mean that once we're all able to, we're *all* going to the town so we can find a ride home. Jack and Vicki go first, find a doctor, pick up more supplies, bring them here, then we all go home. We're done. This is where it ends."

"But we're so much closer now than we were this time yesterday. If Hunter is okay later and we have the means, I think we should stick to our original plan and keep going."

"And risk getting stuck out there, even farther away from anyone who can help if we need it?"

"Other people live out here," Jack interjects.

"But we don't know where," Vicki counters. "I'm with Kai on this one. I wouldn't want to see any more near-death tragedies for a while, either. Can't y'all finish this trip another time? Give yourselves some recovery time first?"

I open my mouth to protest, but a voice from behind beats me to it. "No."

Kai and I turn in our seats while Jack and Vicki look past us. Hunter stands in the doorway to the other room, still wrapped in a blanket. His hair is more scraggly than wavy now, and his color is still unnaturally pale for him.

"We're not turning around," he says. "We did not come all the way out here just to turn around."

"You almost died—" Kai starts, but Hunter cuts him off.

"But I *didn't* die. We're survivalists, Kai. Dad didn't teach us to quit just because things get hard. I'm going to keep going whether you come along or not. Gabi's right—we're too close to give up. If this were reversed, Dad wouldn't have given up on us. You know it's true. Your decision, though. I'm going to Dad's cabin, with or without you, and I'm going to find out what happened to him, *with or without you*. You started this, but I'll end it by myself if I have to." He turns and shuffles back into the other room, leaving Kai staring at the space he was just standing in.

"He knows I won't let him go alone." Kai clenches a fist as he turns back around to face the table. I uncurl his fingers and hold his hand, hoping it'll help him relax. "Stubborn," he says. "Just like Dad."

He isn't the only one.

"So we're going," I say, and Kai doesn't argue. "Vicki? You're going to town with Jack tomorrow, then?"

She nods, and when Jack grins at that, she adds, "So I'd better spend the little time I have left here with my boyfriend." Then she gets up from the table and joins Hunter in the other room. Jack's smile drops away. "Guess I'll go out and get some more wood. Gonna be a long night."

Kai and I sit in silence after Jack leaves, watching the fire crackle and pop. Vicki is talking to Hunter in the other room, but I can't make out what she's saying, and he doesn't reply to any of it. Within a few minutes, Mother Nature forces me up, and I'm thankful for an excuse to do something, get our minds off this, even if just for a moment. "Will you come with me to the outhouse? I don't want to walk out there alone."

Outside, the wind blows constantly, creating soft snow-drifts and whipping my hair over my face. I tuck it under my hood and follow Kai into the brush and trees. The outhouse isn't far, but being in the woods, it feels like we're secluded. I don't see Jack out here, but every few seconds I hear the faint echo of wood chopping.

I finish my business as quickly as I can, which isn't nearly fast enough, trying not to think about the fact that I just peed in a hole in the ground. I've become an animal out here. The farther north I go, the further I recede on the evolutionary timeline. I'll be dragging my knuckles by the end of the week.

"Done?" Kai shouts.

"Yeah." I exit the outhouse. "Let's get inside before my eye-balls freeze."

On the way back, though, we spot a couple of caribou. There's enough distance between us that I think we can scoot past without them noticing, but still, my heart starts pounding. They're huge. Wild. Animals. Kai holds my hand firmly, plants his feet, and whispers, "Don't move." Then he starts creeping toward one of them.

"Kai," I say as loudly as I can without going above a whisper. We're supposed to keep on walking past a little fox, but it's okay to walk right up to a giant caribou? "What are you doing?"

He doesn't answer, just keeps moving. Slowly. Steadily. The caribou finally notices him and freezes in place, eyeing him cautiously. Kai stops an arm's length from the beast and reaches a hand toward it. Amazingly, it hasn't moved, but its breaths quicken, nostrils flaring, releasing little puffs of white mist. I'm still at a distance, but I've never been so close to a wild animal before, not even the bear we saw this morning—Was that only this morning?

Kai sinks his fingers into the fur on the caribou's thick neck. "Oh my God," I whisper, awestruck. He's *touching* it. Like a pet. That thing is as tall as he is and twice as broad. But it doesn't move.

I reach into my pocket and, as quietly as I can, pull out my cell phone. Line up the shot. Wait for it to focus, and . . . *click*. The tiny shutter click echoes like a rifle shot in the silence, and the caribou flinches, turns tail, and runs, its companion not far behind.

Kai stands in place unmoving for a moment, then turns, his jaw slightly dropped. Is he mad I scared it away?

"*That,*" he says, "was freaking amazing. Did you see that? Did you *see* that!"

Laughter rushes out of me. "I saw it. See." I turn the face of my phone toward him.

"Yes!" He raises his fists to the air and lets out a whoop.

"How did you know it would let you touch it?"

"I didn't. But I had to try." He takes my hand and leads us back toward the cabin. "I get why Hunter doesn't want to kill animals. They're magical—that was *magic.*"

"Total magic," I agree. "It was so magical it was practically a unicorn."

"Yeah, well, I'd even shoot a unicorn if I had to."

I fake a shocked face and gasp.

"Stop it," he says, laughing. "It's about survival. Food to live, fur to stay warm, fat burns like fuel, the list goes on. But Hunter doesn't see it that way."

"I know. I don't think either of you is wrong in what you believe, though. Just different."

"I wish he could have seen what we just saw. Make sure you save that picture. I want to show it to him. You know, he tried to get up close to a moose like that once, but then he was afraid it might charge him, so he chickened out."

"Hunter was afraid of a moose? He *is* a moose!"

"I know, right?" Kai's steps slow as a new thought spreads his smile even wider. "Maybe that's why he's so intent on us going now. Maybe just being out here . . ." He lets out a breathy laugh. "You heard what he said—he remembers everything Dad taught us. The brother I used to have fun with is still in there. Somewhere. Trying to get out. I just have to keep reminding him of what he already knows."

"Maybe," I say, not wanting to ruin his high. But nothing in life is ever that simple, especially when Locklear stubbornness is involved. "So you agree, then? We should keep going?"

"Look at where we are," he says, spinning a slow circle to take it all in. The sparkling white mountains. The crisp blue sky. "I don't know what I was thinking before—I *wasn't* thinking. I was just reacting . . . But I got this far, farther than I've ever been, and so close to finding the truth. How can I leave now?"

CHAPTER SIXTEEN

My chest is on fire. I can smell it smoking, hear it crisping and crackling.

Fear thrusts me upward, eyes wide, suddenly alert, scanning the darkened room for any sign of the familiar. Walls made of rough logs and stone. This room is big enough to hold maybe three people and a cat. Kai is bundled in a blanket and sitting on a chair next to a glowing wood burner, his head bent to one shoulder, eyes closed, breathing even.

He's sleeping. *I was sleeping.* It's either the middle of the night or early morning.

The memories of yesterday come crashing down on me. Hunter almost died. Kai and Jack risked their lives to save him. I only *felt* like I would die. Vicki and Jack will be leaving today. Right now they're on the floor in Hunter's room. I'm lying in a cozy bed that smells like old wool, wearing an extra set of Kai's thermal underwear, and decidedly not being consumed by raging flames. It must have just been part of the dream.

The dream . . . My chest sinks on a heavy exhale. *It was only a dream.*

But it felt so real. I was at LAX again, screaming in my mother's face, lashing out at her with words I can never take back. She grabbed at her throat like she couldn't breathe; then the whole dream went up in smoke. Literally. Or so I thought. But I must have just been smelling the wood burner.

I breathe in, just to make sure I still can, and then out. Again, slower and deeper this time.

I push myself up to sit, unable to relax now. The mattress creaks loudly.

"Gabi?" Kai stirs and rubs his eyes. "What's wrong?"

"Nothing, I just can't sleep." Instead of telling him about the dream, though, I go for something less dramatic but no less true. "I'm worried about my dad. I talked to him yesterday, but . . . He's going to notice I'm gone soon. Even he's not that oblivious. And Vicki's mom will notice, too, and so will yours. Do you think they'll send someone after us?"

"Maybe. Not much we can do or not do about that." Kai gets up from the chair slowly, still hugging the blanket around him, and then crosses the room toward me. He leans over me and smothers me with a hug, swallowing me into his fleece-covered embrace. He smells like ashes. Then he sits next to me on the bed, pulls his knees up to his chest, and swaddles the blanket around himself tighter.

It's odd to see him reacting to the cold, trying to stay warm.

This is the boy who waited until after the temperature dropped to almost freezing to jump in a lake with his friends. This is the boy who walked across Alaska in a snowstorm and burrowed in a bank of snow. *Cold* is not in his vocabulary.

"I haven't been able to sleep very well, either," he says. "Was that all that was bothering you?"

I shove my hands under my legs to keep them warm. No getting around this. I'm not going to lie to him or hide anything from him that he wants to know. "I had a bad dream, and it shook me up a little."

"Do you wanna talk about it?"

No, but if I don't tell him, he'll worry about it. And then I'll end up telling him anyway, so he knows that it's nothing to worry about. It's not that I don't want to talk to him; it's that I don't want to talk about this. "It was more like a memory," I say, "but it got twisted. You know how dreams are. They don't make sense."

"Was it a bad memory to start with, or did the dream twist a good one into bad?"

"Bad to start with." The worst. "It was from the day I moved to Alaska."

Kai gives me a side-eye. "Not including recent events, is living here really that horrible for you?"

"No, that's not what I meant. I was still in LA when this happened; it was right before I got on the plane." And there are reasons I never told Kai about it. One, I've been doing my best to forget it ever happened. It isn't a memory I want to relive. Two, I'm not sure how he'll react, not having been there, in my shoes.

My mother deserved all of it and more, after she broke up our family. How do I convey the pain that was roiling in my gut that day with mere words? "I was really mad at my mom. She started all this . . . stuff. With her and Tom, and the divorce, and sending me away."

Kai nods. "So what happened?"

Basically? I couldn't handle it. "The strongest thing I remember from the whole ordeal was feeling helpless and out of control. Like the world was spinning too fast and about to collide with the sun. It didn't really hit me that we were moving from that close to the equator to this close to the Arctic Circle until we checked into the airport with one-way tickets, and Mom didn't have a ticket at all." And I'd been holding back my feelings for too long. It wasn't just the affair and everything it led to. It was years and years of knowing my parents would split eventually and *not* knowing how to prevent it—or if I even should. I kept trying to hold something back that was too big for my hands, and it slipped out of my grasp. Leaving my mother behind at the airport was the final push that broke me. A flood burst through the dam I'd built.

"I'd been trained for most of my life on how to express the right emotion at the right time, on cue, which worked when the scenario was planned. But I've never been good at improv.

I failed that workshop, repeatedly. I need a script or I lose focus. And that's what happened that day. It was all unscripted, unexpected. But once I started, I couldn't stop. It had a life of its own and I couldn't control it. To be honest, though, I didn't *want* to stop. I wanted her to hear every word of it and more. How shallow she is. How everyone sees through her bullshit. How fake all her friends are, that they only like her for her money and fame, and how she *deserves* friends like that. How ugly she is inside, and selfish. How much I hated her, and I couldn't stand to even look at her sometimes. Because she isn't the mother I used to know."

The one I used to love, admire, and look up to. The one I was proud to share the same blood with and say, "See that pretty lady on the TV? That's my mami."

"I told her that was it," I say to Kai now. "I never want to see or hear from her again. I'm done."

Kai watches me for a minute, waiting for me to go on. When I don't, he says, "Wow. You told her all that and just . . . left?"

"Yeah . . ." Why does it sound like I committed third-degree murder when he says it? "She hasn't called me since. That's how I want it. Better if we just go our separate ways, don't you think?"

"Sure, if that's what you really want."

"It *is*," I say a little too forcefully, and it sounds like I'm trying to justify something I know is wrong. But I'm not the one who's wrong here. I'm not.

"*Okay*." He mimics my tone, then smiles. "I believe you. I mean, that's harsh, but I believe you think it's best. I don't know your mom like you do. But . . ." He pauses.

"But what?"

"Well"—he scratches the back of his neck—"you know, what if your mom wasn't being totally selfish by sending you here? Have you ever thought it might be to protect you?"

I've heard that before, from Dad of all people, the only other person besides me who knows who Mom really is beneath the Hollywood facade. Kai's suggestion puts me on the defensive. I'm tired of people arguing with me about how I should feel, no matter how good their intentions. "That's what she *claimed* it was," I say. "But think about it. I wasn't really under fire, was I? No. She was. And still is. This is going to take a while to blow over." *We'll reassess the situation in a year*, she said. Reassess. Like this is just a marketing experiment and we'll crunch some numbers over coffee. "Keeping her innocent victims out of the public eye could only make her look better. People weren't going to attack me or my dad, except maybe to ask us our side of the story. And she knew I would have told the truth. None of this was for my benefit." It couldn't have been. I'm the one who the world has been made to think doesn't exist anymore, while she climbs back onto her pedestal.

"You did benefit some, though, didn't you?" He grins. "If you hadn't moved here, we'd never have met."

I smile at that. "True."

A wolf howl pierces the night, loud and sharp, and we both flinch. It continues for a few more seconds before it recedes and I can breathe again.

"That sounded . . . close."

"It was," Kai admits, then quickly adds, "but you're safe in here." He strokes his thumb back and forth over my hand and tells me a story about wolves that his dad used to tell him, something I can tell is completely fictional and meant to quell a child's fear of a wild animal, but it makes me feel better anyway. I listen to the soft rumble of his voice and watch the fire get smaller and smaller, my eyelids getting heavier and heavier. He adds a couple more logs to the fire without interrupting his story.

When he's finished, he locks his midnight-sun gaze onto mine and says, "Do you mind if I lie next to you? You know, so we can keep each other warm."

"Yeah, no. I don't mind." My voice sounds small and uncertain, but I'm sure I want him in this bed with me. We almost died today, and we're not out of danger yet. I need him close. I need to feel his breathing and his warm skin and his heart pumping and know he's still alive.

He crawls over me and then under the blankets, and we settle against each other. Everything inside me ignites, acutely aware there are only two layers of thermal underwear between us, mine and his.

"Thank you," he whispers. "Thank you for trusting me

with your secrets, and letting me trust you with mine yesterday. Thank you for sticking with me, even when we disagree. Thank you for just . . . being you."

I mumble something in response, not paying attention to my own words. I can feel every hard plane of his body against every soft curve of mine. My heart goes into overdrive, threatening to crack my ribs with every pulse. I've imagined being in this position with him so many times . . . being this close . . . alone. Now that it's a reality, I'm not sure what to expect. Our kiss is slow and tentative at first, then suddenly urgent, like this is our last night alone instead of our first—but in the back of my head I'm trying to figure out what to do with my limbs. We're tangled and smashed against each other in a bed that barely fits the both of us. It's awkward and exhilarating at the same time.

I don't think I'm going to get any more sleep tonight. He's not just keeping me warm. He's set me on fire.

We don't stop kissing until sunlight filters bright through the crystalline windowpane, the wood burner has gone dark, and we hear Jack and Vicki making breakfast. There's a river not too far from here, and they already went out to fish. Now they're cooking. Together. And not snapping at each other. It's weird, but also better than hearing them argue.

Reluctantly, I get out of bed and get dressed. My clothes are starting to stink a little, so I keep Kai's thermal underwear on underneath, even though it's too big. I twist my hair up into a bun the way my mother showed me when I was little.

"Like this?" I'd asked, watching myself in the mirror. "Sí, mi niña bonita!" Mom exclaimed. *Yes, my pretty girl!* Then she took my hand and twirled me in place like I was on display at a fashion show.

I smile at the memory. When was the last time I smiled about something related to Mom? Stretching my lips reminds me that they're swollen and sore from kissing, and I wonder if Kai feels as alive as I do right now. Even thinking of Mom can't bring me down. That's the power of Kai's touch.

When we enter the main room, Vicki is plating cooked fish fillets while Jack sits at the table.

"Good morning, sleepyheads," Vicki says. "You're just in time for breakfast."

It seems like everyone's mood has lifted today.

"Thanks." I sit and she hands me a plate, but I eat my first bite too fast and burn my tongue.

Jack smirks. "You look a little flushed there, Kai. You feeling all right?"

Kai flicks a not-so-subtle glance at me, and my whole head bursts into flame—cheeks, ears, everything. Then he says, "Never felt better," and goes to check on Hunter.

Jack and Vicki exchange a knowing look, and Jack snickers.

"Whatever you two are thinking," I say, "you're wrong. Nothing happened."

"Then why do you look more like a tomato and less like a cinnamon bun the more you try to deny it?" Jack retorts.

I decided to ignore *all* the offensive aspects of his comment. "It's hot in here. Good job on the fire, you're roasting me."

"Not so hot in here, I bet, compared to the scalding heat in the other room."

Now Vicki's giggling. When she realizes I don't find it funny at all, she gives Jack a scolding face, but he just grins even wider.

I finish eating as fast as I can, burning my tongue a second time, then join Kai in the other room. Hunter is awake but sweaty and pale. "What happened?" I say.

"Fever." Kai shows me the digital thermometer—a hundred and two—before cleaning it with an alcohol wipe and putting it back in the first aid kit on the bed.

"The hypothermia weakened my immune system," Hunter says, his voice scratchy. He sniffles. "This is probably just a cold. I'll take some ibuprofen and it'll be fine." He reaches for the first aid kit, but Kai gets him the pills instead.

"We're not going anywhere until this fever is gone and you're back to one hundred percent," Kai says. "You're a med student. You know how important it is to rest."

Hunter doesn't argue, just swallows the pills and then rolls over so he's facing the wall.

"Do you want anything to eat?" I say. "Vicki made fish. There's plenty."

Hunter shakes his head and we leave the room, closing the door behind us. As soon as Vicki sees our faces, she knows something's wrong. "Oh no, what happened? He was fine last night . . ."

"He's got a fever," Kai says. "But you and Jack can still head out. It's okay."

Vicki chews at her bottom lip. "I—I'd rather stay. I wouldn't feel right, leaving him like this."

"Don't worry, Vicks, I'll find a doctor," Jack says. "No hospitals out here, but there has to be someone in town who can come up and check him out. I'll be back in two days, tops. Maybe sooner. Okay?"

Vicki nods and goes into Hunter's room.

"Thank you, Jack," I say. "For everything."

"I'm just doing this for the new plane," he says through a grin.

His default-mode sarcasm doesn't annoy me this time. "You're not a very good liar."

"Never claimed to be, princess."

I smirk. "And I never said it was a bad thing."

Jack straps Kai's rucksack onto his back. It's considerably lighter than it was when I had to carry it, holding only what he'll need for about a day's travel on foot, leaving the rest of the supplies for us here, but he lets out a grunt like he just lifted the moon onto his shoulders.

I hand him my credit card. "Use this to pay for whatever you need. Anything. Okay?"

He nods and pockets the card.

"Be careful," Vicki says.

He stares at her for a moment, as if contemplating whether he should voice a thought, then says, "Before I go, I . . . wanted you to know. I thought we . . . we had somethin' good. I'm sorry I ruined it. Real sorry. And I'm not saying that so you'll take me back, because I know you won't ever take me back." Swallow. Nod. "I just . . . wanted to make sure you knew." He walks out and closes the door, leaving her frozen in shock.

"Vicki?" I lay a hand on her shoulder. "Are you okay?"

"He apologized." Vicki turns to face me and Kai, brows drawn together. "I thought I'd never hear those words from him." After a moment, she takes in a deep breath, grabs the rifle, and opens the door. "I need to get some air."

"Not with a loaded weapon, you're not." Kai takes the rifle out of her hand.

"Fine." She grabs the fishing rod instead and storms out the door.

"She really shouldn't be alone right now," Kai says. He grabs the hatchet. "I might as well get some work done while I'm out there. Yell for me if you need anything or if . . . anything changes with Hunter."

"I will. I'll stay right by him." Satisfied, he leaves, and I start eating the last fish fillet. The one that was meant for

Hunter. No sense letting it go to waste. The fish Vicki made is no less than divine, even better than what I've had at hoity-toity restaurants in LA, and I feel like I should leave a big tip for her again. If I could. Kai was onto something there when he mentioned she should be working as a chef. But no matter how good the meat is, I miss having fruits and vegetables. Fresh ones, not the dried trail mix I found tucked away in Kai's pack. Mami wouldn't believe it if I told her, after all those times I complained about the all-natural diet she had me on—

Mami? I haven't called Mom that since I was twelve. It started as a spur-of-the-moment way of getting her attention, calling her "Mom" like the heritage she'd given me didn't matter—because it felt like *I* didn't matter to her. And that was confirmed when she didn't react at all. I very pointedly called Dad *Papi* during one of those rare dinners that we actually ate together, and turned to her right after and said "Mom." Dad looked stunned. Mom looked bored. So I just kept calling her Mom, and she just kept not caring. No matter what I do or say, it doesn't matter to her. I've known this for years, so why does it still hurt so much?

The reminder sours my stomach, and I push my plate away. Appetite, gone.

I've been sitting by the wood burner in Hunter's room for so long that it needs another log. Kai and Vicki still aren't back.

Okay. How hard can this be? I pick up one of the split logs from the pile in the corner. A splintered edge pokes my finger and I immediately drop the whole thing, not so gracefully, onto my foot. And let out a scream worthy of a horror flick.

I hobble over to my chair, holding my stabbed finger in my mouth, and Hunter mumbles something behind me.

"Sorry! I didn't mean to wake you up. Are you okay?"

"Yeah . . . I actually feel a little better now. Just thirsty. Can you get me some water?"

"Be right back." I go to the "kitchen" and pour him a glass of water from our stash, noticing it needs to be refilled with snow to melt. A quick glance out the front window—Kai and Vicki are out of sight. I'll have to get some myself later, then. But first, Hunter. When I return to his room, he's trying to push himself up, but his arms aren't quite working.

"Take it easy," I say.

He tries again, and I do my best to help him, but it's like trying to lift a boulder with a feather. Finally, he manages to sit up and lean against the wall, letting his legs fall over the long side of the bed. His socked feet poke out from under the edge of the fleece blanket.

I hand him the cup. He takes a few tentative sips. Sighs. Closes his eyes.

"Now I'm cold again." He rubs a hand down over his face, tugs the blanket up to his chest. "Can you . . . ?" He gestures at the fire.

"I'm not sure how."

"Use both hands to pick up the log," he says, his voice starting to sound less hoarse and more Hunter-like. "They're heavier than they look."

My toe found out that much already. I lift the offending log with both hands this time, one on each end. "Now what? Is there a trick to this?"

"Hold one end and put the other right next to the bed of hot coals. Then—gently—nudge the top end toward the fire. No matter how it lands, it'll catch if you do it like that. Right across the middle. Just don't try to toss it in hard, or the hot ashes will flare out at you."

"But won't I burn myself?"

"Not if you go slow."

"Okay . . ." I do as he said. My skin feels like it's melting, but it doesn't burn. It's just a steady heat, no worse than sunbathing on the beach. As soon as I release the log from my grip, though, I yank my hands back. The flames get hungry. Greedy. The log crackles and pops, and moisture hisses out of it.

It worked! I pull the chair up beside his bed and sit.

"Where is everyone?" Hunter says.

"Outside." Where I'm starting to learn how to survive, but one burning log does not a fire mage make. I tell him what they're all doing, and how Jack went off in search of a doctor in the town, and he takes it all in with his usual calm. I used to think Hunter might understand my antipathy toward being a survivalist, back when I thought he was a shut-in, but he's just as adept at those kinds of skills as Kai is. Even Kai mentioned last night that Hunter was a natural at them and they used to have fun together. Which reminds me . . .

"Can I ask you something? Are you up to it?"

"Depends on the question," he says before taking another sip of water.

Fair enough. "Kai said you used to go out with him and your dad all the time, and that you had fun. So why did you stop? Just because you don't like shooting animals?"

"No, it's . . . not that simple."

I didn't think it was, but he remains tight-lipped about explaining the complexities. He feels like a brother to me, but he doesn't wear his heart on his sleeve when I'm around, like Kai does. "Kai told me what happened to your dad, too," I say. "And I'm not sure how you actually feel about this trip anymore. You pushed him to keep going when *he* wanted to stop. Why?"

He sighs, leaning his head back. "Every day since we got the news, I've had this hope, kind of like Kai's, even though I know it's not logical . . . That's why I never told anyone about it. I've had this hope that one day I'll wake up, go downstairs, like any normal day, but it won't be a normal day, because Dad will be there, and then"—his voice catches—"then we can try again. Start over. But if I see where he died, my hope won't survive that. It'd be like him dying all over again, right in front of me."

The weight he dropped hits me square in the chest. He and Kai aren't so different. "Oh, Hunter. I'm sorry."

"No, it's okay." He sighs. "It's okay. I'm past that now. What we've done the last few days has made me realize my hope didn't ever stand a chance. Dad's gone. I'm sure of it. And the only way to get Kai to understand that, too, is to bring him there, make him see what I'd been dreading to see. Dad was a skilled survivalist, but he wasn't a superhero. I guess I got swept up in Kai's hope after we talked about it, but look at everything that's happened to us in just a few days, and we had each other to depend on. Dad was alone. Something kept him from coming home, and the only logical answer is that he's dead. There's no other reason he would have stayed away, for that long, without contact. He loved Mom more than anything. He would have made it his priority to let her know he was alive. I think Kai knows this deep down. He just needs something to make him see it as the truth."

"I got that impression, too, when we were talking about it last night. With a town nearby, your dad could have called—"

"Help!" Vicki screams from outside. "HELP!"

We both jump up, and the shock of seeing Hunter move like that supersedes my worry for Vicki for a moment. He wobbles, then rushes out the front door, in nothing but thermal underwear and socks, and I go to the window. Vicki is running toward the house, legs pumping hard but too slow. Behind her, something large, dark, and furry, with a rack of antlers that dwarfs her, is hot on her heels. It looks like a moose, but that can't be a moose. It's too fast. And angry as a wild dog. Do regular moose get angry like that? Why is it chasing her?

A split second after Hunter went through the door, he reappears, scans the room, and snatches the rifle Kai left beside the table. Then he's gone again. Oh God, he's lost his mind. A few minutes ago he couldn't even stand, let alone shoot. He can't shoot. He doesn't shoot. He *won't* shoot.

But he's going to. To save Vicki.

Unless he accidentally shoots *her*.

She's still far from the house but close enough to see the panic on her face come into focus, eyes wide, mouth open and panting.

Hunter quickly comes into view through the window and raises the gun, sets his shot. Vicki and the moose aren't headed straight for us. He's set at a slight angle, and I wonder what he's planning to hit. How do you take down a charging moose? "Vicki, *move!*" he hollers. Roars. Suddenly filled with vitality, like he hasn't been knocking on Death's door for almost two days.

Vicki catches sight of him, eyes widening even further, then she drops, landing face-first in the snow like dead weight, eerily still. I can't breathe. I'm safe in this house and I can't breathe. The moose is going to stomp her, and we're too far away to stop it. She's going to get trampled to death!

A gunshot thunders through my ears and I instinctively cover them and crouch, eyes squeezed shut. When I straighten to look out the window again, the moose is on the ground, lying as motionless as Vicki. Hunter is still holding the gun up, aimed and ready for another shot, but he doesn't need another one. Killed it on the first try—and I don't think that was luck.

Vicki's head pops up, and Hunter lowers the gun. Did I really just see that? It all happened so fast.

And where's Kai? I thought they were together.

Vicki looks at the moose, lets out a yelp of victory, then grabs her abandoned bucket of fish and comes running up to the house. By the time she reaches it, Hunter is back inside. He collapses onto a chair. "Are you okay?" we say to her in unison. I tackle her with a hug.

"I'm fine, I'm fine!" Vicki shouts, entirely too excited for someone who was just screaming for her life a minute ago. "That moose came out of nowhere! Must have thought I was a threat. I told you moose aren't slow or stupid, didn't I? I told you."

My chest caves in relief, and then I turn to Hunter. "How did you do that?"

"Do what?"

"What do you mean *what*?" I thrust an arm toward the general direction of the dinosaur-sized carcass outside. "That!"

"I didn't," he says, looking fragile again. "Neither of you saw me do this. It didn't happen."

"I'm not going to lie about it—"

"I *don't* shoot animals."

"But you just did." Vicki's tone sounds as confused as I feel. "You killed that moose in one shot. I ain't never seen anyone do that before."

Technically she didn't see Hunter do it, either, with her face buried in the snow, but that's not the point.

"It's not an easy shot," Hunter says, "for most people. Especially on a moving target. You gotta hit it right behind the ear. Not that I did that—no one can know that I did that, okay?"

It's not an easy shot for most people. Like his brother, who prides himself on being able to shoot as well as their dad. What would he think if he saw Hunter, who prefers not to shoot at all, take down a moose as quickly and easily as snapping his fingers? "This is about Kai. You don't want *him* to know."

"Yes, Gabi, all right? *Yes.* What is it with you needing to know the absolute truth of everything?" His voice comes out forced, breathy, and just this side of pissed off.

"I didn't mean—"

"You want to know it all?" he goes on. "Fine. I'll tell you *all* of it. Dad taught us both how to hunt, and he noticed I was better than Kai. I don't know why or how—I wasn't trying to be better than him. I just was. And Dad kept comparing us to each other, telling Kai he should be more like me, and Kai acted like it was no big deal, but I could tell it was. A very big deal. So I stopped. I told them I couldn't shoot animals, that it bothered my conscience, which wasn't a lie but not for the reasons they assumed. Then Dad didn't have me around to measure Kai against anymore, and I . . ." He heaves in a breath, says his next words slower and softer. "I didn't have an excuse to spend time with Dad anymore."

Which means he sacrificed a relationship with his father so Kai's relationship with their dad would be stronger.

"That's it," Hunter says. "There's nothing else to tell. You know the rest. My father hated me because I pushed him away, so much that he didn't even ask me to go on the trip that would end up being his last."

The front door yawns open without the click of the doorknob. Vicki must not have shut it all the way when she came in. We all look at it to see who pushed it open. But who else would it be—

"Kai," I say, hoping he wasn't standing there the whole time. "Where were you?"

He doesn't look at me, his eyes laser-locked on Hunter. "In the woods. I heard Vicki scream, and . . . when I got to the tree line I saw Hunter."

Hunter looks sixteen shades of guilty, like a kid who got caught stealing cookies. But he didn't do anything wrong. "You saw me," he says, his voice breathy and weak. The energy boost he had before disappeared as soon as Vicki was all right, so that now, even just talking is draining him. He props his elbows on the table and leans on them. "You saw me shoot."

"Yeah," Kai says. "You're still good." His eyes glisten when he smiles, and my heart splits. "Really good."

Hunter's eyes are awash with confusion. "Did you hear . . ."

"Yeah, I heard what you said. Every word of it."

"Aren't you mad?"

"No. God, no. I mean, yeah, a little, but not at you. I'm mad that we lost time." Kai crushes him with a hug. "Why didn't you just tell me?"

"How could I—"

"All those years," Kai says. "It could have been different if you'd just told me. I would have found a way to make it work." His tone is drenched in regret, as if Hunter's actions—or inactions—were his fault. He keeps squeezing, like his twin will disappear if he doesn't hold on.

So many problems could have been avoided if they had just talked to each other, told the truth, made their feelings clear. Which is exactly what I did with my mother at the airport . . . so why am I still so angry about it? Why doesn't anything feel resolved?

"I'm sorry," Hunter says, but he doesn't even have the strength to hug Kai back. "I'm sorry I screwed us all up. I thought I—I thought I was doing the right thing."

"So did I. We both messed up. Dad messed up, too. But that's what happens. We're only human."

Hunter pulls back, and his nose twitches as he sniffles. "What did *you* do?"

Kai stammers for a second, no doubt realizing his mistake. *Tell him*, I mouth. Hunter's secret is out now. Kai might as well spill his, too—that he chose Hunter over their dad. Like he said, they both messed up, and they're only human.

"I . . . ," Kai starts, then clamps his mouth shut. Sighs heavy through his nose. Twists his mouth. "I need to get that moose cut up," he says. "We shouldn't waste it."

My shoulders slump, but I get it. He's not ready. Maybe one revelation between them is enough for one day.

"You don't look so good," Vicki says to Hunter.

"I don't feel so good," he admits. "I'm gonna lie back down for a minute . . ." He pushes himself up and out of the chair and wobbles a bit before moving forward.

Vicki helps him to the bedroom—I'm not sure how she's supporting him, though; she's half his size—then busies herself keeping the fires in all the rooms burning while I keep an eye on Hunter and Kai takes care of the moose we'll be having for dinner. For the rest of our lives. Vicki goes out to help him, leaving me alone with Hunter again.

But it's pretty boring work this time. The fires are steady, thanks to Vicki, and Hunter falls in and out of sleep, never alert enough for conversation. Every once in a while he pushes his blankets off, sweat glistening his forehead, only to tug them back up again a few minutes later, shuddering. "It's just the flu," he keeps saying. "I'll be fine in a few days."

I'm not so sure he will be.

Vicki comes back and relieves my watch. She keeps him company but doesn't get chatty. The downward shift in her mood from when Jack left has yet to perk back up. I don't think it's that she cares for Hunter any less, or she wouldn't still be here. It's more like thoughts of Jack are distracting her. I wonder how long she was waiting for that apology from him, and what happened between them. How easily your whole world can change with just two simple words, spoken from the heart:

I'm sorry.

CHAPTER SEVENTEEN

The next morning brings dull sunlight filtered through a quilt of gray clouds, a brisk wind that stings my cheeks, and a creeping dread in my gut. Hunter definitely needs a doctor. He's still not eating, his congestion is worse, he developed a cough and a sore throat overnight, and our limited stock of ibuprofen and Tylenol isn't going to last much longer at the rate he's popping pills to keep his fever in check.

"I may not be a pre-med student," Kai says, "but I do know that stuff will burn a hole in your stomach if you don't take it with food. Come on, Hunter, just a little. Try." We cooked as much moose meat as we could yesterday so it wouldn't go bad, which still left quite a bit for the wolves and whatever else is out there to pick clean overnight, and packed up in baggies what we couldn't eat right away.

Hunter takes exactly one bite of the meat Vicki offers him, then flops back onto his pillow. Five minutes later, Vicki's wiping up puke off the floor.

The usual wrinkle in Hunter's brow has left his face and taken up residence on Kai's. And probably mine, too. I will never again take for granted the convenience of pharmacies and hospitals and ambulance service in the city. Or roads, phones, indoor plumbing, food service, other *people*. We're completely alone out here—and we sent Jack out alone. Our plan seemed good when we first thought it up, but without any way to contact him, who knows if he even made it to town? The weather has been cooperative, but wild animals are always wild. He's been gone for more than a day now and Hunter is rapidly getting worse. Even if Jack is okay, can we wait another day for him to get back? I don't know what other options we have, though.

Vicki is in the other room with Hunter, alternating between keeping the fire going strong and wiping him with a cool wet rag.

"What do we do?" I ask Kai. "We don't know when Jack will return—or if he found a doctor—and Hunter can't travel, and we can't leave him alone to find someone ourselves."

Kai drops his armload of wood, removes his gloves, and rubs his hands together near the fire. "I don't know. This wasn't part of the plan."

"Well . . ." I sidle up next to him and wrap both of my arms around one of his. His chest relaxes on a sigh. "What would you have done if you'd been out here alone and gotten sick?"

"I don't know," he repeats. "I guess I just didn't think it

would happen. Stupid." He shakes his head. "Hunter has his life all planned out, you know? He's always been the smart twin, the sensible twin. He's known exactly what he wanted to do, what he wanted to be, since we were, I don't know, twelve, and I still haven't figured anything out. Hunter just wants to help people, and now he can't even help himself." His fists clench over the fire.

"He'll be okay. Just don't give up on him, or on yourself. You're smart and sensible, too. You can do this. *We* can do this."

Kai presses his palms against his eyes. "I need to think. I can't think in here; it's suffocating. And I need to keep my hands busy. I'm going back out. Do you want to come?"

"Sure—"

But suddenly the door bursts open and Jack rushes inside.

Kai and I both let out yelps of surprise that melt into relieved smiles. And then, just as quickly, I start to worry. He's alone. This could be good news, or bad. Either the town is closer than we thought, or he had to turn around before he got there.

He lifts a pair of sunglasses away from his eyes and squints at us. He didn't have sunglasses before . . . "Oh good, it *is* you," he says, shoulders dropping. He slams the door shut behind him. "I wasn't sure if I had the right cabin. Seemed like it was taking longer to get back here than it took to get to town."

"Thank God you found it," I say.

Jack looks at the closed door to Hunter's room. "How's the big guy?"

"Not good," Kai says. "Did you find anyone who can help?"

"Yes. Nice guy I met at the café gave me a ride up, 'cause I couldn't carry everything I bought—"

For himself or for us?

"—and the rest of them are coming in a big truck not far behind me." He wrestles the rucksack off his back and it hits the floor with a hard *thunk*. Definitely heavier than it was when he left. I take a peek out the front window and see a bright red utility vehicle. A bored-looking man sits in the driver's seat, smoking a cigarette. "I told them where you are," Jack continues, "and then left right away so I could get your stuff back to you and let you know what's going on. They had to find the right people first and gather supplies—it's no thriving metropolis down there, everyone's a volunteer—but they should be here soon. I caught sight of them down the mountain from here a few minutes ago."

"Wait, slow down," Kai says. "Who's 'they' exactly?"

"Medics, police—"

"Why the police?" My heartbeat kicks up a notch. "Are we in trouble?"

The door to the bedroom opens. "What's all the commotion . . . ?" As soon as Vicki catches sight of Jack, she runs toward him and captures him in a tight embrace. "You're back!"

She lets go as quickly as she snatched him. "I mean, I'm glad you're all right."

"Missed you, too, Vicks." Jack winks at her, then turns his attention to me. "Your parents aren't too happy you all took off without a single peep about where you're headed. There's an Amber Alert out on the three of you. I didn't know until I told them your names and they thanked me for helping them find you. Called me a hero, even." Amused grin. "They're not going to let you go any farther when they get here. You're delinquent minors, they said. They're coming to take you all home."

Oh no . . . "We can't go home yet."

"I know you don't want to," Jack says, "but the law's the law. Sorry."

Kai spits out a curse. "This is why Hunter was supposed to stay home. He would have figured out where I was before anyone else—"

"He did," I say.

"—and he could have kept Mom distracted, and whoever else noticed me missing from trying to come after me."

"Including me." I cross my arms. "Did you really think I'd just let you go?"

"I know now that was a bad plan," he says. "I thought I could do this alone, that I *should* do this alone. But I was wrong." He puts a hand on each of my shoulders and looks me straight in the eye. "I was wrong, Gabi. I need you. And I need my brother."

"You can't have us both now, though."

"What are you saying?"

"That we have to get out of here before the police show up. We have to go *now*, Kai, and . . . I guess that means leaving Hunter behind. He'll be all right. Jack said medics are coming."

"I know, but . . ." Kai's gaze flicks to Hunter in the other room. "Gabi, we're in deep—"

I put my hands on my hips. "You're not really thinking of going home, are you? We're too close! And you agreed the other day—we might never get another chance like this."

"Fine. We'll go." Kai starts shoving all the bagged moose meat he can fit into his pack. "Stubborn girl."

"If I am, I caught it from you." I grin.

He flashes a grin right back, and that's all I need to see to know we're okay. We just have to face one more trial on this journey and then we can go home and everything will be okay.

"I'll stay with Hunter until he's ready to go home," Vicki says, earning a sidelong glance from Jack.

"I had a feeling you guys would keep going either way," Jack says. He pulls out a folded piece of paper and a pencil from a side pocket of Kai's pack. "So I picked this up while I was in town. It'll help you get to where you're going faster. You need a path." He unfolds the paper and spreads his palms over it, smoothing out the creases. It's a map, but not the full state of Alaska like the others I've seen. It's zoomed in on the

Fairbanks area. Alaska looks so tame like this, just a bunch of rivers, lakes, plains, and mountains. Fairbanks is a large shaded area. Smaller towns are scattered all over—those are whole communities, and they're just *dots*. And us, little specks moving about, smaller than dust motes by comparison. We don't even register on this.

Jack runs one fingertip along the latitude and another along the longitude, then stops in the mountains north of Fairbanks and marks the point of intersection with the pencil. "This is Ukiuk, the town I came to at the bottom of our mountain. So we're . . ." He draws an X not far from the town. Maybe a quarter inch? How far is that in real life? "Here," he finishes. "This is a public cabin we're in. They know exactly where it is. But no one thought you'd be this far up, so no one was even searching out here."

He pulls a slip of paper out of his pocket, the one Kai gave him with his dad's cabin's coordinates on it, and runs one fingertip along the latitude and one along the longitude, until they meet, then marks a new X on the map. It's almost the same distance from our current location as Ukiuk is, but only a fraction of the distance we've covered already. "This is your final destination," he says. "That's less than a day away on foot, if the river isn't too deep to cross. If it is, you'll have to find a way around, and that could add days to your travel. I packed you some extra stuff, just in case that happens."

I lift my gaze from the map and lock it on Kai. "We have to cross a river? In this cold? Isn't getting wet what messed up Hunter?"

"Are you changing your mind?" He looks offended, as if he didn't change his mind more than once in the last few days. Now that he's firmly set on going, anything less won't do. Like Hunter said, tunnel vision.

And I wouldn't want him any other way.

"No," I say, "I'm just . . . trying to process this." We're really going out there, only the two of us. Me and Kai against the wild. Less than a week ago, I was at home, safe, unaware that he was even missing. Now I'm halfway across the state and about to risk my life to help him. And if we don't find his dad's cabin or another one before dark, I'll be sleeping in snow.

Dad's never going to let me outside to do so much as take out the garbage after this. I can't imagine how worried he is. Mom is probably just annoyed by the inconvenience of having a "runaway child." She had to be the one who tipped everyone off that something was wrong after seeing those charges at the lodge. But she would have never guessed how far I've come.

Too far to not see it through.

Jack traces a bumpy path from X to X, through the mountains, then hands the map to Kai. "Good luck."

Kai studies the map for a second, then adds it to his pack, zips it all up, and hefts it onto his back. "We're not leaving without saying good-bye to Hunter."

"And we're not leaving without a plan B." I turn to Jack. "Can you stick around Ukiuk until we're done? If we're not back at this cabin in three days, send someone out to find us. Three days. Okay? But don't say where we're going before then."

"Ay, ay, princess." He gives me a mock salute.

I follow Kai into the bedroom, and he kneels beside the bed, nudges Hunter awake. "Hey," he says, giving his shoulder another shake. "Hunter, wake up. We're leaving."

Hunter grumbles and rolls slowly onto his side. "Where are we going?"

"Not we—No. You're right. We're all leaving. But you're going home. Me and Gabi are going to Dad's cabin. We have to go *now*, though. There's some people on their way to take care of you, okay? You're gonna be all right. But me and Gabi won't be with you. Vicki and Jack will be. If we don't get out of here right now, the police will force us to go back home. Do you understand what I'm saying?"

"You're going to see Dad. I'm not." Hunter's lips are cracked and peeling. He licks them and swallows, changing nothing about their appearance. Even his tongue is dry. His whole body jerks with a coughing fit for a few moments.

"Yeah," Kai says after Hunter quiets. "I'm going to see Dad. I wish you could come with me."

"He wouldn't want to see me," Hunter rasps. "I pushed him away on purpose . . . and got exactly what I asked for in return—nothing."

His words hit me hard in the chest. That's exactly what I did to Mom, pushed her away on purpose. And I thought I wanted nothing in return, but now I'm not so sure. It's not that I don't want her at all. It's that I don't want the person she is now. If there were a way I could have the mami back that I had when I was little . . .

Hunter coughs again, pulling me out of my thoughts. "I pushed him away so you could have him, Kai. Why didn't you go on that trip with him? He wanted you to go. Why did you tell him no?"

Kai drops his head. He can't avoid this now. Hunter may be slightly delirious from the fever, but even so, Kai won't ignore a direct question from him. "The same reason you pushed him away. For *you*." His voice cracks and he lifts his head. "I love Dad, but I was tired of him coming between us. I miss being your brother. I miss the fun we used to have, whenever we were together, with or without Dad."

"Me, too. And I miss *him*, too." Hunter struggles to keep his focus on Kai, but that doesn't keep a tear from spilling down his cheek. "I miss him every day."

"I'm going to set this right when I see him, okay? I'm going to fix this." He runs both hands up his forehead and into his hair. "You just take care of yourself and get better."

"That's an order, Dr. Locklear," I tease, though I can't keep my tone from wavering. I think Hunter tries for a smile, but it looks more like a grimace.

Kai gives him a quick hug, and then he grabs my hand. "Ready?"

Holding Kai's hand, his warm confidence surging from his fingers into mine, I feel like I could take on anything. "Ready," I say. "Let's do this."

We say our good-byes to Jack and Vicki, and they tell us we're crazy but wish us luck anyway. When Kai opens the front door, cold air blasts me in the face. It doesn't lock me up this time, though. It energizes me.

As soon as we get outside, we see a big black truck with blue flashers spinning on its roof. And it's driving straight for us.

CHAPTER EIGHTEEN

We make a mad dash for the trees.

The roar of the truck's engine thunders over me like an ocean wave, gears grinding as it attacks the incline. They're probably fifty yards from the cabin, close enough to easily catch us even after they stop in to get the others, but these trees are too close together. They can't drive through here. They'll have to go by foot, like us, and I can only hope we've got enough of a head start to lose them.

"No way they didn't see us," I say through panting breaths. "We are in so much trouble."

"Then we might as well have fun with it, right?" There's laughter in his voice, begging for release.

"Just tell me you know where we're going, that we're not running blind."

He lets the laugh out this time. "I know where we're going."

We dart through a maze of naked trees and spindly

evergreens. Many of them have been chopped, evidence of our stay here the past few days.

"Hey!" a gruff voice shouts. "Stop!"

I dare a glance over my shoulder. Two people—men, I assume, by their size and builds—are chasing us at a dead run, maneuvering through the trees as well as we are.

"We can't run forever," I say. Well, Kai probably could. But I'm already lagging behind. Kai tugs me along, urging me to go faster. "I need to catch my breath."

"We're almost there," he says.

"Almost where?"

"At something I found yesterday when I came out to get wood."

The trees break away suddenly, revealing a sheer drop. The bottom is pure white—who knows what that snow is hiding? Rocks? Another ice-covered lake? Straight ahead of us is open air. Behind us, the men are closing the gap. We're trapped. Unless—

"We're jumping," Kai says, grinning wide. I know that grin. It's the same one I see before he does something sure to give him an adrenaline rush. It's the same one I see when he kisses me, like doing that is just as much of a thrill for him as soaring into a freezing lake, or zip-lining through the mountains, or snowboarding.

Kai is as excited about this jump as I am scared.

"Are you insane?"

"A little late to be asking me that, isn't it?" He's still smiling. If this jump doesn't kill him, he is so dead. "This is the only way to keep them from following us."

"That's because no one in their right mind jumps off a cliff!"

"You came with me this far; don't quit now. You can do this, Gabi. I know you can."

Shouts crescendo behind us. How easy it would be to just let myself be caught. To quit.

You can do this, Gabi.

"There's a good blanket of snow on the ground," Kai says, sliding the pack off his shoulders. "It'll cushion your fall, but this is still gonna hurt. The incline can work in your favor, though. Don't try to land on your feet; you could break a leg or force a knee into your face. Tuck and roll." He demonstrates quickly. That stupid grin hasn't left his face.

He pulls two full-head masks out of his pack, hands me one, and then tosses his pack over the edge, throwing it hard to the left so we don't land on it. I count how long it takes to hit the ground. *One-Mississippi—splat.* One second. That's all the time I'll have to get properly tucked before I have to roll.

He pulls the mask down over his head, leaving only his eyes exposed. There's a flap over the mouth hole. I put mine on, too. The inside of the mask is soft and warm, and the outside feels like a Windbreaker. Already, my face is heating up from my own breath. Kai lays a palm on my back. "You ready?" His voice is muffled by the mask.

I could pretend I didn't hear him, but I nod instead. Kai needs me. And Hunter's counting on me to see this through for him.

"Don't do it!" the guy behind us yells.

"Together, on the count of three," Kai says. "One . . ."

Wherever you go, let your heart lead your feet.

"Two . . ."

If you have a really good reason for wanting it, your heart will make you do it.

"Three!"

Oh god oh god oh god oh god—

We leap into nothingness. As soon as I register I'm in a free fall, my heart and stomach somersaulting over and around each other—*tuck!*—I shoulder-butt the ground. All the air leaves my lungs in one big grunt. I'm rolling downhill but not on purpose. Bright white stars flash behind my eyes. My teeth clang hard against one another.

Finally, my body stops, and I'm lying on my back, staring up at the sky.

Everything is still and quiet; the whole world is at peace. Then the men appear at the top edge of the cliff, gesturing wildly and shouting. I hear Kai groan somewhere behind me, followed by the sound of boots shuffling through snow. And the wind returns with a vengeance. It scratches my eyes with icicle blades. I don't know where on the mountain we are exactly, but it feels like we jumped through a portal and came out at the North Pole. On Pluto. I push up to a sitting position. Nothing on me seems broken or unusable. It just hurts everywhere, like a full-body bruise.

Kai opens the mouth flap on his mask and helps me to stand. "Are you okay?"

"Yeah. Just achy." I rotate my right arm and wince, then open my mouth flap, too. "I landed on my shoulder. But I should be okay."

"Let me know if it gets worse or if you lose feeling anywhere." He pulls a couple of pairs of ski goggles out of the pack. "Remind me to thank Jack later for getting all this stuff for us." After handing me a pair, he straps on his, hiding his eyes behind their reflective shading.

I snap on my goggles. Everything darkens but sharpens focus, and blocking the wind from my eyes is a miracle cure. We get as close to the cliff face as we can, taking cover, and then walk briskly alongside it for a few minutes.

"I think they turned back," Kai says, head tilted upward. "We can stop now. Catch your breath."

I lean against the rock wall, panting. "That was awesome, right? I mean, I don't *feel* awesome right now, but I'm sure I'll look back on this later and be like, you know what? In retrospect, that was pretty freaking awesome. How many people do you think can say they jumped off a cliff and survived? I bet Jase never did. I bet he never *would*, either. I'd win back everything he won from betting against me and then some."

He laughs at that. "I'm glad you came after me and we took the rest of this trip together. It's so much more fun when you have someone to share it with."

Facing off with Death at every turn is fun? Okay. If that's what he wants to call it. "I'm glad we took this trip together, too, Kai." The truth of that catches me off guard—I just admitted to liking a wilderness hike in Alaska—and it takes me a moment to shake off my surprise. Focus on what we're doing. "But it isn't over yet. Which way do we go from here?"

He takes the map out and studies it. "That little jump veered us off the path—"

Little jump?

"—but we should get back onto it okay." He looks between the map and the horizon a few times, changing direction. "This way."

I follow alongside him, putting my complete trust in his survival instincts. Something itches by my eye, so I take my shaded goggles off for a second to rub it. The sudden cold and brightness make me gasp.

"Keep those on unless it's an emergency," Kai says. "Not just to protect your eyes from the wind but also from the sun's UV rays. Even when it's cloudy, those get through. Just like at the beach. Ironic, isn't it?"

"Yeah." I snap them back on. I won't make that mistake again. "Any other tips?"

"You know that saying, *If you can't beat 'em, join 'em*?" I nod, and he says, "Don't try to fight Alaska. She always wins. Work with her instead."

I'm not sure how, but okay. "Is that something your dad told you?"

"No. It's something I learned on my own."

"Recently?"

"Yes and no. Like everything else in my life, it's been a process, and the process is longer for some things than others. Learning how to survive in the wild is constant trial and error."

Learning how to survive anything is constant trial and error. Life in the city. Life in the wild. Life with my mother. Life with*out* my mother. None of it has been easy to navigate.

The clouds have parted and the sun is high in the sky, marking the hours we've been walking, but the wind gets stronger the higher we climb. Fierce. Making it feel even colder.

Kai stops at a boulder jutting up from the snow. There's slightly less snow here but more ice and rock. I don't know why anyone would build a house way up here. But it's not even as high as we can go, not even close. The top of this mountain is in outer space.

I plant my tired butt on the chairlike rock next to Kai, huddling close. My fingers are throbbing, my legs are mush, and my neck is tied up in tight knots.

"How are you holding up?" Kai says.

"We've been hiking for hours. How do you think I'm doing?"

"I'm guessing you're hungry." He unzips a side pocket of his pack.

He isn't wrong, but the grumble in my stomach pales in comparison to the rest of what I'm feeling. Still, I take the strip of moose meat from him greedily. It's cold and chewy, like refrigerated leftovers that haven't been reheated, but it might as well be succulent prime rib for all the praises my body sings to it.

Amazing how little a person actually needs to survive. We rest for a minute to let our food settle and our muscles recover, and I think about all the excess I took for granted in SoCal. There was always an overabundance of food at parties, and at home, so much that it often had to be thrown away. And that's just one part of it. Mom rarely wore the same outfit twice. She has a regular bathroom, a sauna bathroom, a vanity bathroom that houses all of her makeup and styling products, complete with a personal stylist at her beck and call. Guest houses, gardeners, maids, chauffeurs, fancy cars, personal assistants, social media specialists, a state-of-the-art espresso machine, top-of-the-line tutors, a laundry service, a personal shopper, a movie theater and a popcorn machine in the basement, swimming pools and hot tubs, the list never ends.

I had all of that, for years, and I didn't need any of it.

A little bit of food. A few articles of clothing. A safe place to sleep. And good health.

That's it. That's all I need.

Kai clasps his gloved fingers around mine. "I like this," he says. "Just you and me out in the middle of nowhere. I can see why Dad kept coming back here, it's . . . indescribable. But I don't think I would like it as much if I were alone, like he preferred." He pauses to take a deep breath in, his body relaxing on the exhale. "Happiness is real only when shared."

"Sounds like another quote," I say. "But that couldn't have been from your dad."

"It is a quote, and you're right. My dad never said it. Alexander Supertramp did."

"Who?"

"Chris McCandless was his real name."

"The guy they made that movie about?" The one Vicki mentioned, I think. I know movies, but I'm not a Hollywood encyclopedia. And movies about Alaska never interested me—before. I'm going to watch more of them now.

"Yeah, that's the one," Kai says. "He came to Alaska alone only to realize that the joy he got out of his adventure was bittersweet. Me and Chris aren't so different. And me and my dad aren't as alike as Hunter thought we were." He laughs, but it sounds sad. "He's still my dad, though. A difference of opinion doesn't change that."

No, there's one more thing I need, something I didn't have in SoCal, because it isn't something you can buy, but I didn't realize it was lacking there until I came to Alaska. Because Kai gave it to me.

Companionship. The real kind, like this, the soul-baring kind.

I thought I had it with my mother, as I followed in her footsteps, watching and learning how to be like her, doing what I thought would make her happy, but it wasn't genuine, not like this feels with Kai. How could it have been, if she was able to throw it away so easily? And, unlike how Kai feels about his dad, the differences of opinion between Mom and me changed everything.

The sun is much lower when we reach the river, which is more like a stream. Not as big as I was expecting but too wide to hop across. And wet. And cold. Two things I'd rather not be together. This is why I didn't jump in the lake with Kai's friends. This is why Hunter nearly died. Wet and cold are a lethal combination.

"We're really close now," Kai says, his tone rising in excitement. "I bet Dad fishes here. This is probably why he always came up in winter. The water would be deeper in spring and summer, when the snow melts. It's easier to cross now."

I hate to deflate his enthusiasm, but: "Is there a different path we can take to get to the other side? Even if it takes us longer?"

"We'll be fine," he says. "I'll make a fire as soon as we're on the other side, and we'll get dry. Then we'll keep moving. We should get to the cabin before dark. Seriously, we're *that* close. He might even be walking around here . . ." He's smiling big now. His cheeks have bunched so much they're creating bulges at the sides of his mask. "You might not get that wet. You've got good boots and your snowpants are water resistant. You jumped off a cliff, Gabi—this is nothing."

This is nothing. The last time he said that to me, I had to roll across cracking ice—and I survived. Okay. Just a quick bit of cold and wet and then we'll be resting by a fire. God, I hope his dad is alive and rebuilt the cabin, like Kai thinks, or we're sleeping outside for sure, even if we do get there before dark.

Kai takes the first step in, and the water covers only the tops of his boots. It can't be more than twenty steps across. As I look down at the riverbank to get my footing, I notice ours aren't the only tracks in the snow. The other tracks definitely aren't human, though.

"What is that from?" I ask, taking Kai's hand.

"Something that was thirsty."

"Obviously." I resist the urge to roll my eyes at him. I know what he's doing. Messing with me so I don't focus on the water, the cold, the wind, this whole crazy thing we've gotten ourselves into. The consequences we'll have to face when we get back home—whenever that is. "Do you recognize the animal?"

He nods, leading me into the water. Only a few steps in, I'm calf-deep, and the riverbed isn't smooth. I can't walk as fast as I want to. Icicle threads slowly weave inside my boots, finding any little crack in coverage. My legs stay dry, though, thanks to the snowpants, and the water doesn't get any deeper. We're halfway across when I realize Kai never answered my question.

Well, no, he did answer it. He just didn't explain. "What were those tracks from?"

"An animal that was thirsty before we got here and that I hope doesn't get hungry anytime soon, and if it does, I hope it stays on that side of the river."

That was avoiding the question. We're nearly at the other side. There's no reason to keep me distracted anymore. "What kind of animal was it?" I press. "Just tell me. I won't freak out."

On my next step, I hit something wobbly—a rock?—and it slides out from under me. My ankle gives, pulling the rest of me downward at an awkward angle. Kai squeezes my hand to keep me from taking a full plunge, and I grab him with my other hand, too. Our opposing forces pull against each other, and for a moment I'm motionless, suspended midfall, and then Kai's strength wins out, yanking me upward. He grunts with the effort, then breathes hard like he just ran a mile uphill.

"You okay?" he says.

"Yeah, but I twisted my ankle. Everything else feels okay."

He helps me onto dry land, then guides me down to sit. He pulls his pack off and props my foot up on top of it. "Did your feet get wet? Being numb would actually help you with this, to keep the swelling down."

"They aren't numb, just cold." Even as I say it, liquid heat flows around my hurt ankle, battling the chill in my toes.

Kai makes quick work of igniting some kindling, then pulls a bandage wrap and the last of the ibuprofen out of the first aid kit. I'm amazed at how easily he can make fire from nothing, how he always knows just what to do. Is there any situation this boy can't handle?

He hands me his canteen of water along with the pills. While I swallow them down, he takes off my boots and wet socks and sets them by the fire. Then he wraps my left ankle, leaving my toes exposed. Okay, *now* they're going numb. And they're so pale . . . If not for the fading red nail polish and distinct shape of my toes, almost identical to Mom's, I wouldn't have recognized my own feet. With my sun-soaked upbringing, nothing except my teeth has ever been this white.

"You sure you aren't the pre-med student?" I say.

Cheeky grin. "I actually learned this from Hunter. When I was fifteen, I sprained my ankle while I was out jogging one day. I wasn't even that far out of our neighborhood, but I hit a bad crack in the sidewalk or something. Limped all the way home. He didn't even say anything when he saw me; he just stopped what he was doing and took care of it. And I watched. And I never forgot it." He secures the end of the wrap with a couple of bandage claws. Lets out a sigh. "I hope he's okay."

"He is. You left him with people who can take care of him. You can't fix everything yourself, you know? Sometimes you have to let other people step in and help."

"I know that now, thanks to you." Kai pulls the hatchet out of his pack and removes the blade guard. "I have to get something bigger to burn or we'll never get warm enough. I won't go far. Yell if you need anything."

"Can you tell me what animal that was by the river before you go?"

"Only if you promise not to worry. Because it might not even be a problem."

"Okay." Although, if something tries to attack me, I can't run with this bum ankle. So I'm *already* worried about it.

Kai stands, looks back the way we came. "Those were wolf tracks. If you see one, stay down, don't make eye contact, and don't scream. Don't do anything that makes you seem like a predator or prey. There's likely more than one out there, and chances are they've been watching us since long before we noticed they were here. If they want to attack us, there isn't much we can do to stop it. They might just be curious, though, and sniff around. So don't take any food out."

"But it might not be a problem?" How can being stalked by wolves not be a problem?

He confirms it with a nod. And then he's gone.

X . X . X

The wolves have opted to ignore us. For now. It's getting dark when we pack up and start moving again, thoroughly dry and somewhat fed. My pace is slower now. I'm hobble-hiking. Kai hums his favorite songs, like we're on a pleasure hike. Well, maybe for him, we are. He thinks he's going to see his dad again and they'll have a tearful reunion, then tell each other stories all night by the fire.

The farther we go, the more my ankle throbs, and the trees have become sparse. Where many trees once stood there remain only splintery stumps. Someone was chopping—someone *lives* out here. Wind whips through the unnatural gaps. The gusts are getting stronger and stronger. One of them nearly knocks me over, and I catch myself on my weak ankle, sending a new sting of pain up my leg. We cross more animal tracks, something Kai can't quite identify. Something with a split hoof, but not a moose; the feet are too small. A mountain goat, maybe? As long as the animals stay hidden, though, I don't care what they are.

We find a faint set of human tracks, too, that's been nearly swept away by the constant wind. Kai doesn't say it outright, but I know what he's thinking. *What if that's my dad?* I don't say what I'm thinking, either. *What if it's not?*

Then I spot someone weaving through the trees toward us. It's a man as tall and broad as Hunter, and I remember what Kai said to me the other day, that his dad is a big guy, like Hunter. My heart jumps and my breath skids to a stop. Could it really be him? His face is completely covered, like ours, but I try to make out the shape of his eyes, his nose. He pulls his wrap down to expose his mouth, which is surrounded by wiry black-and-gray hair. "What're you kids doing out here?"

Kai lifts his goggles, maybe to get a better look at him. "We're looking for Mikah Locklear's cabin. I'm his son. Do you know where it is?"

Not his dad, then. But maybe someone who can help.

"You're his son?" The man sizes up Kai. "Don't look much like him."

"So you do know him," Kai says, ignoring the quip. "I've never been here before. I know we're close, but it would be helpful if you could show us the way?"

He shakes his head. "It's gonna be dark real soon. Not safe for you out here. Why don't you come back to my place and head out in the morning?"

Say yes, Kai. Say—

"Thanks, but no."

Well. There goes that. If this cabin is still a wreck, I'm sleeping in the snow. With wolves. Awesome.

Kai pulls the goggles back down over his eyes. "Can you at least point us in the right direction?"

"Stubborn," the man mutters. "Now I *know* you're Mik's son." Despite the antagonistic response, he points uphill. "Keep going the way you're going. Straight up to the ridge, then a quick right. You can't miss it. Be careful, kid." He covers his mouth again and continues his descent.

Kai sets off, walking faster than before. I can't keep up. "Wait," I say, breathless. He stops and doesn't move again until I've caught up to him, then he continues at a slower pace for me, but he's coiled like a spring. Every step is agony. I don't know how my leg muscles have anything left to give, but somehow we make it to the ridge in what seems like only minutes. Kai makes a sharp turn to the right.

And drops to his knees.

CHAPTER NINETEEN

The wreckage is more intact than I thought it would be, situated on a steep incline. The front is jammed against the mountainside while the back has a deck that hangs over a sheer drop. Not exactly my idea of prime real estate, but I bet the view was stunning.

We'll never know, since that part of the house isn't accessible anymore. It looks like it was cut in half by some giant saw. A dull saw that left rough, splintered edges. The part of the cabin that's missing must have housed the main room, because all that's visible now is one wooden wall with a fireplace in the center, a stone chimney leading up and out the roof, and a few feet of flooring alongside the wall from the front to the back of the cabin, like a ledge. A rocking chair still sits in one corner—there are even pictures hanging on nails and trinkets on the mantel. It's like we're looking inside a one-room dollhouse, but at a cross-section from the side instead of the front.

The slope where the other half of the cabin once stood has been worn smooth by time and wind, and covered in snow. No evidence remains of the search for Mikah's body. And I can see why they didn't risk gathering what's left of his belongings. The rest of the cabin might collapse, and the drop in the back makes the jump we took earlier look like a short hop. I can't see the bottom.

"Kai, I'm . . ." At a loss for words. What do you say to someone whose every hope has been shattered in one big blow? There's no way his dad is still alive. If he was, and he didn't stay here to rebuild his cabin, then why didn't he return home? Or at least find a way to send word to them? It just wouldn't make sense. Which means he's buried under the dirt, rubble, and snow here. We're visiting a grave. I take his hand. "I'm sorry."

"He didn't come back," Kai says. "Why didn't he come back to fix this?"

"Because he's gone."

"I know he's gone, but . . . where?"

"No. *Kai.* Listen to me." I take away his goggles and put a gloved hand on each of his covered cheeks, force him to look me in the eye. "I don't mean he's away. He's still here, buried. He's *gone.* Do you understand?"

He shakes his head furiously, pulling away from my grasp. "He isn't. You're wrong."

"If he didn't rebuild this—"

"No. I can prove he's still alive." He pushes himself up and approaches the cabin like it isn't one strong gust of wind away from falling. "There has to be something here that will prove it to you. I'll find it, and you'll see."

Now he's scaring me. He's lost his mind—or maybe this is his brain's version of a defense mechanism. I chase after him. "Kai, come back. It's too dangerous."

He ignores me and keeps going, all the way to what was probably once the front entryway. "If I can just get to . . ." He tests a step onto the broken floorboards, pushes his weight onto them. And they hold. He takes another step, and another, and then gestures for me to join him. "It's fine," he says. "It's stable. See?"

Kai takes off his pack, sets it on the rocking chair in the corner, and then jumps up and down. My heart leaps to my throat. "Stop! I believe you. I'm coming. Just . . . don't do that again."

He extends a hand and helps me onto the ledge, which is about four feet wide. Plenty of room to stand, but not nearly enough room for comfort. I keep my weight on my right side, on the good ankle, but the other is hurting now even without pressure on it. With part of the wind blocked in here, and the sun nearing the horizon, my goggles are no longer needed. I lift them onto the top of my head. Half of the floor, the part Kai jumped on, is situated firmly over ground. The other half is suspended over the incline by a series of support beams, some of which are bent out of alignment. We just need to stay on this side and we'll be fine.

Unfortunately, in his distressed state, Kai doesn't draw the same conclusion. He edges toward the far end of the wall, using the mantel as a grip.

"What are you doing?" I say, anchored to the safe side. He can jump all he wants this time. I'm not following him.

"There's something over here I want to show you. A picture."

All the walls are decorated with wildlife artwork and photographs. Many of them are completely frosted over with ice crystals. Some of them, the glass is cracked, but certain things in the photo are still visible, like the spread wings of an owl or the yellow eyes of a black wolf. Kai has zeroed in on one of them, but I'm not sure how it's different from the others.

Until Kai lifts it off its hook, turns, and shows it to me.

Even from the ten feet or so of distance between us, I can see the whole Locklear clan is there, all nine of them, although the youngest of them is just a baby. So that couldn't have been taken more than a couple of years ago. Hunter and Kai look younger but still like teenagers. They're standing in their backyard in Anchorage on a sunny day, the river flowing behind them. Maybe their previous duplex neighbor took the picture, or their aunt Claire. Everyone is smiling, even Hunter. My heart aches for them. They don't know yet . . . the family in that picture doesn't know that Mikah is going to die soon.

"These are Dad's photographs. Not just this one, but the animals and landscapes, too. He took pictures wherever he went. We have more of these at home." He sniffles and swallows. The wind kicks up for a moment and I reach for anything to keep me still—my hands find the mantel. The cabin creaks and groans, and I don't take another breath until the gust has left us, whistling a warning to its next victim.

I hate to push him, but this picture isn't proof of anything other than what we already know, that this is his dad's cabin. He's still gone, though.

"What are you getting at?" I don't think even he knows his reasoning anymore, or what he thought he could prove. His mind is bouncing all over the place, trying to make sense of what he's seeing yet still not willing to face the truth.

"We were happy," he says. "We had problems, but we were happy. He loved us. He wouldn't stay away without a reason. He just wouldn't do that."

"Kai . . . He would if he didn't have a choice. If he was dead."

He glares at me like I just insulted his mother. "I thought you were here to support me."

"I *am*." Okay, so that was too harsh of me to say it outright. He doesn't need a reality check; he needs first aid. His scars have been slashed open—but I have nothing to stop the bleeding.

If I can't help Kai now, he might do something crazy and get himself hurt, or worse. I absently finger my rock necklace, thoughts racing, and reluctantly tear my eyes away from him, searching for something, some way to prove their dad is truly gone—in a way that Kai will understand.

And then I see it, hanging from the antler of a moose statuette on the mantel above the fireplace. A rock pendant with the initials *KM* on it. Just like mine, and Kai's—and his mom's. What else did Hunter say about the necklaces . . . it wasn't that long ago, but the days lately feel like years. *Think, Gabi . . .*

It comes back to me in pieces. Hunter's voice, his furrowed brow, having his first ever conversation with me, before this whole crazy journey began. When their dad was home, their parents kept their necklaces together on the mantel. Their mom wore hers while their dad was away. But if their dad kept his on display on the mantel while he was here, only wore it while he was traveling . . .

"What's your mom's first name?" I say, stretching as far as I can without moving my feet, lifting the pendant from the mantel.

Kai's brow furrows, but he answers. "Katarina. She goes by Kat."

"And her maiden name is Martin, right? Same as your aunt Claire's?"

"Yes."

I lift the pendant to check the other side. *ML*. Same initials we saw at the first shelter, next to Kai's, where Hunter added his. *ML*—Mikah Locklear. *KM*—Katarina Martin. Together, even when they're apart. Forever.

"Is that what I think it is?" Kai's tone is suddenly strained.

I hold my hand out as far toward him as I can, letting the chain drip from my fingers. The pendant hangs heavy at the bottom, swinging and twirling until it settles. Motionless. Dead.

"No." He shakes his head, eyes glistening, then looks at the pendant, then at the wreckage all around us, like he's seeing it now for the first time, then back at the pendant. He drops the picture of his family, and glass shatters at his feet. His breaths become ragged. "Gabi . . . I can't . . ."

An iron weight presses onto my chest and my throat closes up. I can't save him from what he's about to go through. "I'm sorry. I'm so sorry. I wanted him to be here for you. I really did believe it was possible at first, but not anymore."

"No," he says again.

"If he were alive, he would have come back for this. He wouldn't have left behind something so important to him. Kai, I'm sorry," I repeat. "This is your proof. He's gone."

"*No.*" It comes out more like a squeak than a word this time.

"Come back to me. I'm not going anywhere; just come back over here where it's safe." I reach for him, but he's lost in his grief. He doubles over, pushes his fists onto his thighs, and finally—*finally*—lets himself cry.

It's the worst sound I've ever heard, the sound of mourning from somewhere so deep inside I think even the marrow of his bones sheds tears, releasing all the pain he's ever felt over all the things he's lost with this realization—his dad, the time they could have spent together, the things he had yet to learn from him. Tears sting my eyes, too, and fall freely. I know he needed to face this, but it still hurts to see him crumble.

And something inside me is crumbling along with him—my belief that what I said to my mother was the right thing to do. Was it how I truly felt? Yes. Was it necessary? No. What if those are the last words I ever speak to her? I don't think I could bear it. I thought I wanted her out of my life, but even a world away she's still been with me every day in my thoughts, and not all those thoughts have been bad. I don't want to lose her, not like this. Not permanently.

I settle back against the wall and slowly drop to the floor, on the opposite side of the cabin from Kai. I ache to hold him, but I can't get myself to go across to him. Wood creaks and the wind continues its assault. Maybe it's just my imagination, but it felt like the wall shifted. Safer to stay put.

The sun has abandoned us completely by the time Kai stops crying, drained and quiet, in a heap on the floor. A ghostly glow has cast over him—the moon. At least we'll have *some* light to help us find that other man's cabin, assuming his offer to let us spend the night still stands.

"Kai," I say gently. "I know you don't want to leave, but we can't stay here all night." My feet fell asleep, staying in the same position for too long. I slip his dad's necklace into the pocket of my coat and then zip it closed, shaking out my left foot as it prickles back to life. The needles stab into my injury, and I endure the sensations with gritted teeth.

Kai looks up at me, his eyes dead and hollow—and then suddenly very focused and alert, looking past me. "Gabi, don't move. Stop moving your foot."

I set my foot down, which only intensifies the needle pricks and the pain of torn ligaments, or whatever I did to myself, and then I start to look over my shoulder. "Holy sh—"

"Don't move," Kai repeats. He hasn't gotten up, either. "Don't even look."

He must not have heard my reaction. "I already saw it." Just barely, though, before I turned my head back toward Kai. The glow of yellow eyes. The wolf *did* follow us, and it waited until dark to strike. Or maybe this is a different wolf, and our noise alerted it to our location.

Either way, we're trapped in this broken house. If it comes in here . . .

"What do we do?" Besides panic, because I'm already there. "What do we do?"

"Just stay still. Stay against the wall. Don't draw attention to yourself." He pushes himself up slowly, eyes locked on the wolf. Didn't he just tell me not to move—what is he doing? Using himself as bait?

Well, there's a slight problem with that plan, besides that it ends with Kai getting eaten and leaving me stranded out here alone. To reach him, the wolf has to get past me first.

Kai growls at the thing. Actually growls. "Come here," he

says, never breaking eye contact—staring it down in challenge. "I'm the one you want."

Don't do anything that makes you seem like a predator or prey, he told me before. Way to take his own advice. He's gone into full-blown predator mode. But we're equals in this. There has to be a way to save us both.

And I'm the only one here to do it. I'm the only one standing between Kai and a wolf.

This whole trip, I've been relying on other people to get me through. Because knowing what needs to be done isn't the same as knowing how to do it—and I know how to do nothing out here in the wild. But now, I have no choice but to try. I have no choice but to be brave, and I'm scared out of my mind. Is it possible to be both?

I rack my brain for any survival clues Kai might have dropped in the past few days. The first thing I hear in my memory is:

Don't try to fight Alaska. She always wins. Work with her instead.

How do you work with a hungry wolf?

A *hungry* wolf. That's it.

It's hungry, just trying to fill one of its basic needs, like anyone or anything else in this world. "Kai—"

My new plan dies on my lips, as a giant lump of gray fur leaps past me, then lands on the flooring by the mantel. It ignored me, like Kai wanted. But now it has him cornered, and that side of the cabin dips with the added weight.

"Gabi, get out of here! Run!"

"I'm not leaving you!" Not when I can offer that beast something more appetizing than my boyfriend. In the wolf's opinion, not mine.

I fumble with the zippers of Kai's pack, my fingertips buzzing with adrenaline. As soon as it's open, I smell it. Cooked moose meat. Kai packed a lot of it for this trip.

The wolf turns its giant head toward me, nose sniffing the air. Yes. *I'm* the one you want. Not him. Come and get it.

Kai has other plans, though. He takes advantage of the wolf's distraction and kicks it square in the ribs, knocking it hard. Not hard enough to push it off the broken flooring—this wolf is as big as he is—but hard enough for it to lose its balance. Paws scramble, scratching across the floor, until its hind legs slip over the edge. It bites at the leg of Kai's pants to keep from falling, bringing him down with it. The cabin creaks and shifts again, and I brace myself against the wall. As they slip toward the edge, Kai punches the wolf in the jaw, and it quickly disappears from my view. The wolf's howls and ear-piercing yelps get quieter and quieter in its descent, only to be replaced by Kai yelling as he slips down.

He catches himself on the ledge with a pained grunt.

"Kai!" I scramble through his pack. Wasn't there a rope in here? He lifts one foot up high enough to catch the floor above, but when he tries to pull himself up with it, the board breaks and his foot slips down again. Crap crap crap. This place is falling apart around us.

My heart pounds against my ribs like a mad gorilla. The sound of blood rushing through my ears is almost deafening—but still, I hear it. Something low and guttural. I pop my face toward the trees, and immediately wish I hadn't.

More pairs of yellow eyes, catching the light of the moon, all on me.

Black, gray, mud-colored, and a white wolf at the lead. I can only hope there's enough meat in here to satisfy them.

"Gabi, help!" Kai screams, still scrambling to get up. "Grab the rope!"

Now he asks me for help. Now, when I can only do one thing or the other.

Help him. Or help myself.

Get the rope. Or get the meat.

"Hang on, I'm coming!" I find the rope, finally, and yank it out. The lead wolf—the big white one—lunges toward me, head low, eyes intent. I throw Kai's pack as hard as I can, which isn't very hard, because the cinder blocks are still in there, apparently. The bag lands with a *thud* only a few feet away, stopping the wolf in its tracks. It bares its teeth at me.

For a moment I wonder if I made the wrong choice. The wolves are going to come after us anyway, and I just tossed all of our supplies away. Even if I can get Kai back up to safety, how will we survive?

I don't know. But I won't find the answer if Kai drops to his death now. Together we can face anything, right? We've come this far—God, we've come so far. Faced Death head-on. Faced every threat imaginable. Faced our own personal demons. And we're still here.

The stuff I went through with my mother is nothing compared to this. *Nothing.* Why did I think it was everything? Why did I think it was irreversible? Unforgivable? Life is constant trial and error, and I've made enough errors in this trial. It's time to stop expecting my mother to change back to who she was before. It's time for me to change myself. Who I am *now*.

I can do this. I can be brave and scared at the same time, no matter the challenge. I can have a mother who makes mistakes, doesn't always love me the way I need her to, and still be okay. And right now, I can save Kai *and* myself.

I brace my shoulder against the lip of stone where the hearth connects to the wall and throw him one end of the rope. He lets loose one secure hand to grab it, and for a moment I think he might pull me right over, the corner of the hearth cutting into my shoulder, but the pressure is gone as quickly as it appeared. He's up. He's safe.

Safe for only one second before the cabin starts falling out from under him.

"Kai," I scream. "Run!"

He pushes to his feet in a blink, one step, then two, then he grabs my arm as he's running, and we take a giant leap toward stable ground.

We land and turn to see the cabin collapse, leaving only the corner we're standing in at the front end. Then the snarl of wolves steals my attention, and I snap my head back toward the woods. They're fighting over the meat in the pack—that's what they wanted all along, not us. The lead wolf snatches it by one of the straps and starts dragging it away.

And now I feel like I might puke, as my brain realizes the danger has passed, unsure what to do with this excess adrenaline. This day . . . this everything . . . it was too much.

Kai cradles me in his arms. We huddle silently in the corner for a few minutes. Our breaths fall into sync and my heartbeat slows.

"The wolves took our stuff," I say.

He sniffs a laugh. "Actually, you gave it to them."

"We're screwed."

"Completely screwed," he agrees. "Unless that guy we passed before turns out to be the good-est of Good Samaritans and lets us crash at his place and borrow his supplies."

"Good-est?" I must be on the brink of hysteria, because after all that's happened, I can't stop laughing at the dumbest thing. "Good-est is not a word."

"Anything can be a word." He pulls a mad face, but it breaks quickly and then he's laughing, too. "We are insane."

"The insane-est."

"The most-est in trouble-est when we get-est home. Est," he adds.

"You can't do anything without going overboard."

"Nope. That's just me. Take it or leave it."

"I'll take it," I say. His lips meet mine, transferring heat and goose bumps and a future with no limits. Together. In Alaska, or anywhere.

I'm so lost in him, I almost miss it—but then it becomes too strong to ignore. The rumble of helicopter blades overhead, accompanied by an even fiercer wind than we encountered on the exposed mountainside. Kai and I look up in unison. A bright light shines down on us, blinding me, and I turn my head away.

"Is there really a helicopter up there, or am I delirious?"

"There's really a helicopter up there," Kai says. His tone is just as confused as mine.

A man in a harness drops down on a line. He tells us that, one at a time, he's going to pull me and Kai up to the helicopter. Kai insists I go first, because of my injury. My ankle. I almost forgot. It's like my brain doesn't know which signals to focus on anymore; there are too many. And suddenly I'm very, very cold. Shaking so hard my teeth chatter.

When I get up to the helicopter and see Hunter, I collapse in relief. "Y-y-you're okay."

"And you're in shock," he says, wrapping a warm blanket around me. "Just relax. Everything's okay now. We're going home." He looks out the opening of the helicopter, and I assume he's watching them rescue Kai. But then he rubs his palms against his eyes and catches his breath. Pulls back inside.

"He's gone."

My heart jumps, thinking he means something happened to Kai, but then they start pulling him up to the helicopter with the line.

"You mean your dad," I say.

He shakes his head, as if clearing away confusion. "I knew he was. It's just . . . seeing it—knowing Dad is under there somewhere." He turns to look at me. "Is Kai okay? After seeing this?"

"I wouldn't say he's okay," I tell him, muscles melting as they soak up heat. "But he will be. He's not denying it anymore. He knows your dad isn't coming back."

He nods and swallows. "When I got to the hospital in Fairbanks, after a few hours of fluids and a bowl of broth, I started to feel a lot better." He coughs, still not completely well yet. "The whole time, they drilled me and Jack and Vicki with questions about where you and Kai ran off to. We didn't tell them anything until they agreed to take me along to pick you up. Sorry if that was overstepping, but I couldn't go home until I knew you guys were safe . . . And . . . yes. I did it so I could see the inside of a rescue chopper, too." Sheepish grin.

"You did the right thing. I wouldn't have made it another day." I take off my boot and show him Kai's handiwork with the bandage. "Your brother did that, and he learned it from watching you. He needs you, Hunter, even if he doesn't say it."

He smiles big, his eyes glistening. Kai and his rescuer arrive, and once Kai is safely inside the helicopter Hunter tackles him with a hug. They say nothing to each other, not with words, anyway. And then we veer off, leaving the wreckage behind.

Dad meets me at the hospital in Fairbanks, and although I'm ecstatic to see him, my gut clenches. Time to face the music.

"Your mother was right," he says. "I am a bad parent. I didn't know you ran away until she called me back and explained what she meant about the credit card." His face is all hard edges, but his forehead is creased with worry. I did that to him. He's not a bad parent; I'm a bad daughter.

"I didn't run away. I didn't mean to be gone longer than a few hours, and then . . . things got out of control." I thought they were under control at the time, but looking back, it was more like surfing a tsunami and hoping you don't wipe out— I'm surprised we survived. And I thought I was done crying, too, but fresh tears pour down my cheeks as freely as the IV drip in my arm. "I promise this will never happen again."

"No, it won't. Because I'm never letting you out of my sight again."

"Never? Not even to go to the bathroom?" I tease. But it feels so good to joke with him like we used to that I might start crying again.

"You know what I mean," he says. "You deserve a better papi than I've been lately." He hugs me for an eternity, squeezing me hard.

Finally, I grunt. "I can't breathe."

"Sorry." He clears his throat and lets go. "I'm just glad to see you're okay, querida." He hands me a plastic bag. It's full of my clothes. *Clean* clothes. I could kiss him. Then he says, "As soon as you're cleared by the doctors here, we're taking the first plane home."

I don't question which home he means. I shift my gaze from Dad to Kai, who's sitting on the ER bed next to mine, then look at Hunter and Vicki talking and smiling at each other in the chairs across the room. Even Jack stuck around the hospital to make sure we made it back okay. Alaska is my real home, because home is where your family is. The people who stick their necks out for you, not the ones raising the ax. This may be one of the coldest, most brutal corners of the planet, but it's the warmest home I've ever had.

CHAPTER TWENTY

Thanksgiving brings with it a few inches of snow and a few prayers that Kai won't reject what I'm about to offer him. While everyone, including my dad, congregates around the Locklear dinner table, Kai and I escape out the front door. It's only seven p.m., but the sun went down hours ago, before we even sat down for dinner. "Close your eyes," I say, leading Kai across the driveway to my garage. He steals a kiss, kicking my heartbeat up from anxious to exhilarated, and then shutters his eyelids. "No peeking."

"Yes, ma'am," he teases.

The garage door lifts slowly, hinges creaking. The automatic lights blink on and the scent of gasoline greets us. I tell Kai to wait while I squeeze around Dad's car and retrieve my gift. It's black and silver, sleek and shiny, and nearly as tall as I am.

"Okay," I say. "Open your eyes."

He cracks one eye open, then the other, his smile fading as he realizes what it is.

"I was planning on buying my own snowboard," he says. "I mean . . . thank you. It's really great of you. But, Gabi . . ."

"This isn't for you. It's mine."

His face quirks in confusion.

"You're going to teach me how to snowboard this winter, just like you said you would when we first met. But you're not teaching me for free. So . . . once you've *earned* enough to buy your own, then . . ."

Kai isn't the only person I'm taking lessons from. I've been going to the Grinning Bear Lodge for cooking lessons from Vicki whenever I can, and Hunter's been teaching me first aid. This snowboard arrangement can't really be a surprise to Kai. Ever since we got back home, I've been trying to learn how to do things for myself. I even wash dishes now.

A grin tugs up into one of his cheeks, and I hand him the snowboard.

"This is nice," he says. "Better than my old one. You're gonna love snowboarding." He smiles fully again. Boyish. Giddy. He's practically bouncing on his toes. "How did you know what kind to get?"

"Hunter helped. It's going to cost me a full weekend of babysitting the next time he wants to get out of the house, but I would have done that anyway. I like this new version of him."

"It's not really a new version," Kai says. "He's going back to his old self. Finally."

Hunter said the same thing about Kai when we were out

snowboard shopping. Funny how we all went through the same experience and I feel like I'm even further from the person I was in SoCal now, but the Locklear twins are back to who they were before we met. Mostly.

The front door opens and Hunter trots down the steps to the driveway, cell phone in hand. His thumb-tips tap the screen. "Hey, Kai," he says without taking his eyes off the phone. "You're up next. Mom needs help with the pies."

"I'll be right back," Kai tells me. "Pie emergency."

I tuck the snowboard back into the garage and then close the door. Hunter is still out on the steps, staring at his phone.

"Something wrong?" I say.

"I got a text. From Dakota."

"Oh." It takes me a second for the name Dakota to ring a bell. "You mean your ex?"

"Yeah. She wants to know how I am. It's just weird, you know? I haven't talked to her in almost a year. I don't know what to say."

"I'm not a communications expert, but you could start with maybe telling her how you are?"

"Actually, I was thinking of not replying. I don't want to encourage her. I heard she's single again. This isn't just a 'hey, how are you' text. She's baiting me."

So he still doesn't want to get close to anyone. Okay. One step at a time. He's not a total shut-in anymore. That's a good start.

"Do what you think you should," I say. "Just remember, she's not the only one out there wondering about you. I talked to Vicki this morning. She said to say hi."

He shoves his phone in a coat pocket. "How's her new position at the lodge going?"

"Why don't you ask her yourself?" I leave him with that and head back into the house.

The mantel has a new photograph added to it now, the selfie of me, Kai, Vicki, and Hunter that I printed off my phone. Also, there are two identical rock necklaces displayed in the center, each with Kai's mom's and dad's initials.

All the kids are at the table, wide-eyed, as Kai hands them each a slice of pie. Dad keeps them laughing between bites with stories about the post office. Who knew mail fails could be so entertaining? He volunteered to take a babysitting shift after work three times a week so Mrs. Locklear has regular breaks, and being around the kids has brought out a fun side of him I haven't seen since *I* was little. He's been in a better mood in general since I came home. He even helped me convince Mom to buy Jack an upgraded plane.

Mom. I still haven't called her. Emailing her for a favor doesn't count. We need to *talk.*

And it has to start with me. I'm not the same person I was four months ago—or even four weeks ago—the kind who expects other people to do the hard stuff for her. The kind of person who expects other people to change instead of changing herself. We're all human, like Kai said, and that's all we can be. Screwups are inevitable. It's what we do in the aftermath that really matters, even if we don't figure out what to do until months or years later. It has to start with me, or we'll be in this standoff forever and I won't ever have a mother again, of any kind.

I kneel by the couch and give Diesel a good scrub between the ears, then cross the house into the kitchen and out the back door. The laughter and chatter from inside rings in my ears as they adjust to the outdoor silence. It's peaceful out here, the only sounds coming from the rippling river and the light breeze rustling in the branches. The freshly fallen snow sparkles like a blanket of diamonds. I can't remember why I used to hate it here so much. I still prefer to be warm, but the cold doesn't bother me like it used to.

Mom doesn't answer her phone. She probably doesn't have it on. I saw something on the news this morning, right before the Macy's parade, that *the* Marietta Cruz is volunteering at a homeless shelter today by serving them Thanksgiving dinner. Newsworthy or not, it did make me think. I don't know if she's just doing it for publicity or if she's genuinely trying to be less selfish now. Time will tell.

Part of me is relieved that she's too busy to answer her phone. The scared part, not the brave part. I had no idea what I would say to her; I just know I have to say *something*. Maybe I should start with a text, anyway. Get things started slowly, on the neutral ground of our wireless connection.

The back door opens and shuts behind me. "Gabi," Kai says.

"I'll be there in a sec."

"Look up."

"Hang on. I'm texting my mom."

"Really?" His footsteps shuffle through the snow, closer. "That's great!"

"Yeah," I say, smiling. "I'm stuck, though. How do you strike up a conversation with someone after trying to disown them?"

"Go with your gut, but keep it simple. It's only the first step. You've got the rest of your life to build on it."

There's a reason I met Kai, and in moments like this, I remember—it's how well he understands things. How he knows just what to say at just the right time. Because he gets it—life, the world, secrets of the universe that escape most other people. He sighs and I wonder if he's thinking of his dad, how he doesn't have the same opportunity to fix things with him like I do with my mom.

I start to turn to face him, but he threads his arms around me from behind and gently nudges my chin upward, forcing me to lean back on his chest and sink into his embrace. But that isn't what takes my breath away. The sky is exploding with color. Purple, green, and yellow swirls against an inky black sky. The sun didn't die. It just went backstage for a while so something else could have the spotlight.

"The northern lights," Kai says. "They aren't always easy to see here, because of the city lights. I didn't want you to miss them."

"Wow." The word doesn't do justice to the awe thrumming inside me. "It's beautiful."

"You'll be an Alaska girl yet."

Too late—I already am. And there's still so much left for me to explore.

"I was with my dad the first time I saw the lights, and he said they're like a sunset, or a snowflake, never the same thing twice." Kai breathes in deep and lets it out slowly, making me rise and fall with his chest. "I wish he could see these now. They're perfect."

"Yeah. Perfect." I snap a picture of Alaska's newest gift to me and send it to my mom with a text. Wish you were here, Mami. It's gonna be a bright winter.

ACKNOWLEDGMENTS

My eternal gratitude goes to the following people, some for making this particular book possible and others for supporting me as readers and friends:

Laura Bradford, my agent, aka Superwoman; Emily Seife, my editor, and everyone else at Scholastic Press; Kelly Said, my critique partner, and everyone else who has ever helped me improve my stories; Stacy Cantor Abrams and everyone else in my second family at Entangled Publishing; everyone in my other second family at Kohl's; everyone in my first family, either through blood relation or marriage; the YA author community; and the YA book reviewer community.

You, the person reading this, whoever and wherever you are, thank you.

And last but by no means least, my husband and son, to whom this book is dedicated. Only they know just how much of my "blood, sweat, and tears" went into working on this story, because only they are the ones with me *every day*, tirelessly supporting me, encouraging me, never giving up on me, and for that I am forever indebted to them.

ABOUT THE AUTHOR

Lydia Sharp worked a number of different jobs, everything from retail management to veterinary medicine, before turning her passion for stories into a career. She is now an editor for Entangled Publishing and writes young adult novels with lots of kissing and adventures. *Whenever I'm with You* is her debut, and she lives in Ohio with her husband and son. When not completely immersed in a book, Lydia binges on Netflix, pines for fall, and hosts mad tea parties in Wonderland. For details about her books and more, visit lydiasharpbooks.com.